The Gilded Shackle

Book 2: Tested

C.T. Griffith

ISBN: 978-0-692680-58-2

Edited by Elaine Roughton and Sylvia Griffith
Cover Art by Karyn Lewis Bonfiglio
Cover Design by Angelique Mroczka
Typeset by Angelique Mroczka

Printed in the United States of America

For my aunts, Marilyn and Judy.

Contents

Chapter 1: Chosen

Marne drew a deep, ragged breath, his voice soft but rich with sad, childish longing. "I wish I knew," he answered, resting his sharp chin in his hand, his elbow on his knee. "All I know for sure is that I'm no more an Aoife than you are."

Teine couldn't help but nod his agreement, wordless with wonder. But Marne's response only multiplied his questions. He was dying to know how Marne managed to hide his true appearance so effectively. Why had he spent the ride to the tower bundled up in a duffel bag like some kind of luggage? And how did Marne repair and light the candle? Was it magic? Teine was so tangled in his own thoughts, it took him several awkward seconds to realize he was still standing there, mouth agape like a simpleton.

"Would you mind bringing the tray in?" Marne asked gently. "I'd get it myself, but I'm really supposed to stay in bed."

"Oh, yes. Sorry." Teine shook his head, then hustled to bring in the tray. Once he realized the tiny dank bedroom was several degrees warmer than the rest of the storage cellar, he closed the door behind him.

Marne had cleared the bedside table of the spare candle holders and a model glider to make room for their food. "There's a chair over by the table you can use," he told Teine, pointing into one of the dimly lit recesses of the room. "It should be big enough for you. We can both just eat here. I see no reason for formality."

Teine fetched the chair, wondering at the incredible oddity of the situation. How many Humans had ever dined at the same table as their master, even if it was only at a bedside? Masters and servants eating together was unthinkable. Was it only Marne's unique situation that made it possible or would it be a regular part of the life he was going to lead? Should he pick up crisps out of the bowl with his hands or should he simply try to pour them onto a plate? Was he supposed to be serving Marne his dinner, and if so, how was that to be done properly? Brow furrowed with worry, Teine sat in the chair, folded his hands in his lap and waited for direction.

Marne raised an eyebrow, then gave a quiet chuckle that sounded far more sympathetic than mocking. "You really are out of your element, aren't you? Don't worry. When there's no one around to impress, there's no need for the show," Stretching to reach the cover on one of the bowls, Marne set it aside, then poured them both tea from the steaming earthenware pot. With surprise, Teine watched as Marne filled his own tea last, as though Teine were a guest. He also noted that, despite Marne's focused look of concentration, his frail arms were shaking from the exertion by the time he'd topped off the second cup.

"Here, master, let me," Teine offered, emboldened by the strange boy's subtle kindness. "Please instruct me if what I do is not to your liking. I've only learned the basics of setting a table, but I would welcome the opportunity to broaden my horizons."

Marne chuckled, "I'm not easy to offend. And please, Teine, no formalities. I haven't the energy for them." With a sigh, Marne settled himself back on the pillows, his cup of tea steaming near at hand.

Somewhat perplexed, Teine decided the best course of action was to simply wing it. Marne had made it clear that it would be fine for Teine to do as he liked, within reason. Hoping he looked somewhat skilled, he uncovered the small basin that held the damp, citrus-scented towels for washing before their meal. He started to reach in and take out the towel for Marne before he realized that would be unsanitary, and offered the whole basin instead. Nodding his approval, Marne selected a cloth and began to diligently wipe his face and hands. Teine did the same, the ritual words of formal evening prayer on his tongue. But from the way the young master was eying the consumables, he suspected it would be fine to dispense with the prayer as well and get directly to the food. Using a wooden ladle on the tray, he filled a bowl with savory beef stew, heaping it high with chunks of seasoned meat and tender vegetables. With a flourish, he then offered it to Marne.

Eyes wide, Marne shook his head, warding the bowl off with both hands. "I wish," he sighed. "It looks heavenly. But perhaps I'd better just try the broth first." Nodding, Teine set the first bowl aside, thinking about how good it would taste once he got to it. Mindful of the young master's wishes, he filled the second bowl with a generous amount of broth, then, as an afterthought, added a couple pieces of carrot and potato, mashing them flat with the ladle. Marne accepted the bowl as offered, taking it in both hands and giving it a long, anticipatory sniff before reaching for his spoon.

More items remained on the tray, and Teine was determined to make a good impression. He carved up one of the red pears in the bowl, thoughtfully removing both the core and the skin, and placed it on a plate. He then added a couple of slices of buttery farmer's cheese, and on a whim decided to shake a few crisps onto the plate for good measure. But his shaking was a little overzealous, and he ended up covering the entire plate with the tasty little lemony cookies.

"Oh rats," he muttered, trying to shake some of the excess crisps off onto a second plate. He looked up to see Marne watching him, his odd eyes sparkling with humor over his bowl of broth.

"It's perfectly acceptable to use your hands on the crisps if you've just washed," Marne told him. "But, I was hoping for dinner *and* a show..."

Teine snorted, embarrassed but amused at his own discomfiture. "You don't want to see what I do for my next act, believe me," he countered, vividly imagining himself flinging crisps everywhere while trying to shake them back where they belonged. Leis was right: although Marne was physically frail and the strangest-looking creature Teine had ever seen, he was a fair-minded, witty little fellow.

"I hope it involves making a lot of that food disappear." Marne sipped a spoonful of broth, then nodded in satisfaction. "Honestly, this is excellent, but I don't think I'll make much of a dent in what she gave us. I hope you're hungry."

"I'm always hungry." Sensing he had Marne's approval to tuck in, Teine brushed most of the crisps off onto the second plate with his hand and offered over the fruit and cheese. Marne hesitated, and Teine felt oddly elated when he took a piece of pear and immediately ate it. "Say the word if you want more."

"I will. Just focusing on one thing at a time."

The pair of them fell to dining, with Teine consuming about five times the volume in about half the time as his more finicky companion. He ate to keep his mouth busy, hoping to avoid some of the awkwardness, and praying he wasn't breaking any major rules of etiquette. Marne, for his part, seemed relaxed and serene as he nestled into his pillows, listening to the muffled sounds of the storm outside and sipping broth from his spoon. Teine was still fascinated by Marne's alien appearance, but didn't want his curiosity to offend. That, alone, was an excellent reason to remain silent. He was dying to ask so many questions, but he didn't want to disturb the easy silence that dining together provided.

He filled the time between mouthfuls by carefully observing the room. The solo candle didn't provide much illumination, but Teine was able to make out strange markings in a glittery kind of paint on the floor and the walls. They looked similar to the ones stitched into Marne's traveling bag, but it was hard to be sure in the dim light.

Teine's mind was racing like a hound slipped from its collar, darting from conclusion to conclusion as he tried to take in everything. He wanted to sketch: the way the candlelight fell on the rocking horse caused a shadow on the wall that gave him an idea for a new composition with soldiers and their mounts riding through a canyon, their looming shadows looking more fearsome than the contingent itself. He wanted to paint: only his jealously guarded oil paints would be able to capture the depth of Marne's mysterious iridescent eyes. And he wanted to write: the things he'd seen in the last few hours challenged nearly every belief he'd had about Aoife, magic, and what was possible in the world!

The core truths of the world he'd now entered were far stranger than Teine had ever imagined, and his awareness of the situation was truly alarming. The ongoing need for secrecy was obvious. Even a rumor of the young master being some strange, alien, magic-wielding creature could send half the Humans at Solmurry into a panic, and it wouldn't matter how many of them had played with Marne or listened to him read them stories when they were nurslings.

Living among and educating themselves with Aoife had managed to raise Humans out of some of their baser tendencies toward superstition and xenophobia, but they were still only Human. Not even the avalanche of books Teine had read, packed full of tales of fairies, adventure, and magical creatures, had truly prepared him for this, and he was more open-minded than the average Human. Most likely, Marne would be reviled as a demon, rendered helpless by any means possible, and then either killed outright or given over to the Church. Even Lord Solmurrian being home at the time would not guarantee Marne's safety.

The situation begs one burning question, Teine thought. *Who knows about Marne? Does Leis? Does Lord Solmurrian himself know that this creature is not his own flesh and blood, but perhaps a changeling of some sort? Maybe Lord Solmurrian's real son is locked away in a faerie realm while an impostor lives in his place.* The thought gave Teine a shiver of dread, but he found it hard to sustain any feeling of fear when he looked at the child across from him struggling to thrive on thin broth and peeled pear slices. Teine had always trusted his instincts, and nothing about Marne seemed particularly dangerous, other than the power he had over the course of Teine's life.

He was about to refill his bowl when Marne spoke. "I want to ask your opinion on something rather important." The boy set down his bowl and reached for his tea.

Teine blinked twice. *His opinion? The day was getting stranger and stranger.* Wordlessly, he nodded and continued dipping out his second bowl of soup as though his betters asked his opinion every day.

Encouraged, Marne regarded Teine over the lip of his steaming cup, his strange reflective eyes serious. "Now that you've seen how deep this rabbit hole goes," the boy began. "Did I make the right choice?"

Teine smiled at the *Alice in Wonderland* reference, before he realized that Marne was talking about *him.*

"After all," Marne continued. "While most noble families have their secrets, we at Solmurry have more than our fair share of skeletons in the closet."

Unwilling to answer hastily, Teine considered the question. Out of all the boys who were his age-mates, he could think of no one at Solmurry who had the right combination of interests, temperament, and abilities to be the guardian of such terrible secrets.

Only Marcus stood out as even a remote possibility. Marcus had a more developed physique than Teine, tending toward strength and bulk. When Teine thought "Display Model," it was types like Marcus that automatically came to mind. Additionally, his friend had a good nature, a sense of fair play, and the right temperament to enjoy the work. But he lacked...

Teine drew a blank. What *did* Marcus lack, anyway? He seemed the logical choice. Convinced that Marne wasn't trying to trap him into saying the wrong thing, Teine decided it was best to answer his question with another question.

"Why did you defy your father on this?" he blurted out, unable to contain himself any longer. After his meeting with Lord Solmurrian, Teine couldn't imagine *anyone* willfully defying the hot-tempered Aoife noble on anything. He was truly frightening. "Marcus would have been a more logical choice. Why not him?"

Marne didn't answer for several long seconds, and Teine began to wonder if Marne was beginning to have doubts about his choice. As much as Teine would have jumped at the opportunity to return to his old life and the chance to see which of his carefully-laid plans would come to fruition, he now found himself torn.

Could it be that he actually *wanted* this life, now that he knew it would be an adventure beyond his wildest imaginings?

"Marcus never would have asked that question," Marne answered. "That's why I selected you."

In the dim candlelight, Teine could see the boy was visibly fatigued, exhaustion showing in every line of his young, frail body. Marne set down his cup, pushed the food away, and sank back into the cushions.

"Marcus never would have asked that question." Teine supposed that was probably true. Marcus was content knowing what was, without ever questioning *why* it was. Suddenly, Teine couldn't help but feel very special. Chosen, even. All his life, Teine had watched the world around him and tried to learn from it. Apparently, someone had noticed. He was about to express his gratitude when he realized Marne had fallen

asleep. Rising, he pulled the heavy wool blanket up around his frail charge's shoulder and whispered, "Thank you."

Chapter 2: Light, Sight, and Flight

April 11, 3131

Teine woke to the unaccustomed sound of dishes rattling. Blearily, he opened his eyes. The elderly kitchen Bess had brought down a fresh candle and was bustling around the small, windowless chamber, stacking the dinner dishes onto a tray and generally tidying up. After the long night, Teine was confused, disoriented, and more than a little stiff from sleeping in a chair.

Marne had slept fitfully. Although Teine was used to dormitory living, with the usual snoring and murmuring of many sleepers in one room, he had barely gotten a moment's rest. The strange child must still have been suffering the aftereffects of his illness, as he had tossed, thrashed, and babbled feverishly most of the night. After having awakened for the third time, Teine had wondered if Marne might be chilled. He had added his own blanket to Marne's, hoping the extra warmth would help him rest more comfortably. It seemed to work. Eventually both boys had fallen deeply asleep, and now Marne was still sleeping.

Teine stole another look at his patron's alien features to assure himself that he hadn't dreamed their conversation. Although the child was still odd-looking, his unhealthy flush had faded overnight. He seemed to be resting comfortably, with his arm draped over a well-worn stuffed model of a Holidocrith, made of suede leather and threadbare velvet. One of its yellow glass eyes was hanging by a thread and it seemed to have lost an ear. Teine smiled, remembering the stuffed bear he'd kept for years. The poor thing finally fell apart right after he'd been transferred to Mastiff Cohort.

Teine rose slowly, twisting his neck this way and that. As he rubbed the sleep from his eyes, daylight streaming in from the open door made him wonder if he'd slept too long and missed breakfast.

"Good, I'm glad you're awake," the matron told him, shaking him free of his drowsy memories. Her face was wizened, but friendly. "The storm petered itself out around dawn, and Lord Solmurrian has come calling to take brunch with his brother and son. Best get to tidying yourself up in case he wants you to present yourself before mealtime."

"Where do I go for a good washing up?" he murmured hastily, trying to collect himself before Marne woke up. "After moving all that furniture yesterday I'm sure I stink to high heaven. I'm surprised the Aoife can't smell me from here."

She chuckled and handed him the tray with the previous night's dirty dishes. Just as she was giving him directions to the servants' washrooms, the electric lights came back on, flooding both the shelter room and the main basement storage room with light. Teine could hear muffled cheering from upstairs.

"That's a relief," the old Bess quipped. "It's a lot easier to cook over the electric range than the wood stove."

"I can only imagine," Teine replied before taking his leave. Marne muttered something, stretched in his sleep, and rolled over to hide his face from the morning light.

"Breakfast in a half-hour," she told Teine's retreating backside. "You'll be dining in the kitchen with us."

Teine decided to take his bath in the new quarters he would share with Marne, enjoying the large tub, the privacy, and the nearly unlimited rush of hot water. His close-cropped auburn curls made shampooing easy, and he found he even had time to shave the copper-colored stubble from the few patches on his chin and cheeks. Afterward, he wiped his face with a towel and examined his handiwork in the mirror. "Not bad, for a first-timer."

Determined to make a better impression on Lord Solmurrian this time, he dressed carefully in one of his new outfits. The deep green tunic with a black hem, matching black trousers, and his new leather ankle boots were easily the finest clothes Teine had ever worn. He checked his reflection several times to be sure he hadn't missed anything shaving, and that his hair was tidy. Finally satisfied, he headed to the kitchen to join the rest of the servants, stopping only once to survey the storm damage through one of the windows.

From the amount of debris in the courtyard, Teine guessed that they'd lost at least one tree. The new day looked clear and beautiful, though, and he hoped his duties might take him outdoors for a bit. Although he'd had plenty of exercise toting furniture down the stairs the previous day, he couldn't help but feel a bit cooped up. Despite the wild carriage ride to the tower, both his hospital procedure and the storm itself had kept him indoors too long.

By the time he made it to the kitchen, Kenneth and his boys were already seated and feasting on fresh buttered biscuits and jam while waiting eagerly for more substantial fare. Teine could hear low tenor voices and the occasional soprano interjection from Marne filtering in from the formal dining room. Thus alerted to the presence of the noble Aoife, Teine took his place where Hamoni indicated, at the end of the table opposite Kenneth. The positioning wasn't lost on Teine, or Kenneth's two boys, who scowled before returning their attention to the food. Servants were usually seated in order of rank, and Teine's placement at the foot of the table instead of on one of the sides spoke volumes about his status within the household. It was all Teine could do to avoid grinning when he realized that he wouldn't be taking orders from anyone, except possibly Kenneth, once he learned his way around.

The matron was putting the finishing touches on stuffed omelets and fruit compotes for Lord Solmurrian, Madric, and Marne, while Hamoni was heaping a gigantic pile of scrambled eggs into a serving bowl.

"I swear," the Aoife girl groused, "I feel I've been cooking since sun-up. As if I don't have enough to do today. I thought the Rangers and refugees would *never* leave!"

Teine was momentarily sorry he didn't get to say goodbye to the Aoife children he'd been playing with, but he still didn't miss the irritated glance the kitchen Bess gave Hamoni. He had the impression that the Aoife girl was somewhat of a complainer but the Human servants didn't feel they had the authority to upbraid her. With an irritated sigh, the old woman loaded a tray with the omelet plates, then added a small vase of flowers, some silverware, and the teapot. "Here, Hamoni. You can serve—"

She didn't have a chance to finish, as Madric appeared in the doorway, his hair tousled. He was still wearing the clothes he'd had on the day before and was carrying an empty bread basket. "We've decided to take our meal on the dining terrace, Pasha-my-dear," he told her playfully. "Hamoni can serve us out there, when it's ready. Are there any more biscuits?" he added, holding out the basket like a beggar child offering a hat for loose coins.

Teine made a mental note of the kitchen matron's name, now that he'd finally heard it. It'd be easy to remember, as he and Leis had had a character in one of their earlier stories with the same name. Likely, they'd heard someone mention this Pasha at one point or another, and it had stuck. He watched with interest as Pasha refilled Madric's bread basket with a fresh batch of biscuits while the magician waited patiently.

"Perhaps I'll even get to eat some of these," Madric joked, eyeing the steaming pile with eager eyes.

"I take it Marne's feeling better?" Hamoni asked with a grin.

"And then some," Madric added, his expression jovial. "I don't know whether to be alarmed or relieved. He was bold enough to snatch the last one right out of his father's hand!"

"Saints preserve us!" Pasha chortled. She added an extra layer of biscuits to the basket for good measure. Hamoni picked up the tray with the omelettes and followed Madric out of the kitchen.

Teine could hear Madric returning to his brother and nephew on the dining terrace overlooking the courtyard, while Pasha brought the scrambled eggs and a plate of fried ham to the servant's table. There was no standing on ceremony; as soon as all the items were on the table, everyone simply helped themselves. Teine hesitated, looking at Hamoni's empty spot for a moment before digging in. He didn't have to wait long, as the Aoife peasant came flouncing in and plopped herself down on the bench next to Pasha a moment later.

"It took him long enough," Hamoni grumbled. "I can't believe he did it again!"

Teine, unsure of what or whom she was speaking, decided to remain silent.

"You've got to be kidding," Kenneth replied, keeping his volume low so as not to be overheard. "Again? I've seen Aoife take more active interest in the lives of their *servants* than that man takes in his own son. It's shameful."

Teine couldn't help himself. After swallowing what he was chewing, he asked, "What did he do?"

Hamoni eagerly turned to face him and hissed in his ear, "He was home for three whole days, and didn't even make the time to see Marne. Even when he was in the hospital and nearly died!"

Teine shoveled in another fork full of eggs and chewed while he contemplated the information. Even though he and Master Solmurrian hadn't gotten off on the best foot, Teine was surprised and more than a little saddened. Perhaps Madric had stepped into the boy's life to fill the void left by his father's disinterest? Though, on second thought, Madric, the magician, was very interested in magical oddities—an appellation which certainly described his nephew. Teine's heart sank. *But*, he rallied, *it could explain why Marne still had a nanny, although that was also easily explained by Marne being so child-like.*

Even with so much evidence, Teine was reluctant to condemn Lord Solmurrian without further information. Not every Aoife parent was an attentive one, but that didn't mean they didn't love their children. He was equally reluctant to automatically cast Madric in the role of the completely altruistic doting uncle; Madric had surely reaped benefits from having his nephew there to study.

But judging from the conversation going on among the other Humans, some things were abundantly clear. Madric's people loved him. Lord Solmurrian's didn't. And Marne needed companionship and possibly even protection far beyond what a nanny could offer. Teine's role in the grand scheme made itself apparent with a resounding crack of sudden insight: he realized that he wasn't privileged above and beyond the other Humans. Instead, he was in training to be a companion to Marne in the style to which the child was accustomed.

The other Humans assumed his silence meant shocked outrage, and they all began offering examples of how Lord Solmurrian neglected his son. From what Teine was able to sort out of the hastily whispered conversation, this sort of thing happened all the time. It seemed that months might pass between the Lord's visits home, and even when he was at the Solmurry Demesne, he treated his son as an obligation that was strictly optional. By contrast, Teine's own sire, who only saw him a few times a year, always greeted him with pride and enthusiasm and would have leaped at the chance see him more often. That Lord Solmurrian had opportunities to see his son and passed them up boggled Teine's mind.

"At least he lets him take all the classes he wants and visit with Madric whenever they wish," Hamoni finished, with grudging approval. "It's a good thing that boy has an uncle who cares, otherwise..." She trailed off sulkily, and Kenneth nodded his agreement.

"So..." Teine asked, looking back and forth between the adult servants for guidance. He'd felt he'd found a real treasure trove of information and advice as to how to best perform duties that hadn't even been spelled out for him. "What do you think I should do? I don't want to get the master angry at me, and I want to do a good job, but no one has given me much in the way of instruction."

Before anyone could answer, one of the bells fixed above the kitchen exit chimed once.

Hamoni groaned and rose from her place at the bench. "I swear, I only just left them! What more could he..."

Then the bell chimed again, several times in a row, as if whoever was ringing it was frantic.

When the bell stopped Teine was surprised to see the sudden, tense expressions around the table. "Easy, easy," Hamoni assured them, her voice calm and carrying over the bell. "Remember, we have a very demanding guest. It might not mean what..." The bell started again in earnest, ringing without stopping. Hamoni swept dramatically from the room in a swirl of long skirts, heading out through the dining room. Without a word, Pasha got to her feet, grabbed a small picnic hamper down from one of the shelves and began filling it with portable foodstuffs.

Hamoni was back in an instant and had gone pale under her golden complexion. "Teine! Report to the dining terrace at once. Take your bag. Do you have shoes on? Good! Now, go!"

"What is it? Raiders?" demanded Kenneth, rising to his feet so suddenly his big belly lifted the table an inch before dropping it to the ground with a plate-rattling din. Both the Human boys stood up so fast they knocked their bench over.

"Worse," Hamoni hissed. "Inspectors."

Red-faced with rage but wide-eyed with alarm, Kenneth swore under his breath. "Those swiving sons of whores! Can't they just leave us alone?"

Although the headman spoke softly, his harsh words fell hard on Teine's ears. Although boys his age often cursed in play, Teine rarely heard strong language being used in earnest. Throwing his satchel over his shoulder, he fled the room, spurred on not by the tone of anger in Kenneth's voice, but by the fear he heard there as well. He rushed into the formal dining room looking for the door that led to the terrace. Movement caught his eye, and he could see Madric, his brother the lord, and Marne through the leaded glass windows on the doors leading outside to the dining terrace. Marne and his two Aoife relatives all seemed to be staring at something in the distance. Marne had even climbed up on a chair for a better vantage point.

Hurrying out onto the terrace, Teine craned his neck to see what the others were looking at. A distinctive scarlet and gold carriage, pulled by white horses, was edging up the winding driveway toward the tower. "It's a bloody lucky thing we decided to dine up here rather than down in the courtyard," Master Solmurrian was telling his brother. "Otherwise we wouldn't have seen them until they were upon us. But if only you'd done your job, we wouldn't be in this mess!"

"I don't want to hear it now," Madric growled, with real menace. Teine saw Marne catch his eye, his expression pleading. "I told you, the storm interfered..."

"Can't we put him back in the basement?"

The pale, barefoot child looked both helpless and frightened, and Teine realized with a start that Marne still wore his strange alien features, unguarded for the whole world to see.

"If I've told you once, I've told you a thousand times..." Madric roared at his brother. "They *always* check the basement. Always! And there's only one way in and one way out of any room here. You know as well as I do that they suspect something. There's no hiding him this time, unless he..."

Teine tuned them out the instant he realized the enormity of the situation. Inspectors from the Church would be there within minutes and Marne was unable to be hidden away, either with the use of crafty magics or in a room no one would find. That really only left one solution, and Teine's eyes scanned the terrace. After a moment, he cleared his throat.

"Does that path lead to the beach?" he whispered to Marne, pointing. From the terrace, a stairway led down to the bowl-shaped courtyard. Stairways led out of the courtyard in many directions, but Teine could see that one in particular led down to a sandy beach, where he could see foamy waves lapping the shore.

Marne nodded wordlessly, his strange eyes wide and frightened as a kitten's.

Teine bit his lip as a plan came to mind. He hated speaking up and interrupting the angry lord, but it was worth the risk. "I can take him to the beach. *Right* now."

Suddenly the two Aoife men stopped arguing and turned to look at him. Master Solmurrian glared, but Madric grinned. Then both spoke at once.

"That's a good idea. Hide him in plain sight," Madric crowed.

"You fool, that will never work," Master Solmurrian growled.

Madric put his hand on his brother's arm, nodding at Teine in a way that indicated he'd better get moving. As Teine shuffled his shoulder bag into a more comfortable position with the strap across his shoulder muscle and chest, he beckoned for Marne to climb on him in piggyback fashion. Like a monkey, Marne crawled onto the Human boy's broad back, wrapping his skinny legs around Teine's waist. Although the child weighed hardly anything, Teine could tell that some of Marne's weight rested on his satchel, providing the boy with a little extra security and a bit of a seat.

"It's a good plan," Madric was convincing his younger brother. "They aren't interested in Marne. They're here for me and my work, as usual. They probably think they're being kind, checking on our safety after such a bad storm. If the boys go down to the beach and play in plain sight, it'll look very natural and likely not even be noticed."

"If we see anyone coming that we don't recognize, we can make a run for it," Teine added. The carriage had now rounded the bend.

For several long seconds, Master Solmurrian scowled at Teine but Teine did not back down. "Go, then. They're almost upon us," he finally agreed.

"Wait!" cried Hamoni, banging open the terrace door hard enough to rattle the glass in its panes. "Take this!" Either she'd been eavesdropping or she'd anticipated Teine's idea but either way, she was prepared. She pushed the small hamper that Pasha had packed into Teine's hands and threw a white sun-cloak over Marne's fair head and shoulders. Now they really looked prepared to play on the beach.

"Thank you," Teine told her gratefully. "Wish us luck."

"Luck. Now get going." Madric snapped, hurrying them along. "Be careful, but act natural. Don't come back until we send someone for you."

Teine noticed Marne looking at his father for acknowledgment or direction, but the master didn't meet his son's gaze. Instead, he shielded his eyes from the sun and stole a glance toward the carriage, muttering, "Getting closer now. Better hurry."

Inwardly, Teine grimaced at the master's brusque dismissal, but kept his tongue and nodded in acquiescence. With no further comment, he turned and headed down the steep stone stairs, carrying the hamper under one arm and doing his best to support Marne with his other. The cobblestones of the courtyard loomed far below. He felt awkward about witnessing the master's coldness toward Marne. He was just wondering how the child dealt with his feelings when, surprisingly, Marne chuckled. Taken aback, Teine asked, "What's so funny, master?"

"Faithful steed," Marne giggled, "And don't call me master. You won't do it again, will you?"

Teine grinned. Faithful steed, indeed. It was the most whimsical, childlike thing the boy had said yet. Teine returned the jest in kind, replying, "Neigh," and prompting more laughter from his charge. The pair descended the stairs from the terrace to the courtyard. Once they made it to the bottom of the stairs, Teine increased his speed, breaking into a fast jog.

"The pun is the lowest form of humor," Marne intoned. "But I like them anyway." They breezed past the decorative fountain, and Teine jumped in alarm when a watery figure rose up out of the pool and made a swipe at them.

"Was that...?" Teine started to ask, but he'd just gotten to the next batch of stairs, which led down to the beach, and concentrated his efforts on a rapid and safe descent.

"A water elemental," Marne confirmed. "His name's Foosh, and he lives in the fountain. He's always cranky after a storm, but you can meet him later."

Shaking his head in wonder, Teine hitched Marne higher up on his back and pushed aside the remnants of a fallen palm tree as he sped down to the beach.

Chapter 3: Hiding in Plain Sight

A couple hours later, when Marne had wrapped himself in his sun-cloak and dozed off in the shade of a battered palm tree, Teine had time to sit down under another tree and crack open his journals and sketchbooks.

It had been an eventful morning, he reflected as he ground his bare toes into the soft white sand. This was the nicest beach he could ever remember having visited. Directly below the tower, it was protected by a cove with craggy stones jutting out like sharp teeth to impale any unwary or overly large sailing vessel. There were no sounds other than the rhythmic pounding of the surf and the occasional call of a songbird. There weren't any sharp rocks in the sand, but there were plenty of colorful seashells for the hunting. Small, silvery fish could be clearly seen in the shallows.

A pile of interesting stones and seashells, a half-built sand castle, and the seagull-picked remnants of their snacks stood mute testimony to the enjoyable time they'd had before Marne had grown weary. The two boys hadn't spoken much, but the knife-edged pressure of the situation had forged a bond between them. When they'd noticed figures on the dining balcony watching them, Marne waved cheerfully as if he hadn't a care in the world. Teine suppressed a nervous giggle at the impulsive gesture, which made Marne laugh outright. And though the circumstances seemed dire, the laughter itself lifted some of the tension. Teine was surprised at how comfortable the silence had been, and how similar Marne was to many of the other intelligent boys he'd known.

He'd expected Aoife to be different, somehow. But then again, Marne wasn't exactly an Aoife.

What was he? Teine had been pondering that question all morning, but was practical enough to admit that if Marne himself and other educated minds hadn't answered that question after a century, it was unlikely that Teine would have an answer any time soon.

Allowing his thoughts to drift pleasantly, Teine opened his sketchbook and made quick field drawings of a couple of birds he'd never seen before. After coaxing them closer with the leftover crumbs of their lunch, he was able to record the shape of their bills, and what colors went where on their feathery bodies. He was so absorbed in his work, he didn't hear the footsteps approaching.

"Hey, you!" Hamoni called out. She'd taken off her sandals and was approaching him on tip-toe, with the hem of her skirt hoisted enough to show her petticoats and dainty ankles. The wind whipped her mane of hair into a frenzy, exposing the graceful curve of her neck and the delicate points of her ears. Even if she was an Aoife, Teine was beginning to think she was the loveliest girl he'd ever seen. The beach suited her.

"The inspectors cleared off half an hour ago, so it's safe to come back." As Marne stirred at the sound of her voice, Hamoni wrinkled her nose at Teine. "You probably should have left your shirt on. You look like a lobster in a pot."

If Teine hadn't been so sunburned, she might have noticed his self-conscious blush. "It was a new shirt, and I didn't want to get it dirty," he explained as he assessed the damage. Sometimes, it just didn't pay to be a redhead. He suspected he'd be really uncomfortable later.

"Did Father leave, too?" Marne asked, stretching and yawning. Alarmed, Teine blinked twice. He hadn't noticed before, but Marne's teeth were different, too. Like most Aoife, he had larger canines than Humans did, but it seemed this trait was exaggerated in the boy. It made his sleepy yawn look positively threatening, especially if one wasn't expecting it.

"No, he's still here. I suspect he and Madric will still be verbally fencing when we return," Hamoni answered.

Marne sighed. "Ah, the manly arts of small talk and sibling rivalry." He glanced at Teine, with a knowing expression on his youthful face. "They pretend to like each other, for my sake. And they're not even good at it." After rising to his feet, Marne shook out his sun-cloak and draped it over Teine's reddened shoulders. "I think you're well-done."

Suppressing a chuckle, Hamoni nodded. "Agreed."

Unlike Teine, Marne had benefitted from his time in the sun. Most of the time he'd been out, he'd been sitting on his sun-cloak, not wearing it. The child had already begun to tan, and the faint golden brown looked far healthier than his earlier pallor. He seemed well-rested and almost chipper. Teine suspected whatever his ailment had been, he was on the mend.

They gathered up their belongings and Teine carried the lot. Together Hamoni and the two boys made their way up the steep stone stairway back to the tower. Although they were heavily shaded from the early afternoon sun by trees and undergrowth, going back up was far more exhausting than their frantic trip down to the beach had been. After only a minute, Teine looked back over his shoulder to see how Hamoni and Marne were doing and realized he was leaving them both behind. Having never gotten a chance to compare his long strides to the smaller, daintier steps of Aoife, Teine was appalled at how much he'd outpaced them. Immediately he retraced his steps, scooping Marne up to carry him piggyback. Although his tender skin screamed in protest, it was fitting penance for his earlier thoughtlessness. With the extra burden, it was easy for him to slow his pace to walk next to Hamoni.

"What happens now?" Teine asked. He didn't care which of them answered. It felt odd to come from a highly regimented life, where he had a schedule and a calendar he was expected to keep, to a life where his schedule was dictated by the whims of others. It wasn't unpleasant. But even if he had more leisure time than he was used to, and more quality entertainments available during that leisure time, he still liked to know what to expect.

"Madric wants to see both of you back in his workroom," Hamoni told them. "Kenneth and the boys got the mess from the storm mostly cleaned up and have gone into town for new glass. It's a pleasant day, so we thought we'd finish Teine's evaluation."

"What about my bracelet?" Marne asked, resting his pointy chin on Teine's shoulder. "I feel rather naked without it." Teine could feel how cool the boy's skin was against his, and he was beginning to fear for his poor sunburned hide.

Hamoni frowned. "We think we've figured out the problem. We *think*," she emphasized.

It was Marne's turn to frown, and he did, biting his lip as if he were nervous. "What happens if it doesn't work?"

"It'll work. You worry too much."

"It's *my* face," Marne reminded her. "That means I'm allowed to worry." The boy sounded very grave, indeed.

* * *

Half an hour later, Teine was back on the stool in Madric's workroom. The room itself was much the same as it had been first time he'd seen it, except that most of the windows had been broken out and had not yet been replaced. A cool breeze that smelled of the ocean teased his hair, and Teine also caught the scent of the lush flowers growing in the courtyard. Hamoni sat at her desk with Marne's bracelet, writing in a stiff new book that she had to hold open. Marne sprawled on the floor with the bucket that contained the water elemental between his knees. It sounded like he was talking to it, trying to coax the watery being into activity by offering it a small model boat.

Lord Solmurrian had gone into town with Kenneth and his boys to buy replacement glass for the shattered windows. As the tower was part of the Solmurry holdings, its repairs were the responsibility of the estate.

Although Teine was privately appalled by the Aoife lord's indifference to his son, he'd made a conscious decision not to let it bother him. Marne seemed fine. He was a tough little fellow. Teine was pondering over the tower staff's gossip about Master Solmurrian's neglectful parenting when Madric stepped over and peered at him intently. Apparently the examination was beginning where it left off.

The magician stared at Teine, his piercing blue eyes serious. Teine could feel the heavy weight of judgment in the Aoife's gaze. The moment had arrived: Teine would find out if he had any latent magical abilities. After the excitement of the last day and Madric's descriptions of the monastery, Teine wasn't sure *what* he wanted the verdict to be.

"I can't remember for the life of me," Madric finally admitted, "What were we speaking of, when we were interrupted?" Teine let out a breath he didn't realize he'd been holding. "All I remember is that there was some finer point that seemed very significant at the time. And now it completely escapes me."

Teine wracked his brain, replaying the events he remembered. The excitement of the storm, the breaking glass, and everything else seemed to have trumped any memory he'd had of the details of their conversation. "Me neither. Sorry."

"So, did Teine have any magic?" Marne asked. When he glanced up at them, the toy boat in the bucket began to heave violently, as if in a miniature storm on a miniature sea. Marne didn't notice, but the instant he looked back, the elemental splattered him in the face with stray droplets. "I suppose I deserved that," the boy sighed, wiping his face with his sleeve. "At least he didn't make me look as though I've wet my pants." Distracted by Marne's antics, Teine smiled down at the boy.

"All the usual tests were negative," Madric confirmed, "But because of his bloodline and what he said that I can't remember, we'll retest him again next year. Besides, by then the test procedure for mind magics should be completed at the University."

"That'd be more useful than the standard tests, for him," Hamoni piped up.

Marne nodded his agreement, then abandoned his watery playmate to go look out the window.

Suddenly, Madric clapped his hands together with glee. "I remember!" he crowed. "Premonitions! You knew your Amagorra was going to be ill!"

Although he was unwilling to contradict Madric, Teine couldn't help but wrinkle his nose at the thought. His inner skeptic just couldn't endorse Madric's interpretation of the events without actual *evidence*. "That could just have been coincidence, don't you think?"

The Aoife magician didn't seem to mind at all. In fact, he fairly beamed. "Possible latent talents, a good head in a crisis, and a skeptical, scientific mind! You're quite a find, lad. Marne did very well in choosing you."

Teine suspected he was blushing under the burden of such unexpected praise, but with his sunburn he was sure no one could tell. "Thank you," he replied, in what he hoped was a gracious, not conceited, tone. "But what about my bloodline? Do we have magicians?"

Madric continued to stare at him thoughtfully. "Yes and no. It would depend on how you define 'magicians.' Some don't consider mind magics to be magic at all, but a gift directly from the Gods."

"Can he borrow a book, Uncle?" asked Marne, looking back over his shoulder at them. "There are some good examples in that Greeves Academy text, and the writing isn't too far over the top. He can read up, then you can answer any more specific questions he has, once he has a good basic foundation of knowledge on the subject."

"I have that one in my room," Hamoni volunteered. "I'll get it for him later."

"Get the one on divining, too," Marne added, without looking back up.

Madric blinked once. "What does divining have to do with this?"

"Nothing." Marne plucked the boat up out of the bucket, then wagged a finger at the watery being. "Play nice," he scolded, before replacing the toy. To Madric, he added, "Nothing except…"

Teine could see the boy floundering for an excuse, and although he had no idea why Marne wanted a book on divining, helping Marne get what he wanted was part of his job. "It's for me," he interjected.

"You?" Madric raised an eyebrow.

"Yes, sir," Teine nodded, feigning an earnest expression. "I'm writing some action-adventure stories with my sister, and I want them to be exciting, but also accurate. Having access to real information about the different kinds of magic is a… a dream come true."

Madric chuckled, his features changing from skeptical to indulgent in an instant. "Stories, eh? Are they any good?"

"I think so, but I might be biased."

"They're good!" Marne chirped. "But they'll be print-worthy if he can do the magic parts better. Might even make them some money."

Madric pondered for an instant, before nodding his consent to Hamoni. "Divining now. Then anything else he wants to read later." Turning back to the boys, he shot a stern look their way. "But I reserve final veto before you try to distribute or submit them anywhere. I owe it to the craft to be sure you're accurate, but not scaring people unnecessarily." He rubbed his chin, eyes lost in thought for a moment. "Stories like that would fill a big need right now. Too many people fear magic, and their fear is fueled by their ignorance. If I vet the magic parts for you, I'll be the one in the line of fire if "The Big, Orwellian Theocracy" decides to complain."

Teine was privately taken aback by the unexpected turn their conversation had taken. His mind whirled with all the sudden possibilities. He had to fight a sudden urge to flee the room, seek out his notebook, and begin charting all of the exciting plot ideas that had just leapt, unbidden, into his mind. Then, another thought surprised him. *Has Marne already read our stories, or was he just following my lead? And did Madric just agree to edit—and endorse—our work? Leis is going to faint dead away!*

Madric, however, was unaware of the storm he'd just caused. Beckoning to Marne, the magician changed the subject. "All right then, nephew of mine. It's your turn on the hot seat." He gestured for Teine to stand, and Madric lifted Marne up and placed him on the examination stool. "So, tell me how it went this time."

"It lasted longer, I think," Marne began, rubbing his wrist unconsciously where the bracelet would normally sit. "And I didn't have a single person comment on it, so perhaps the shielding worked better this time and no one paid it any attention."

Teine had drifted over to take Marne's spot at the window to enjoy the view, but was listening intently to the conversation. It was all so fascinating. This window into the secret world of magics was so unexpected and so... well, words escaped him. He supposed it must be commonplace for the people who dealt with it every day, but for the vast majority of people it was unheard of. He felt very privileged to be a party to such radical conversation.

Madric scribbled a few notes in a book, taking down Marne's response. "Did you see anyone looking at it directly, as if they could see it?"

Suddenly, Teine put the pieces together and realized they were talking about the bracelet that Marne wore. "I remember seeing it," he volunteered—then immediately wished he hadn't, as all three of them turned to look at him sharply.

"What did you see?" Madric asked him, point blank.

Teine swallowed, hoping he hadn't gotten himself in trouble. "That chunky gold bracelet, with the engraved pattern on it. It caught my eye because it looks too big for him."

Madric and Hamoni exchanged a look that Teine couldn't read, before Madric spoke again. "We'll definitely have to test him again sometime." Marne simply sat on the stool, swinging his feet and looking interested.

Teine found himself blurting out his questions. "Does everyone magic have hidden jewelry?" he asked. "Or is it only for special occasions? Is *all* of Marne's jewelry supposed to be hidden?" he asked, giving Marne some serious scrutiny in case there was something he'd missed earlier. "Because I see his necklace and ring, too."

"No, no," Madric assured him. "Marne's bracelet is a special case. We crafted the masking spell into it because the bracelet is so crucial to hiding Marne's features and inhibiting some of his—"

"Wait a second," Hamoni interrupted. "*What* ring?"

Madric blinked, seemingly blind to the existence of the ring that was as plain on Marne's right thumb as was the nose on his face. "Yes, Teine, what ring are you speaking of?"

Teine, and Marne too, pointed at Marne's right thumb. "This ring." Marne took it off and set it on the edge of Madric's desk. "I've had it forever. It was my mother's."

"Well, I'll be damned," Madric muttered under his breath, blinking at the ring that, for him, didn't exist until just then.

Marne shrugged. "You can have a look at it, if you want. Just don't break it or keep it. I want it back. It was my mother's," he repeated.

Like a hawk pouncing on a field mouse, Madric swept up the ring and went to one of his workbenches, Hamoni trailing in his wake. The two of them pulled out some instruments, plus a bag of fine powder, and then began talking about "original magics" and guessing at the approximate age of the item in question. Their general consensus was that it was "very old, and primitive."

Teine, feeling overwhelmed and more than a little confused, padded over to stand next to Marne. Marne looked up at Teine, his expression mildly reproachful.

"I wish you hadn't told him about the ring."

Teine frowned. "I'm sorry. I've never met anyone with even one magic item of their own before. You have *two*! And one of those was even made for you!" He hated the idea of so casually betraying something Marne would have liked to keep to himself. "So," he asked sheepishly, "How long have you known the ring was magic?"

The strange boy sighed, a wistful expression on his alien features as he nodded. "I've always known. But it was nice to have a secret that was mine alone."

Although Teine had never had any secrets of his own, he understood. "I'm really sorry."

Marne shrugged it off. "It's all right. I know you didn't mean to. Besides, now that the secret's out, maybe I can learn more about it. It feels… important… to me, somehow." He watched Hamoni and Madric for a minute, then asked them, "Can you read the inscription?"

"There's an *inscription*?"

The boy sighed, then grinned at Teine with a subtle hint of mischief in his alien eyes. "Yes. On the inside."

Teine couldn't help but wonder, so he asked, "How many other people know about that ring?"

"Your Amagorra noticed it, when she first came to work in the nursery," Marne told him. "Other than that, just us, and my father. He gave it to me when my mother died."

"But weren't you only a baby then? Or am I remembering wrong?"

"I remember *everything*," Marne insisted quietly. "I even remember Mother wearing it. She looked at it often, as if it were important to her, too."

Teine was becoming more intrigued by this story the more he heard, and he didn't even care if it was true or if Marne was making up details to fill in the natural gaps in a young child's memory. Then again, perhaps whatever kind of creature Marne was really *could* remember everything. "So, why can't people see these things? How does that kind of magic work?"

Marne glanced over his shoulder, as if to be sure Madric and Hamoni were still deeply involved in their examination, then he leaned closer to Teine. "I don't know all the details," he confided. "But I'll tell you what I do know, as I understand it to be. The art of making things appear different than they are or concealing them completely is called 'illusion.'"

Although Teine had heard this before, he didn't dare interrupt the young master to tell him so. He had a feeling that Marne's explanation would be simple, to the point, and useful to him in the future for all the stories he planned to write with Leis.

"Illusions are one of the most simple and therefore most durable magics, but they can be easily thwarted if a person is alert to their presence. For example, now that Madric and Hamoni know about the ring, they'll probably always be able to see it." Marne hopped down from the stool to look out the window, before continuing. "It wouldn't surprise me one bit if that old ring was around for the last big Awakening... or longer." Marne read the skepticism on Teine's face and added an earnest, "It just *feels* that old."

"So, what does it do?"

Marne shrugged artlessly. "I don't know. It might have had another magical function at some point, or it even still might. But it could be so old that the illusion is the only thing that's left. Or," he continued, looking thoughtful, "It could continue to Awaken, like some of the other items that are turning up. I have strong feelings for it, it's my most prized possession, so who knows?" Marne gave him a sidelong, mischievous grin, rubbing his hands together in mock villainy. "It could even be for 'ruling them all.'"

Teine chuckled, "If you ever call it 'Precious,' I promise you, I'm going to skip tattling to Madric and just get straight to running away from home."

Marne grinned, careful to keep that mouthful of dangerous-looking teeth well hidden under his shy smile. "You read those books, too?"

Teine nodded fervently. "I had a hard time getting used to all the racial slurs, but I suppose some people might actually talk like that in uncivilized lands. I don't think any of the races were called by their proper names even once."

"I wondered about that, too. Do you suppose the people in those stories were like us? Er... us Aoife, I mean. Some people believe they're historical, and not fiction."

Teine thought about it for a second. He'd had a similar debate with Seymour once after they'd both taken the same Ancient Literature and Mythology class. He decided it couldn't hurt to be bold with his opinion. He was beginning to trust Marne enough to risk disagreeing with him. Considering the gulf between their stations in life, that was really saying something.

"I think they're fine examples of epic storytelling," Teine ventured. "But I believe they have to be fiction."

Interested, Marne turned from the window and tilted his head toward Teine. "I agree with you, but I'm curious as to your line of reasoning."

Just as he was about to explain himself, Teine noticed that Madric and Hamoni had abandoned their tinkering with the ring and were approaching with both the ring and Marne's bracelet. Suddenly, he felt very self-conscious. It was one thing to share his personal theories with another boy, albeit one that owned him. But it was quite another to broadcast his opinions loudly to adults and his betters.

"Ah, I'm quite relieved," Madric said. Without further preamble, he picked up Marne and plunked him back on the examination stool. "I'm hoping that if Marne gets someone he can talk to about some of his interests, he'll stop pestering his father to let him go to the University."

Marne submitted to the hoisting, but wrinkled his nose at Madric's suggestion. Even with his odd features, the expression was whimsical.

"I've already taken all the classes I want from the tutors I can get out here," Marne explained. The tone of his voice broadcast his frustration very clearly. It was the voice of a child who'd had his plans thwarted, but was desperately trying to avoid giving the appearance of whining. "All three Ancient Literature classes were great! But the fourth is only taught at the University level."

"Someday, someday," Madric consoled him, then changed the subject deftly. "So, how's your imaginary friend doing? I haven't heard you talk about her lately. Do you still see her?" His eyes danced with merriment. "Have you gotten her to show up for any of the little tea parties you throw for her?"

"We *all* take tea in the afternoon," Marne returned, raising an eyebrow. Teine could do nothing but marvel at Marne's sudden change in demeanor. The instant before, he'd been a supplicating child trying to win a key adult over to his point of view. Now, he was an adult taking offense at another adult's mocking. "If I choose to set a place for an absent friend, in her memory, it doesn't diminish my experience to the status of 'a little tea party.' If you had a good friend like mine, you'd do it too."

"Easy, easy," Madric consoled. Teine noticed the magician's smile was still slightly patronizing. "I stand corrected."

"Also," Marne continued without missing a beat. "Just because we only get to see each other when we're asleep doesn't mean she's imaginary. Besides, *all* realities are at least somewhat valid. That's the core principle behind why magic works at all."

Madric sighed, wiped the smile off his face, and seemed to face the remainder of his dressing down with good humor. "So you've told me."

"And to answer your question: yes. I saw her last night."

Hamoni and Madric exchanged a look, then suddenly Hamoni began scribbling madly in her book. Madric's features had folded into a thoughtful frown. Teine could sense right away that something in the conversation was a matter of some gravity, at least to Hamoni. Madric still seemed more amused than serious.

"Well, that rules out possession, at least," Hamoni muttered, heaving a sigh. "The warding in the basement would prevent it."

Marne gave an annoyed little snort. "I'm not possessed, Hamoni. I might be some kind of strange monster that no one's ever seen before, but I'm not possessed." Then, he turned to Madric, defiance in his eyes. "And she's *not* imaginary, either."

"And that puts us back at square one," Hamoni sighed. She handed the bracelet and ring to Madric, then excused herself from the room, closing the door behind her with some force as she left.

"Pshaw. All the drama," Madric muttered, waving the departed Aoife girl away. Then he turned to his nephew, trying to diffuse his discomfiture. "You're not a monster, Marne. You're just…"

"Just what?" Marne interrupted. Teine had watched Hamoni go, unable to stop himself from feeling badly for her. Obviously proving Marne's imaginary friend to be real was very important to her. He decided he might ask her about it later. But it was Marne's reply to Madric that pulled him firmly back into the conversation. "Deformed? A freak? A *Changeling*?"

"I was going to say *special*. Unique," Madric volunteered. His tone was surprisingly gentle, and Teine was touched to realize that the magician cared very deeply for his nephew, regardless of who or what he was.

While they'd been talking, Madric had absently slipped Marne's ring over his own finger and was pulling it off to give back. When Marne took it and put it on, Madric gasped.

"Did my eyes deceive me, or did that ring just change size to fit you?"

Marne shrugged. "Your eyes told the truth." He was starting to look bored.

The magician's eyes rolled back in his head, and Teine was afraid for a moment Madric was having a seizure, until he let out a whoop of joy and did a little dance. Marne tilted his head inquisitively at his uncle, then gave Teine a little shrug and shook his head in mock exasperation.

"Can I borrow your ring again?" Madric asked, holding out his hand with an eager, elated expression on his face. "If I can figure out how that sizing enchantment works on a metal item, I can fix your bracelet so it will fit snugly and not bang around."

Marne nodded with real enthusiasm, and within an instant had pried the ring off his finger and given it back to Madric. "Would it help to see its workings?"

"Do you think you're strong enough to show us?" Madric asked. Skepticism and concern warred for control over his angular, handsome face. "The ring didn't seem important enough to bother with, until we realized it could change size."

Marne paused to give one of his trademark shrugs. He'd been wrestling the bucket and water elemental up to the table, but was having trouble on his own. "Sure." Without missing a beat, Teine reached over and grabbed the bucket by the handle, lifting it the rest of the way.

"Thanks," Marne grinned, casually dodging a flick of droplets from the elemental. "Spritz will want to see everything."

"A quick peek is all we'd need to get going," Madric answered. He looked thoughtful, as if trying to plan something out. "All right, here's what I think we should do..." He was interrupted by a polite chime from a wooden box that hung on the wall. "Oh, damn it all! Looks like your father's returned from town." The magician looked as disappointed as a convict who'd been offered a pardon, only to find he was going to be executed after all.

Teine stole a quick glance at Marne to see if the child had any enthusiasm at the prospect of seeing his sire, and was unsurprised by Marne's seeming indifference. "I doubt he's in any hurry to seek me out," Marne replied. "So, we probably have a few minutes before I'm summoned. If he calls for me at all."

Madric seemed to think quickly. "All right then, here's what we do," he said. "Marne, give me a quick look at the threads on that ring, then run off to find Hamoni and show her, too. Once she's seen, tell her we're going to work on your bracelet and send her up here. Then, if you're tired, you can take a nap in the Blue Room. I had Pasha bring your things up from the basement this morning."

"Maybe later Teine and I can set up our own rooms." Marne suggested. "If they're mostly cleaned out, that is."

Nodding, Madric glanced back and forth between his nephew and Teine. "That's a good possibility. Now, show me the ring's workings, so you can get going."

Obediently, Marne hopped off the stool and advanced on his uncle to place the ring in the palm of Madric's hand.

The magician seemed outwardly calm, but Teine couldn't help but notice Madric's hand trembling ever so slightly. His own stomach did a sympathetic fluttering of excited butterflies.

Marne covered Madric's large hand with his own tiny one, hovering less than an inch above the ring without touching it. Then, he closed his eyes to concentrate. Teine found himself holding his breath. After three heartbeats, Marne whispered, "Now," and opened his eyes.

Teine gasped in wonderment and skittered back two steps at what he saw.

Chapter 4: The Fabric of Magic

The area surrounding the ring, Madric's, and Marne's hands exploded with translucent, gossamer threads of color. Even though he had retreated a couple steps initially, Teine began moving closer to get a better view of the spectacle. Once the initial shock wore off, he flushed with a heady rush of discovery and excitement. "The fabric of magic," he whispered.

The phenomenon illuminated more than just the magic of the ring. Some of the threads of light and energy wrapped around and through both Marne's and his uncle's hands. The spectral energy strands that suffused and interlaced Madric's hand glowed with a rich green, like the color of immature cornstalks reaching toward the summer sun. Marne's slender hand, above his uncle's, was augmented with threads of painfully vivid blue.

Their individual threads seemed to pulse in time like two heartbeats. Marne's electric blue fluttered fast and irregular like the beat of a butterfly's wings, while Madric's green was slower and steadier.

Teine looked into Marne's odd alien eyes. "Is this...?"

Marne nodded solemnly, "This is what *everything* looks like to me. This just lets you see it, too."

Then Marne pulled his hand away. The bright blue vanished, leaving Madric's green and the threadwork that must have belonged to the ring itself. The ring's threads were made up of many multicolored strands of varying thicknesses and subtleties—if anything made purely of magic and energy could have a thickness.

"It won't last long. Put it on so you can see," Marne prompted.

Madric shook himself and cleared his throat. "All right, then. Let's see how this works." He took the ring off his palm and slid it over one finger.

The whole woven pattern expanded, the colored lights flowing like rivulets of quicksilver. The magic seemed to make the physical silver malleable enough to accommodate Madric's bigger finger, then able to contract slightly for a perfect fit. The faint threads brightened in a subtle rainbow of complex knots.

"There, there!" Madric shouted, pointing to the ring with his other hand. There was a hunger in the magician's eyes that made Teine's stomach flutter with unease. It almost looked like envy, as Madric glanced from his nephew to the magical effect the boy had created. "Did you see the red? Could that be the enchanter's auric signature? Could it be…"

"I wish I knew," Marne sighed. "I still have no idea how to interpret it." The boy's voice was breathy, as if he'd exerted himself considerably. When Teine pried his eyes away from the ring, he could see that Marne was back to his drawn and slightly peaked state. He immediately planned a dash down to the kitchen for refreshments for the boy as soon as possible.

Madric frowned with disappointment when Marne had no new insights for him. But by the time the threads had faded, the Aoife magician had scribbled two pages of notes and seemed at least momentarily satisfied. With a smile and a pat on the back, he dropped the ring into Marne's waiting hands and propelled him toward the door with a gentle shove.

"Go find Hamoni," he told his nephew. "Give her the ring and show her exactly what you showed me. Then go take your nap. And hopefully, if we're lucky, by the time you wake up we'll have enchanted your bracelet so it can size itself as well."

Teine found himself frowning, despite Madric's jovial mood. Was the man completely oblivious to the fact that Marne looked as though he could fall over at any moment?

But Marne didn't seem to mind. "That would be nice," the boy agreed, starting toward the door. "As it is now, the bracelet's so burdensome that I find myself wondering where the ball and chain are attached." Marne glanced over his shoulder to see how his joke had been received.

Teine couldn't help but grin back at him. Marne was a clever and personable little fellow. He fully expected that Leis would pronounce him "adorable" once she got to know him—if she hadn't already. He was about to comment on the ball and chain joke when he realized Marne was holding the door for him.

"Oh no," Madric intoned, shaking his head. "Go on. Teine will catch up later. I need to speak with him."

Marne's shoulders drooped, but he did as he was told.

"Gosh, he sure looks tired," Teine muttered, watching Madric from the corner of his eye. Madric nodded, and they both watched the door swing shut.

"Yeah, he always has it rough in this weather." Madric nodded. "He's dragging for a few days after every storm. Maybe you should take better care of him."

Teine felt the heat of indignation creep up his neck. He turned to Madric, mouth open to defend himself, but found Madric grinning. Teine raised an eyebrow at the magician. "You're having me on, aren't you?"

"What was your first clue?" Madric chuckled.

Cheeks flaming with embarrassment, Teine changed the subject. "So, what did you need to speak to me about?"

The Aoife shrugged, an expression so like his nephew that Teine had to keep himself from grinning. Madric gave one of his office chairs a shove with his foot, sending it rolling over to Teine. "I figured your head would be about ready to split with questions, and thought now might be the time to offer you answers to anything that I can. You'll get precious little of that, once you get back to Solmurry proper."

"I was afraid that might be the case." Teine sighed and took a seat.

The magician fetched a bottle and a couple of goblets from a rack on one of the shelves, then hopped up on the examination stool with his back against the desk. He leaned back, resting his elbow on his desk while he poured each of them a drink.

"Well, don't fret too much. My brother will be on his way again after a few days, and when he's gone things get back to normal pretty quickly. His trips home are mercifully brief and infrequent. But when he's around, it's better for everyone to mind their manners and stay out of sight as much as possible," he advised. "His very presence can be toxic to a person's sanity."

"Hmmm," Teine replied, trying to appear more nonchalant than worried. Following Madric's lead, he took a small sip of the wine, savoring the special treat and wishing he didn't have quite so much on his mind. Even though he was new to Demesne-level politics, he really did trust Madric. But Teine could feel deep in his bones how dangerous it was to place himself in opposition with the master by allying himself with the lord's elder brother. With a small sigh, he decided it was time to steer the topic onto less treacherous grounds.

"So, tell me," he began. "Is there a reason that the master doesn't want to see his own son?"

Madric scowled, toying with Marne's bracelet. "I ask myself that all the time. I think it's partially because he sees Marne's appearance as a deformity, and he overlooks everything else about him because of it. But what he says is that he's just too busy."

"Could it be that he just doesn't like being at Solmurry?" Teine volunteered. "I'd think it'd be much more exciting to be at Court, with the Prince. Wouldn't *most* people choose to be there, if it were an option to them?"

"Oh-ho! You've got a good eye," Madric cheered, clapping his hands together a couple of times in applause. "And you're right. My brother keeps some very interesting company. You could say he's been tempted into town. After all, there are three Solmurry shipyards to visit, plus an open-armed welcome at Court in Empyrea any time he wishes. It's probably much more comfortable to live a carefree life and have other people manage your obligations, wouldn't you think?"

Teine agreed. If Lord Solmurrian had no great love for his son— and so far it seemed he didn't—it would be easy to leave the daily workings of Solmurry in the hands of competent servants and set about the serious business of merrymaking and politics.

"So, how much do you help out with running Solmurry when he's not around?" Teine asked.

"As little as possible," Madric answered. His eyes were suddenly steely. "It's not my problem. He made his bed, and I'm sure not going to lie in it for him."

"How do you mean?"

"Oh, I forgot you're too young to know," Madric waved a hand airily. "Once he'd married and I hadn't, he made sure the Church found out about my magic. By the time they'd broken me down to the point that they thought I could be trusted outside the cloister, our father had died and Marne had been born. Then *he* was Lord Solmurrian and it was too late to contest." The magician sighed and shifted position so his other elbow rested on his desk. "Not that I would. I don't regret that he took it from me. I could do the job, but it's not my preference. What I regret is *how* he took it from me, and how terribly he's mismanaging it."

Teine rubbed his chin thoughtfully, enjoying the new stubbly feeling that had come from shaving. It grated in a most satisfying manner across his fingertips as he contemplated the turn his conversation with Madric had taken. He'd heard rumblings of discontent before, from the other Humans, but he'd never taken them seriously. It was Human nature to complain about their bosses. Apparently it was Aoife nature, as well.

Madric looped Marne's bracelet over a finger, twirling it as he continued. "I never wanted to run the whole damn thing by myself, anyway. I'd always assumed we'd just be partners. And back then I was never more than just a dabbler in magic, not worth as much notice as I got. But for that I got fifty years locked in a cloister with a shaved head, surrounded by three hundred other lost souls." He gave Teine a look, then sipped from his glass.

"I'll tell you, Teine, it's the Solmurrian name that sold me out to the Church, even more surely than my grasping little brother. Thanks to the Capite, anytime our family name gets attached to anything involving magic, the whole Empyrean sits up to watch."

Teine blinked, then sat up ramrod straight in his chair, opening his eyes wide to stare at the puzzled magician. He managed to hold the pose for three whole seconds while Madric stared back, before Madric burst into laughter.

"Ha ha! I get it! You're part of the Empyrean, and you're watching me! Very funny!" Madric waved his hands as if to dismiss Teine's mock scrutiny. "You can keep on staring. Unlike my famous ancestor, Aleric Solmurrian, *I'm* not planning to rise from the dead to fight any wars for our Doyen Prince. And hurrah," he grumbled. "We have another one who thinks he's a joker. Once you and Marne have time to get to know each other, you'll get along fine."

Unable to keep the grin from his face, Teine relaxed and took a sip from his wine. "Speaking of Marne," he prodded, feeling a dangerous sense of camaraderie with this magician who was so far above his station.

"Here it comes," Madric sighed, rolling his eyes.

Teine blinked, "Here what comes?"

"The deluge of questions."

"Sorry to be so predictable," Teine countered. "But what do you expect? Nobody prepared me for this! What is he? Is he some kind of inherently magical being, or is it just some set of deformities and a weird coincidence? How in the world have you been able to keep a secret like this for so long, with so many potentially weak links and attention from the most dangerous kind of people?" Teine elbowed his wine glass, then froze with his arms in the air at the sound of breaking glass.

Madric had snatched the bucket containing the elemental out of the way just in time. But now he looked forlornly at his broken wine glass on the floor. His relaxed countenance was gone, but it hadn't been replaced with anger. Instead, he reached up and brought Teine's hands back to the tabletop, gently pressing his palms to the cold, smooth granite. "Easy." The Aoife magician's expression was kind, but somber.

"Sorry," Teine breathed.

Madric shrugged, then glanced over to the water elemental in the bucket. "Water elemental, or wine glass. It was a very tough choice."

The water elemental chose just that moment to spritz the magician in the face. Madric squinted, wiping the water from his eyes. "There's gratitude for you."

Teine took in a deep breath, then released it, managing a chuckle at the end. "You probably should have chosen the wine glass." Grateful for the break in the tension, Teine left his hands on the table to prevent himself from smashing any more stemware.

"Indeed," Madric flicked the droplets he'd wiped from his face back at the elemental. "Worthless creature."

Lowering his voice to a conspiratorial whisper, Teine leaned in toward Madric, "But what happens to *you* if Marne's discovered? What happens to Marne? Surely, there would be consequences for both of you." His questions just tumbled out, giving Madric no time to answer. Just thinking of that good-natured, frail child at the hands of Church Inquisitors made Teine feel physically ill. If Madric had loathed the attentions of the Church, how much worse would Marne fare? "Am I wrong, Madric, or would the bread and water diet alone kill him?"

"Probably," Madric agreed, his expression carefully neutral. "They're of the 'scourge the body to save the soul' school of thought."

Teine focused on the cold of the granite radiating up from his palms and struggled to maintain the calm that Madric had just modeled for him. "I swear, sir," he told the magician. "I mean no disrespect, but this seems to be a precarious situation for everyone!"

"I don't think *you're* in any personal danger," Madric assured.

"That's not what I meant," Teine retorted. "I'm worried about Marne. How can we protect him? What are we going to do?"

Chapter 5: Shackled

"That's what I was waiting for," Madric replied. "You said *we*."

"I did?"

"You did," Madric offered his hand to Teine, as if they were equals. "Welcome to the team."

Teine blinked in surprise, then pulled his cool hand from the granite and placed it in Madric's without another thought. The Aoife's grasp was so warm, by comparison that it burned. But Teine smiled. In that fiery handshake, a partnership had been forged. He knew what side he was on: the side that kept Marne safe.

Just then, the door to Madric's study slammed open. Madric broke the handshake and retreated guiltily, as if caught in an act of treason. But it was only Hamoni.

The Aoife girl swept in, shutting the door behind her, and paused to dramatically lean up against it as if in a swoon. Her cheeks were flushed, her hair tousled, and her eyes bright. She was breathing as hard as if she'd run all the way up the stairs, and looked for all the world like a girl who'd just had a passionate liaison and was now ready to tell all the steamy details.

"Oh, my heavens!" she squealed. "Madric! Did you *see* it?"

Madric's lopsided grin said yes, he had. "It's not exactly the magic bullet we need, but it's good to have in the arsenal." To Teine, he added, "We'll get started right away trying to replicate the sizing effect so we can add it to Marne's bracelet."

Hamoni jerked her chin at Teine. "What about him? Is he in?"

Madric nodded smartly. "Marne couldn't have made a better choice. No need to shelter him any further. Teine's got some good ideas and an outside perspective that will be very useful."

"Excellent!" Hamoni practically danced over to Teine. He thought she was going to shake his hand, like Madric. Instead, she hugged him tight and reached up to kiss him on the cheek. "You're part of the family now!"

"Hamoni!" Madric scolded, his voice sharper than Teine had ever heard. The Aoife magician's brow was wrinkled in genuine consternation. He pointed firmly to a chair on the other side of the room. "Sit down over there and contemplate the error of your actions. It's unfair to treat Teine that way. You'll only confuse him and make him uncomfortable."

Hamoni's lapis blue eyes filled with tears. Absolutely crestfallen by Madric's harsh words, she retreated to the chair he indicated to weep silently into her hands.

Teine's eyes prickled with sympathy for her, and guilt gnawed at his belly, but overall he was very grateful Madric had intervened on his behalf. He was old enough to have taken the mandatory classes on basic Human sexuality and understood why he'd been secretly thrilled by her attention. Over the last couple of days, he was starting to recognize some of his feelings for Hamoni were becoming a bit inappropriate. He was going to need to guard his thoughts and actions carefully. As an intact male he had certain responsibilities, and he wanted very badly to be worthy of the honor Marne had bestowed on him. Allowing himself to get all wound up over a completely unattainable Aoife woman seemed the worst possible way to start.

Madric went to the window and glanced out, seemingly oblivious to the microdrama in front of him. "Damn."

"What's wrong?" Teine asked.

"My brother's buggy is outside, and the horse is still hitched. It means he's probably planning to collect you and Marne, then head back to the Demesne," Madric scowled. "I'm sorry about this, Teine. I wanted to give you the whole history on what's gone on, and answer your questions in the kind of detail this complicated situation deserves."

"But we're going to have to rush?"

Nodding, Madric reached for the heavy gold bracelet, turning it over and over in his hands as if it would help him formulate a plan.

"I'll tell you what I can right now, and then I'll have to get to work on this. When I dismiss you, find Marne right away and remind him that I said he's not feeling well, and he must take a nap. I don't normally encourage malingering, but this time it's not a stretch. He does look a bit peaked, and we *do* need to delay your departure until the enchantments on the bracelet are complete."

Teine nodded his understanding, but was a bit puzzled by all the secrecy. Madric continued before he could give voice to his curiosity. "If my brother thinks Marne is still ill, he'll be likely to either take Kenneth and go hunting for a few hours, or if luck is truly on our side, he'll give up for the day and return to the Demesne. I've already mentioned I'm planning to come back to Solmurry proper tomorrow or early the next day, so he has an out." The magician gave Teine a long-suffering grin. "The first and most useful piece of advice I can give you is that my brother must always think whatever he is doing at the moment is completely his idea."

"Got it," Teine confirmed. "I'll remember that if I have the occasion to speak with him." He was suddenly very grateful he'd had both Vosh and Seymour as friends. Between Vosh's headstrong assurance in his ability to do no wrong and Seymour's deliberate flouting of authority, Teine had left the nursery with a fair amount of practice in wrangling willful people. "It seems avoiding him as much as possible would be the wisest policy."

"Right. Try not to interact with him, if you can at all help it," Madric confirmed. "Truly, no good can come of it. He's been on a tear all day and drinking heavily of my wine on top of it. I'm hoping if we can make things dull enough here, he'll be off to seek diversion elsewhere."

"Madric, I must ask," Teine blurted out, then caught himself.

The Aoife tilted his head, watching him carefully. In the expression, Teine could see both the magician himself, and his nephew. The two seemed more alike than Marne and his sire. "What is it?"

For a brief instant, Teine almost chose the easy way out. An airy and quick "never mind, it was nothing" would work nicely to prevent him hearing things he possibly didn't want to know. But he plunged ahead. "Why not tell Lord Solmurrian the truth?" he asked. "About the bracelet, I mean. Surely he knows how crucial it is to Marne's safety? He can't just leave it behind if it's still not working, right?"

Madric blinked twice, Teine's only clue to having caught him completely off guard. "He knows of the bracelet and understands its necessity," he confirmed.

Teine still had a head full of questions, but he remained silent. Perhaps Madric would feel the need to elaborate. Several seconds ticked by while Teine remembered the momentary shock and unreasoning fear he'd felt when confronted by just a glimpse of Marne's true face. He could only imagine the panic and terror that could ensue if the boy's strange deformities suddenly became common knowledge.

"This is *exactly* why we need the outside perspective," Madric murmured. "Long-lived people have the danger of falling into patterns—not just what we do and where we live, but how we relate to the other people in our lives. My brother and I have been deceiving each other for so long, I'd forgotten the simplicity of just telling the truth." His sigh was almost a groan.

Rubbing his temples as if massaging away a headache, he continued, "The worst that could happen is that I'll get an earful for not having it ready, and he'll lay around and wait, getting into things, terrorizing my people, and generally making things uncomfortable. It would be best if he leaves, and either returns later or allows me to give you boys a ride home tomorrow. We can probably accomplish that while staying completely on the side of truth." Something indefinable had changed in Madric's overall expression, and Teine was trying to place it when the magician added, "Thank you."

"You know it wasn't a personal judgment?" Teine asked, quickly. "Or any attempt to change the status quo? I'm just trying to understand the waters in which I now swim!"

"Shark infested, as they are."

Teine laughed, unable to hide his nervousness. He'd spent the last couple of days trying to tread water with a head full of questions. Now he was getting the most satisfying answers he'd had so far from this particular conversation.

"I *do* feel as though I need a life preserver." He wished he could get out one of his notebooks and take some notes. He was trying not to feel overwhelmed, but at the same time he felt as though he were soaring. His life had suddenly gotten as complicated as any of the hundreds of novels he'd devoured in his leisure time. And now, the game was afoot! It wasn't a game of Teine's choosing, and so far the rules were a bit unclear, but it did sound like things were going to be far more interesting than he had ever dreamed.

"So, Madric," he interjected, leading with his next most important question. "What exactly does the bracelet *do?*"

"Yes, yes. I'd better explain that," Madric agreed hastily. "It's gone through many changes over the years, as I've perfected my enchanting skills…"

Hamoni coughed quietly in the corner, the first peep she'd made during their whole conversation. Teine had almost forgotten she was there. Madric shot her a dirty look, and she averted her gaze as he continued.

"But the bottom line is that the bracelet has two very basic functions now. Both are crucial to Marne's safety. One, as you've already guessed, is to make Marne pass as a normal Aoife child."

"It does a good job at that," Teine agreed. "I never guessed…"

"Good, good." Madric cut him off with a wave and an apologetic smile. "So sorry, Teine, I would love to hear your observations, but we've really got to make this quick."

"Sorry."

Madric casually waved his apology away, and turned the bracelet over in his hands. "You need to know something important about this function before I explain the second function. In the past, the illusion component of the bracelet was very straightforward. It made him look like an Aoife child. The problem was, it was static. The illusion never changed."

At first, Teine was puzzled. That didn't sound like a problem, unless…

Madric practically read his mind. "It wasn't a problem. Until his circumstances changed. The first time we took him out in a rainstorm, we discovered the flaw in a static enchantment like that."

Teine nodded in understanding. "Marne would have looked dry, while everyone else was getting soaked."

Nodding, Madric continued without missing a beat. "The bracelet did allow Marne some freedom that he hadn't experienced before. He could play outside the Demesne on sunny days. He could meet many of the Humans that lived here at the time. His world expanded beyond just the care of his nanny and the handful of people in on his secret. The original enchantment on the bracelet was the best I could do at the time. It was very far from perfect but it was better than nothing. That is, until..." Madric paused, looking like he might censor himself.

"Whatever it is, you can tell me," Teine urged. "It's all right. I'm *in*."

The magician gave Teine a sad smile. "It worked, until the day Marne got hurt. He and I were on holiday, riding in a public park in the city. He's a confident rider, and was way out ahead when something spooked his pony. He fell." The Aoife's jaw was clenched tight, and his hands balled into helpless fists at the memory. "I spurred my horse to catch up, hoping he was all right. Fortunately we were in a secluded area of the park, but one Human woman beat me there."

Teine frowned. "That's not good."

"She rolled him over before I could dismount and began looking for his injuries. The bracelet prevented her from seeing exactly how he was hurt. I had to take it off him before I could see, and I didn't even think to send her away or warn her. She took one look and began screaming. I've never heard anything like that to this day."

Teine could think of nothing to say, he'd become so lost in Madric's story.

"Marne had a concussion, a broken arm, and there was a lot of blood. You realize," he arched his eyebrow in a warning. "Not even his *blood* looks the same. And the poor woman! Fate punished her for her inherent goodness and concern for an injured child." Regret was evident in every line of Madric's features. "You might guess I had to silence her."

Teine paled. He couldn't tell if he was more unnerved by the knowledge that he'd touched a creature whose blood didn't even look like blood, or by the actions that Madric might have taken to protect their secret from a warm-hearted stranger. "Did you have to...?"

"It might have been kinder," Madric sighed. "Over the years I've done many things I'm not proud of. This is one of them. I'd just been researching spells that altered the memory, and although I didn't have anything solid I did my best to make her forget what she'd seen. It drove her mad. Completely, utterly mad. She didn't even see the end of that year before she hanged herself."

Unable to help himself, Teine groaned in sympathy for Madric's predicament—and the poor woman's too! Madric's remorse seemed genuine, but it didn't change things one bit. He shook his head, wrestling with his sense of incredulity at the company he now kept.

"I found the bracelet and got it back onto his wrist. He stayed unconscious as I carried him back to the Hospitality we were staying at. It was two full weeks before he was well enough to travel home. We'd averted disaster for the moment, but it was clear I had a lot to learn and a lot of work to do on the bracelet."

"Could you enchant a smaller one? Something that would actually fit him on its own?"

Madric shook his head. "That was one of the first ideas I'd had, but in the end we were stuck using the bracelet you see today." He grinned, a wry smile without any humor behind it. "It takes special materials to prepare an item for enchantment. Silderwort powder, purified enchantment salts, and the like. As I wasn't officially doing any enchantment work for the Empyrean at the time, I would have needed to fill out many forms to request a purchase of those items. It would have guaranteed bringing an Inspector to my door. But we had this old bracelet that had been prepared to carry enchantments in ages past. Since no one had reported it, it didn't officially exist. We pressed it into service. I would have preferred to fit Marne with an item that was easier to hide, but in the end this bracelet has been an excellent choice and has served us well."

"So, what all does it do?" Teine asked. "Now that you've been improving it?"

Madric glanced to Hamoni, who was still in her assigned chair but listening intently. "Hamoni," Madric began, fixing her with a stern glare. "Why don't you give Teine the details while I gather the necessary components to attempt this sizing enchantment?"

Hamoni nodded obediently, rising and joining them by Madric's desk. Madric began rummaging around in the cupboards under the desk. "Now that Madric has official recognition as an enchanter we have easier access to the materials," she explained. "But they watch the amounts we go through and we have to account for every speck. We've been saving and hiding spare materials for a long time to start afresh with a new bracelet, but I'm afraid it's going to take decades at this rate."

"Decades?"

"There's a black market for just about everything," Hamoni clarified. "But you can't be sure you're getting quality, and it's very risky. So this bracelet is going to have to do him for a while. It could be quite some time before we have another option."

"So, what's the second function?" Teine repeated, eagerly. His head was swimming with possibilities for his stories with Leis. Many of the things they'd guessed about magic were wrong. The new information he'd learned today would help give his writing a bit more realism.

"It's a little more complicated than a plain, static illusion," Hamoni said. "The old enchantment wasn't very subtle. It told you what to see."

"Instead of telling you what you see, the new magics let your eyes glide right over Marne and see only what you *expect* to see," Madric finished.

Teine mulled this over for a brief second. "So, if you expect to see a normal Aoife boy, that's what you see," Teine guessed. "That's how it worked on me."

Hamoni nodded, "This suggestive type of illusion is effective and durable, but it has some unusual side effects, and those side effects tie into another enchantment woven into it."

Teine wished for the hundredth time he could take some notes. "Suggestive illusion—how does that work?"

"Well, there's the enchantment to make him look how you expect him to look, and then there's the enchantment that makes you simply not notice him or think of him much at all," Hamoni explained. "So it's not just your eyes that glide right over him, but your whole mind as well."

"So," Teine thought out loud. "It makes it not just harder to notice him but also harder to remember him or any of the details about him, as well." He shifted uneasily in his chair, uncertain of why the idea of that enchantment bothered him. "That's... just wrong, somehow."

Hamoni smiled. "That's not a perfect description, but it's the short version. It's also helping people forget he's not aging normally."

"I'm not sure I like the sound of that," Teine sighed. "But it does explain some things." He was relieved to have some explanation for how a house full of kind, caring servants and good people could leave a sick boy alone in a basement for days. Now he understood it wasn't entirely their fault; they simply couldn't remember him.

"Please try to understand," Hamoni begged. Her expression was both worried and earnest. "We love him, we really do! He's just so much safer if everyone pays him as little attention as possible."

"Even us?" Teine asked, trying not to sound accusatory. "Even his own father?"

Chapter 6: The Team

Madric rose to his feet and set a small wooden humidor on his desk. "Yes, even his own father." The magician sounded uncharacteristically stern. "*Especially* his own father. My brother is a weak-minded fool. Have no doubt—he loves his son. But his lack of discipline and insight, plus his fondness for toadying to people of power, puts us all in jeopardy, every day." With an irritated sigh, he slammed himself down into his chair and began pulling wrapped bundles of delicate twigs out of the humidor and sorting them into piles. "As far as the bracelet goes, we're still working on improvements," Madric added. "In time, I hope we can refine the enchantments so they work better, for longer, and with fewer side effects."

"There's something else the bracelet does," Hamoni volunteered. The Aoife girl was looking at Madric for permission to continue. Madric gave it to her in one subtle nod.

"The bracelet..." she winced, as if even saying it out loud was tempting fate, "Puts a damper on him. Marne has something we've never seen anywhere else. It's latent, but very potent. His aura, alone..."

"Ha! I knew it!" Teine crowed, careful to keep his voice down despite his glee at being right. "That's why he has to be bagged or locked in the basement during the magical part of the storms! He attracts them!"

Madric nodded with a wry smile and clapped his hands together. "Give the boy a prize." Then he paused, blinked once, and turned to his assistant as if something had just occurred to him. "Yes, actually. Hamoni, give the boy a prize. That Castellarian textbook on the mind magic disciplines. The Greeves Academy edition. He can take it home with him. Oh, and that book on divining, as well."

Hamoni nodded obediently, but didn't move.

"Chop, chop! Move along!" Madric snapped, clapping his hands together. "Don't keep the boy waiting!"

"But—" Hamoni began to protest, gesturing at the bracelet.

"We can work on it when you return." Hamoni nodded crisply and left the room in a swish of skirts, closing the door behind her so Madric and Teine could continue their discussion undisturbed.

"Thanks," Teine told him. Mind magics sounded like a fascinating field of study, and he knew less than nothing about them.

"Marne can probably answer most of the basic questions you have on that subject. The boy is very well-read."

Teine sighed, "It sounds to me like he's going to have to be. Latent talent, you say? What kind?"

Madric dipped his head in a rather humble pose. "I have absolutely no bloody idea. I've never seen anything like him. I would never say this to his face, but he's a complete sport of nature. He can accurately mimic some of the basic spells he's seen me do, like mend."

Well, that explains the candle, Teine thought.

"And sometimes his touch drains the enchantments right out of things. And sometimes it awakens magic items long dormant."

"Like that suit of armor that was chasing people around?"

"Heard about that, did you?" Madric chuckled. "Yes, we successfully blamed that one on the storm, but it was him. I swear the boy can talk to some kinds of animals, too, like a Druid of yore," Madric sighed, looking exasperated. "If it weren't for the Solmurry Luck, I'd swear he was a Changeling. But I can't deny how much he feels like our own flesh and blood, no matter how he looks."

"Solmurry Luck?"

"The Solmurrian men seem to have a special place in the world—as Fortune's playthings," Madric chuckled, as if reliving a memory. "His father has it, I have it, our grandsire had it, and Marne seems to as well. I swear to all the heavens, sometimes I think it's the only reason he hasn't been discovered. Fortune must have some other dirty trick in store for the poor boy."

"But isn't it *good* to be lucky?"

Madric's chuckle turned into a full-blown laugh. "Ah, Teine. Sometimes I forget you're so young! And Human, to boot." The Aoife wizard leaned over and patted Teine companionably on the shoulder. "You'll soon learn that not all luck is *good* luck."

"Oh, great," Teine sighed, giving Madric a quirk of a smile. "Burst my young and impressionable bubble."

"Apparently it's part of my job description," Madric countered. "But, cheer up! Is there anything else you still want to know, or have I overwhelmed you?"

Teine spent several seconds thinking, trying to catalog all the answers he'd received that day. He scraped his memory for any other loose ends that needed tying up and was met only with a tangle of impressions and his desperate need to sort out all the new information. "Only one thing pops into my mind," he nudged. "And it's not crucial, it's more a matter of curiosity."

"Fire away," Madric encouraged. "Don't know when I'll see you again or if we'll be able to speak freely."

"So," Teine began, unsure of how to phrase the question. "What's the story with Marne's 'imaginary friend?' Do you think she's something dangerous?"

Madric snorted with surprised laughter. "I don't think she *exists*." He glanced over at Teine and gave him a measured look. "Here's how it is. Marne's over a hundred years old. Most boys his age start putting away childish things about then, and start looking toward the future. But Marne's not most boys. His age seems to be immaterial, and although he's very intelligent and well-read, he is—in almost every way that counts—still a child."

Teine smiled at the memory of Marne trying to build a sand castle on the beach earlier that morning, and how he'd broken into gales of defiant laughter when he thought the inspectors might be watching them.

"I can see your point," Teine agreed. "Marne is a bright, creative child whose father ignores him and who has no one his age to play with. Of *course* he might have an imaginary friend. But why is Hamoni so sure Marne's friend is someone real?"

The magician rolled his eyes in exasperation. "I'm not sure she really is, but when she first came to work for me, we made a ridiculous bet. Remember how I said there were things in my life I wasn't proud of? Well, this bet is one of them."

Intrigued, Teine leaned forward in his chair. Was there nothing about Madric that wasn't interesting? He still couldn't believe an Aoife would talk to him with this much candor, especially about his personal life. Madric was rapidly becoming one of his favorite people.

"So?" he goaded. "What's the bet?"

Madric held up both hands as if to ward off Teine's disapproval in advance. "Really, I'm not sure I should tell you this. I knew it was wrong an instant after I said it and saw she was taking it seriously. I was being sarcastic."

"Go on."

"Ugh," the Aoife groaned, putting his head in his hands. "I told her if she could prove that Marne's imaginary friend was real—be it an evil spirit, possessing demon, native to another plane, or whatever—I'd buy out her contract, make her a free woman, and marry her."

Teine's eyes widened. Although common-born Aoife had more status in Empyrean society than Humans, noble-born Aoife rarely, if ever, married them. It was an outrageous idea.

"I know," Madric sighed. "Awful. I wish I could take it back, but I don't know how."

Teine ran his hand over his chin, once again enjoying the grown-up feel of the stubble growing there. "I can't think of a single thing to help you," he replied, after giving the matter some serious consideration. He was beyond flattered at the confidence Madric had shown him, and was truly warming to the Aoife's openness and quirky sense of humor. Teine had a hunch that Marne wasn't the only one who was short of people to talk to. Everyone surrounding Madric was either his servant or a backstabbing politico. Neither situation was ideal for good conversation.

"Well, then," the Aoife picked up the bracelet and groaned, rising to his feet like an old man. "I'd better get to work on this. Remember, our best-case scenario is you and Marne staying here while my brother goes home. We don't want him prowling about, drinking my good wine and cuffing my staff."

"I'll do what I can, sir," Teine replied.

The magician waved him off. "Eh, the 'sirs' are for people who need to hear their titles to feel important. I'm too damn important as it is.

Just call me Madric. Besides, boy," he added. "We're all in this together."

Chapter 7: Ranger Report

Teine turned from closing the door to Madric's office as Hamoni came up the stairs. The Aoife girl's eyes were hooded, her expression guarded as she studied his face. Teine's stomach did a nervous flip-flop. Anything he said or did at this point could be wrong.

As she passed, she pushed a heavy textbook and a lighter tome into his hands, and then walked by without comment or further acknowledgment. A moment later, she went into Madric's office and shut the door.

Teine tried not to feel disappointed but failed. She was clearly upset at being dressed down for her behavior and it seemed she might even be blaming him for it. And to top it all off, he'd totally forgotten to ask her where Marne was.

"My first few days as a Man, and I'm not off to the best start," he grumbled, absolutely certain that Men didn't normally get flustered when a pretty—and completely unattainable—girl snubbed them. Trying not to dwell on his disappointment, Teine headed down to the kitchen to inquire after Marne.

Pasha, predictably, was bustling around, preparing the evening meal. But she knew exactly where the young master had gone.

"Hamoni moved him up to his new room," she chirped, while her little kitchen knife flashed and the discarded ends of the dinner tubers went bouncing into the rubbish bin. While Teine was in awe of Pasha's kitchen skills, he eyed the cattail-like tubers she was peeling with skepticism. They were common, but he'd never seen anyone eat them. Despite her wrinkled and slightly arthritic old hands, Pasha was making short work of a big pile of the vegetables, dicing them with a careless efficiency that made Teine wince. "It's still a mess, but we got the bed set up. He's resting."

Teine knew exactly what she was talking about. Marne hadn't wasted any time. He must have already moved into the suite that Teine had spent the previous day cleaning. There was still a lot of furniture to be discarded, in addition to the pieces that he himself had selected, but he hadn't had a chance to put it all together yet. He hoped he'd guessed well and that Marne liked his choices. Thanking Pasha, he cajoled two apples out of her and headed back upstairs to let Marne know what Madric was planning.

"Be careful, you," Pasha told Teine, catching his sleeve as he went to leave. "Lord Solmurrian is about somewhere, and he's in a foul mood. Best go to the boy, stay nearby and out from underfoot. No need to borrow trouble."

"Yes, ma'am," he agreed, with a little more enthusiasm than was necessary. Even on his worst day, Teine was not the 'borrowing trouble' sort. He suppressed his natural inclination to give the old woman a playful wink, then headed off to find his young master.

As he was about to mount the stairway, Teine passed one of the windows that could be opened and caught the tone of masculine voices calling out in greeting. He peeked out in interest, then pulled back out of sight to listen at his leisure. Normally, he'd never have considered spying on one of the Aoife to be an honorable or particularly wise endeavor, but the circumstances seemed to warrant unusual action.

Master Solmurrian was speaking to Kenneth and one of the Royal Rangers, a golden-haired Aoife gentleman riding a handsome white destrier. His armor was so intricate and gilded that it had to be far more decorative than functional. The Ranger was the most powerfully-built Aoife Teine had ever seen, nearly as broad across the chest as a Human. He cut a dashing figure mounted on his fine horse, and Teine would have liked to have been able to take a sketch of him right then. As he watched, the Ranger leaned down and offered up a battered, muddy bowler to Lord Solmurrian.

"One of the farmers bade me pass this along while I was in the neighborhood," he said.

The lord wrinkled his nose. "Do I have to? I've been hoping he'd lose this dreadful thing for years." The two of them laughed heartily.

Teine recognized the hat right away. It was the bowler that had blown off Madric's head on their way to the tower. Somehow he knew Madric would be delighted to have the muddy old thing back, battered though it might be. When the magician had told him about their family being "lucky," Teine had been privately skeptical. But the unlikely reappearance of Madric's hat had definitely given him something to consider.

He settled in to listen to a few minutes of idle banter, amused by how similar conversations between Aoife were to those of Humans. The two nobles chatted for several moments, the topics ranging from the weather over the past few days to how their favorite fabal teams were doing over the season. They had just begun a lively discussion about next season's lineups when the Ranger caught Teine by surprise.

"You know, Alain, if you're heading back to Solmurry proper today I'd be remiss if I didn't offer you a personal escort."

"Pshaw!" With a chuckle, Lord Solmurrian seemed to dismiss the Ranger's concerns. Without the visual reference to go on, Teine was alarmed to realize how similar Madric sounded to his brother. That was a piece of information he meant to keep in mind for future reference. "What are a few ragged outland Human scum? I'm surprised they've lasted this long. Soon the wildlife in the forest will make a meal of them or they'll finish themselves off with their inevitable backstabbing."

"Indeed," the Ranger agreed. "But the Doyen himself has spoken often of his affection for you and your family." Teine looked down at his arms, then rubbed the gooseflesh away and concentrated on listening. "These outlanders are far more than mere peasants. For all their weedy and ill-bred qualities, they've managed to survive thus far. That ship we sank was no merchant carrier, to be sure. It's likely they were soldiers."

Teine blinked in alarm. Outlander Human soldiers, marooned practically in their backyard, and no mention of it on the news? If it were known Teine was sure there would be talk of little else. *Perhaps it had only just happened,* Teine silently comforted himself. *Too soon to make a broadcast...*

"...unfortunate, indeed." Teine blinked, struggling to catch up to the conversation. "Willis the True has long been a trusted friend of Solmurry and I hope she recovers from her wounds. Her valor in service to our family is the stuff of legend."

Oh! Willis! Teine remembered her from the road on the mad dash to the tower during the storm. It was the first time Teine had ever seen a Holidocrith up close and in person, but she was every bit as formidable as he'd heard. Anything that could injure her seriously had to be considered a threat.

Perhaps Master Solmurrian had come to the same conclusion because he paused as if re-considering the Ranger's offer. "Will my boy be safe here, if I leave him? He's been ill, you know."

"Probably, I would guess," the horseman replied. "Safer here than on the road to Solmurry after dark, to be certain. Would you like me to wait, so you can see if he's well enough to travel now?"

"Thank you for your generosity," the master replied. "Would you care for some refreshments while I check on my son?" The two of them continued to chat while the Ranger dismounted and handed his stallion off to Kenneth.

Teine didn't wait to hear any more. Checking the strap of his satchel to be sure it was secure on his shoulder, he barreled up the stairs to tell Marne the news.

Chapter 8: Real News

The open playroom between Marne and Teine's new rooms was much as Teine had left it. Furniture he'd chosen was scattered randomly around the main room of the apartment, but the door to Marne's side of the suite was slightly ajar. As Teine approached, he could hear the familiar sound of furniture being dragged across the floor. Expecting to find Marne had rallied some of the staff to help him, he was surprised to see the boy himself was manhandling a nightstand over to the wall. It looked like laborious work and Teine had a moment's admiration for Marne's initiative. It was unusual to see any of the ruling class willing to do for themselves. And there was Marne, climbing on furniture, trying to do a Human's job rather than wait for someone to do it for him.

"What are you doing, Mas..., er, Marne?" he asked.

"Hanging a tapestry," Marne replied.

Some enterprising servant had set up Marne's bed, a massive old four-poster that was big enough to sleep a pair of Humans. Marne looked as though he'd moved everything else he could by himself. The boy seemed cheerful and pleased with his progress, though he had a pallor under his tan that Teine disliked immediately.

While Teine watched, Marne picked up a rolled tapestry that had been resting on one of the chairs, tucked it under one arm, and climbed on top of the nightstand. Standing on tip-toe, the alien-looking child was barely able to reach the hook that had been set in the wall, but he managed to get the rope where it needed to go and watched in pleasure as the tapestry unrolled to the floor. It was a pastoral scene of a unicorn and a Holidocrith laying down together under a stylized pear tree.

"Hey, that's a beautiful piece!" Teine commented. "I've always favored the traditionals, but that minimalist modern style is really starting to—" He shook his head and whisked himself into the room, closing the door behind him. "Never mind. Your father's on his way up," he told Marne, closing the distance between them in a few rapid steps. "He's going to want to take you back to Solmurry right away, before nightfall."

Marne squeaked in alarm, "I... I can't go unless the bracelet is finished! Surely he'll see the sense to that?" Before Teine could offer him a hand, Marne jumped down from his perch. "And I suppose Father has found something to be upset about. Let me guess: new activity from the band of shipwrecked outlanders?"

Teine nodded, feeling confused. *New activity? Didn't that mean that there was old activity, too? How had the news not reported that?* He hesitated, uncertain as to what he should tell Marne. The child was fond of Willis and Teine hated to be the bearer of bad news. Instead, he decided on the straightforward approach.

"I just spoke to Madric. He's still working on your bracelet, and he'd like to work in peace. Your father has a Royal Ranger here right now, offering to escort him. So we just have to get him to leave without you. I was thinking..." He stopped, catching himself. "No need to make this more complicated than it needs to be," he told himself, out loud. Then he addressed Marne directly. "Would he see the sense in leaving you here, if the spells on your bracelet are incomplete?"

Marne nodded, watching him with a quiet intensity. "The only real challenge is getting Father to go now, without me. Which I doubt will be any trouble at all." Flopping down on the disorderly bed, Marne heaved a sigh that seemed far too large for his slight frame. "That's better than him hanging around, waiting for the bracelet to be finished," he added, in a very small voice. He then turned away, kicking off his house shoes and gathering his ragged stuffed toy Holidocrith into his lap. He cradled it for a moment, then lay down completely.

Teine leaned forward, sympathetic to Marne's disappointment. However, his father's apparent disinterest was the only thing they had working for them. "Let's just be boring," he suggested. "If things aren't interesting here, he'll just go, won't he?"

Marne didn't answer, shrugging his shoulders and hugging the toy tighter.

"All right, then. Boring it is." Teine looked around, saw the trundle peeping out from under Marne's bed, and pulled it out. He flopped down on it and opened the larger book Hamoni had given him. "This is me, being boring."

The two of them lay in silence for a while, Teine flipping pages and skimming the contents. The book looked interesting, and he was eager to give it a proper read later, when he wasn't so unsettled. After a few moments, Marne rolled over on his side and peered down at Teine. "Is this bed all right for now? You'll have your own room over there the next time we visit."

Teine looked down at the trundle he was lying on. "It's great, Marne," Teine assured him, glancing away from the book to look up at Marne's odd but earnest face. It warmed his heart to know his new master was a gentle soul who cared for his comfort.

At the same time, Teine now had worries the likes of which he'd never experienced before. Marne's safety, and by extension his own, were likely going to be in constant jeopardy. Just hearing about the outlander bandits had been a shock, even without all the new insights into the Church, politics, Marne's health, and magic.

Marne's brow wrinkled into a frown and he crooked his elbows to prop his pointy chin on his fists. "You don't look like it's great," the boy observed. "It's alright to tell me if something's wrong, you know."

Teine chewed his lip for a second, debating. To share all his worries with Marne would be overmuch. He was, after all, a child in need of protecting. So he settled for just a piece of them.

"About the outlanders," he began, keeping his voice low. "How long have they been around? I haven't heard anything on the news. Are they new? What's going to be done about them?"

Marne sighed, "Is that all that's worrying you?" he asked with an air of superiority, as though he were the older sibling comforting a youngster.

"Well," Teine confessed, not sure whether to be annoyed or amused. "That's not all, but it's a start. You also seemed sad and I didn't know how to cheer you up."

He was rewarded by the smallest of shy smiles. "Don't worry," Marne told him. "This bandit thing has been going on for weeks. We think they crashed down the coast about forty or so miles away, and have been making their way north while still eluding capture." His expression was lit with enthusiasm, and Teine understood how and why a small, sickly child might be enamored with the idea of pirates running amok nearby. "I bet, if they're still traveling north, they'll be passing through Solmurry's wildlands soon."

"What?!" *Pirates in Solmurry?* Teine thought. *How had the news not covered any of this?* "That must be why the Ranger was insisting on escorting your father back to the Demesne." Eying his young master, Teine raised an eyebrow. "Why haven't I heard anything about it?"

"You're Human," Marne yawned mightily, granting Teine an up-close view of those sharp, un-Aoife looking teeth. The boy looked for all the world like a sleepy kitten as he hugged his stuffed Holidocrith.

"They don't play the real news on the radio, since it's pretty much just for Huma… oh, wait, I think I hear my father coming!"

Marne and Teine both moved quickly to get into position. They both sensed it wouldn't be wise to be seen gossiping together like a couple of milkmaids. Teine opened his book at a random page and attempted to look boring as he heard the footsteps outside the door. Marne snuggled into the pillows and adopted the peacefully drowsy expression of someone recovering from illness, just as the door opened and Master Solmurrian peered around the corner.

Teine shuffled himself around so he could be in a position to stand and greet his betters, as was customary, but the lord made a "hushing" gesture and motioned for Teine to stay where he was. "Marne?" the Aoife Lord asked, speaking softly.

"Yes, Father?" Marne shuffled the covers around a little and sat up, blinking and rubbing his eyes. Teine thought the boy did a good job looking as though he'd been caught napping. He suspected that Marne might make a formidable faker—not really a bad skill to possess under the circumstances.

Master Solmurrian strode lightly into the room. Even though he wore the hard-soled riding boots favored by the equestrian Aoife gentlemen, his steps barely made a sound. His brow was furrowed by genuine concern for his son. He seemed to be a completely different person than the terrifying man who had threatened Teine in front of all those noble Aoife just two days ago. Stepping over Teine as though he were not there, the lord sat on the edge of Marne's bed. "I see Madric hasn't finished your bracelet," he began, his brow wrinkled with irritation. "How long have you been sleeping?"

Marne shrugged, glancing at Teine. "I'm not sure, Father. Was I sleeping?" He stretched and yawned, causing his toy Holidocrith to fall off the bed, bounce off Teine's head, and land on his open book.

Making a show of checking how many pages he'd "read," Teine played along, "About a half an hour or so, sir."

Frowning, Lord Solmurrian leaned over the bed, looking down with a perplexed expression at his son. Teine held his breath as the Aoife brushed the bangs out of Marne's face with his slender hand. "You feel clammy to me," he told Marne. Then, he turned sharply to Teine. "Make sure he gets an extra blanket."

"Yes, sir. Right away, sir." Teine started to rise once more, but was again gestured to sit still. The master's expression had changed from concern to annoyance, and he reached down to extract Marne's worn toy Holidocrith from where it had fallen on the trundle mattress next to Teine's elbow. The Aoife lord examined the toy critically, taking in the worn-out suede covering, missing ear, and exposed stuffing. Finally, he tucked the toy under his elbow and turned his attention back to his son.

"I suppose it's for the best to leave you here for one more night," he told Marne, looking past Teine as though he didn't exist. "If Madric isn't done with your bracelet, we really have no choice." Teine kept quiet, grateful to Madric for his instruction on how to deal with the lord. Left to his own devices, he was certain he would have spoken up and botched things badly.

"I have important business back at Solmurry and an escort waiting for me," the lord declared. "I'll go on this afternoon without you. Madric can bring you to Solmurry tomorrow when the bracelet is finished and you, young man, are better rested." He ruffled Marne's hair, an affectionate smile creasing his usually cold countenance.

"Yes, sir," Marne replied. Although his own father seemed oblivious, Teine could see unfallen tears in the boy's strange, sad eyes. Marne didn't have a chance to get out anything else before Lord Solmurrian had turned on his heel and left, with the worn toy Holidocrith still tucked under his arm.

Chapter 9: Holidocrith Trouble

"I can't believe he took Holly," Marne whispered.

Teine didn't know what to say. He gaped at the closed door, completely bewildered. Although it was only a toy, regardless of his age, Marne was still just a child.

"I mean," Marne continued, rolling over so he could see Teine. "It's not like it's the first time he's taken her. But he always told me first. Maybe that means she really is the last one." Lying on the bed, Marne was nearly the same height as Teine was while reclining on the trundle, so they were nearly face-to-face. The boy rubbed his red, puffy eyes with the back of his hand, his tears welling up but not spilling over. Teine took in the set of his jaw and the determined expression on his small, strange face, and realized his young master was holding back a flood of sadness.

"The last one?"

Marne nodded solemnly, taking deep, regular breaths to control the sobs that threatened his composure. "The last Holly. He thinks I don't know, but I do."

Teine waited for Marne to go on. When he did, his voice was a little steadier.

"I've had a Holly the Holidocrith for as long as I can remember. The company that made them doesn't even exist anymore." Marne sighed, a wistful smile on his angular, alien face. "Whenever she'd get worn out, Father would come to me and say he had to take her away to get her mended so she didn't fall completely apart."

That makes sense, Teine thought. After all, he'd managed to completely destroy Bosco the Bear in about ten years, give or take. Marne was a hundred years old. "But," Teine asked, rubbing his chin stubble as he remembered. "Couldn't you just fix her yourself? Like that candle?"

Marne shook his head, mouthing the word no. "It doesn't work that way," he breathed. "I tried. Broken is different from worn out."

"But you'll get her back, right?" he prompted, fishing around in his bag for a handkerchief. "He'll get her fixed up and then bring her back to you?"

Marne shrugged, taking the handkerchief that Teine offered and using it to dab his eyes. Teine had never seen anyone cry like that before, looking so devastated without breaking into wails. The boy looked as though someone had killed his best friend. "No, he won't," Marne told Teine. "If I'm lucky, he'll bring me a new one. He's been hiding a whole bunch of them in the vault for years. If I'm unlucky, that was the last one..." he choked back a quiet sob. "And I'll never see her again."

Teine nodded along with Marne's explanation, remembering what it was like to be a child with a favorite toy. He'd been attached enough to Bosco to warrant a whole bucket full of tears if someone had taken him without warning. There was probably nothing anyone could have said to make him feel better.

"I'm sorry." Marne buried his head in the pillow and Teine could barely make out his tiny, "You shouldn't have to see this," that followed.

"That's all right." Hesitantly, Teine reached out and patted his young master on the back. Although he was unsure of the protocol in this situation, it seemed like the right thing to do. "You think he has a new Holly for you?"

"I don't think so," Marne whispered. "If he did, he'd probably just tell me he was going to get her fixed up again. He doesn't know that I know he had extras. He'd keep giving me a new one when the old ones would wear out, but he always made out like it was really just the same old Holly." He sighed, sniffled, and wiped his nose with the handkerchief.

"I think this is the last one and he's just decided I'm too old to be playing with toys. I know it probably sounds stupid to someone who is nearly a grownup, but if this is really the last Holly left, I just can't bear the thought of her thrown out with the rubbish or tossed in the burn pit."

Teine nodded. Some people kept old toys not so much because they needed the toy itself, but because they wanted to honor it for the service it had rendered and enjoy the old memories. He remembered clutching Bosco tight when he had the flu and being grateful for his company. He also remembered crying himself to sleep the week of his ninth birthday when Monty of Solmurry, one of his good friends, had accidentally drowned. All his tears had been absorbed by the threadbare hide of his old bear. An old toy was more than just a possession to be discarded. Old toys were really old friends. It was about loyalty. Of course a cherished old toy deserved a safe place where it could be kept from harm, remembered fondly, and possibly even be shown to your own children someday.

Suddenly, it was absolutely clear what Teine had to do. The thought of it left a huge knot of apprehension in his throat. He closed his book, rolled off the trundle, and rose to his feet.

"Where are you going?" Marne piped, his voice rough from tears.

Teine held out a hand to silence him. "I'll be back." Before he could change his mind or balk at the utter folly of the task he'd just set for himself, he headed out the door.

He made his way up the stairs toward Madric's workshop. It was only a guess, but it seemed the most likely destination for Lord Solmurrian, if he wanted to be on the road as soon as possible. *He's gone to check on the bracelet,* Teine thought, crossing his fingers on both hands in an attempt to make it true. He slowed to stealth once he reached the landing at the top, trying to decide the best way to approach the irritable Aoife lord. With all the horror stories he'd been hearing about the man, he was certain his self-imposed mission wouldn't be as easy as just walking in and asking for Marne's toy outright.

The door to Madric's workshop was partially open and Teine was in clear view of Hamoni working at one of the benches. The utter impossibility of what he saw rendered him completely immobile and dumb. Hamoni was doing magic—*real* magic!

Marne's bracelet was suspended in a cloud of steam and electricity in some kind of device. The enchantment machine was composed of two hoops joined together at right angles to form a rough cage. Below that was an oil lamp. Although Teine had seen many oil lamps before, this one had something new. Instead of a regular flame, an unmistakably humanoid form made completely from fire danced on the wick. Teine immediately thought of the water elementals Madric kept contained. *Was this a fire elemental?* Dangling on fine golden chains attached to the twin loops of the device, a shallow glass basin of water boiled vigorously, generating the steam that filled the magical enclosure. Arcs of captive lightning crackled from one hoop, through the steam to Marne's bracelet, over and over again in varying patterns.

Standing beside this device, Hamoni sang something in words Teine didn't understand, while gesturing with clipped precision at Marne's bracelet. There was something about her countenance that was so radically different, he had to look twice to be sure it was actually her. Even her voice, normally so cheerful and full of fun, sounded alarmingly powerful and arcane.

Unable to break his trance, Teine continued to watch, his fear of Lord Solmurrian and the urgency of his errand for Marne completely forgotten. The sight of Hamoni working actual magic had rendered him insensible. It was beautiful. It was powerful. It was real. And it was happening right in front of him!

The light touch of a hand on his back brought Teine back to the moment. He startled and whirled guiltily, expecting the Aoife lord, but it was only Marne. The boy's eerie eyes reflected back the light emanating from the partially open door, and a small grin played on his lips.

"First time?" Marne whispered.

He's asking about the magic, Teine thought. He nodded and spoke as softly as he could, "Except for seeing you fix that candle, yes."

The pair of them watched in silence for a moment. "It's called 'cantillating,'" Marne told him. "Casting magic with the aid of gestures or the spoken word. Cantillating. Cantillation. To cantillate."

Teine thought back to that night in the basement. "But you don't do it that way?"

Marne shook his head wordlessly. He breathed in, as if to say something, but by then Hamoni had noticed them. Eyes wide with alarm, she stiffened without hesitating or breaking the rhythm of her chant. But her aura of power was gone, and in its place was just a frightened Aoife girl mouthing nonsense words.

The sound of muttering voices carried from a part of the room Teine couldn't see without opening the door further. *Oh, ha! Found him!* he thought, as he snuck a quick peek into the room. Marne squeezed in for a look as well.

Madric and Lord Solmurrian had been just outside his field of vision, leaning over another of the worktables. *So they're in here after all,* Teine thought. *And apparently it's fine for Hamoni to be working on Marne's bracelet.*

The two brothers were bent over a worktable, their heads close together as if they actually liked each other or were conspiring about something of gravity. But while the tone of their conversation sounded quite ordinary, the topic had taken a turn toward the grim.

"So, any news on Willis?" Madric asked. His tone was casual, but his wrinkled brow confirmed his worry. "Hamoni told me she'd heard Willis took a beating last night. Outlanders?" Before his brother could answer, the magician wiggled his fingers toward his desk, then snapped and pointed. "There. There. Oh, hand me that penknife, will you?"

"Outlanders," Lord Solmurrian confirmed, his lips set in a firm, irritated line as he fetched the tool and passed it along to his brother. "Apparently they savaged her quite badly."

Madric growled something under his breath that sounded like "bastards." Bending closely over the table, he wielded the penknife in a poking motion at an unmoving form lying on the table. "That's… unfortunate." Was it Teine's imagination, or did the magician's voice just break?

"It'd be a shame to have a bona fide war hero like her done in by low-life outland scum," Lord Solmurrian agreed. "They must be fairly competent fighters, though, to have done as much damage as they did."

"We just saw her the other night. She seemed so happy to visit with us," Madric sighed. "They must be camping practically in our backyard. It's good you have an escort lined up. I hope the farmers are staying safe."

Lord Solmurrian nodded. "When I get back to the Demesne, I'll have to see about getting a few more Holidocrith to patrol this area until the outlanders are rounded up." He drummed his fingers impatiently on the work table. "As for Willis, she'll be lucky if she pulls through, much less keeps her eye. From what I understood, they've sent for Prior Vihah. Hopefully Vuaren can bless her and help her heal that much faster."

"Well, at least there's that." While Teine and Marne watched, Madric stopped prodding with the penknife. Instead, he began making motions as if he were gutting a fish, to the sounds of suede leather tearing.

"No!" Marne whispered. Teine agreed. Willis's fate sounded horrific. But as he followed Marne's gaze to the table, he recognized a striped suede leg—the toy Holidocrith. They'd been too late to save Holly.

He couldn't help but feel as though he'd let Marne down—and all because he'd been staring at a sight that was likely to become commonplace. The heat of embarrassment roasted Teine's ears and cheeks. And he recognized the dark humor of discussing a brutalized Holidocrith while doing the same to its stuffed miniature. He regretted that Marne was there to experience the whole show.

At the table, oblivious to Marne's distress, Madric was working away and snorting his disdain. "Prior Vihah." His lip curled into a sneer. "Vihah might be able to save her life, but she still won't be able to tell him what she saw. It's a shame we've got to keep Marne... ah... there's the little bugger!"

Teine startled, momentarily afraid they'd been discovered. Instead, Madric fished something out of the stuffing-packed body cavity of the toy and held his tiny trophy between two fingers to show his brother. Holly the Holidocrith lay there, her one ear limp, her exposed glass eye hanging by a thread, and her stuffing innards spilling out of her belly. Teine reckoned she couldn't look any deader if she'd actually been alive at one point.

Lord Solmurrian wrinkled his eyebrows together, inspecting the heart-shaped stone with his usual sour frown. Completely disregarding Madric's success, he made an impatient gesture over his shoulder toward Hamoni. "Will this take much longer?"

Teine decided then that his mission had failed and his best maneuver would be to retreat to their quarters and admit defeat. He put a hand on the dejected boy's shoulder and started propelling him gently toward the stairs when Madric caught his eye. The magician gave them not only a hard glance, but a subtle shake of his head as he mouthed, "Go away."

Teine nodded. This hadn't turned out well, and it didn't take an expert on children to realize the best thing for Marne would be to return him to his room for that nap he'd been needing.

"What do you want?" Master Solmurrian suddenly demanded, striding forward and throwing the door open to meet the boys on the landing. His expression was stormy, and Teine's heart leapt in his chest. Marne squeaked with abject terror and tried to shrink against Teine, but his father yanked the two boys apart. From his vantage point by the worktable, Madric groaned and put his hand over his face as if he didn't want to see what would happen next.

Teine was taller and heavier than Master Solmurrian, but the Aoife lord caught him around the wrist and Marne by the collar, dragging them both into the room without ceremony. "Not a part of my House two whole days, and you're already teaching him the fine art of sneaking around and spying," he snarled.

Teine flinched at the accusation, his fear melting immediately into indignation. How unfair! He hadn't meant to sneak or spy, much less involve Marne in anything shady. He'd only gotten caught up in watching the magic and had forgotten to announce himself! But when Master Solmurrian slammed the door to Madric's office, then shoved his own son backwards toward a chair hard enough the boy practically fell into the seat, Teine realized he wasn't the cause, or even the *target* of the Lord's wrath.

Marne was.

In fact, Lord Solmurrian was pretty much ignoring Teine, except for the ever-tightening grip on his wrist. Teine stood helplessly, wondering why his feet had suddenly turned to stone and his tongue to ashes.

"We weren't spying!" Marne straightened in the chair and rubbed his hip, where he'd landed. "We were just..." His eyes were wide and frightened as he tried to placate his father before his uncle cut him off.

"Take it easy, Alain," Madric interjected. "I don't think we've discovered high treason here. I told them about a couple of books earlier. They were probably just waiting their turn to speak. Am I right, boys?" The magician nodded his encouragement.

Teine didn't know what to say. Madric's lie had been smooth, convincing, and grounded in the truth, but it was still a lie. Teine simply could not make himself confirm it. He could count on one hand the times in his life he'd been in trouble. He could also count on that same hand the number of times he'd been completely tongue-tied. But they'd never happened together!

Marne spoke for both of them. "Y-yes, Uncle." he stammered, his fearful eyes darting from face to face. Hamoni's magical verbalizations continued unabated in the background, adding to the surreal quality of the scene. "They sounded good. I was hoping we could have them now."

Lord Solmurrian raised an eyebrow, his skepticism evident. Madric suddenly burst out laughing. "Honestly, Brother!" he chortled, momentarily drowning out even Hamoni's recitations. "You spend too much time at Court. You see high treason where there are only silly children at play. Come, now. Let's be done with this!"

"Done!"

Teine was flooded with relief, and gulped in a deep breath, not even realizing he'd been holding it. But it wasn't Lord Solmurrian breaking the tense silence. It was Hamoni. The Aoife girl dropped her hands to the table as though she could no longer hold them up. The electrical activity that held up Marne's bracelet ceased and the dancing figure in the lamp flame slowed its frenzied movement. Freed from its enchantment circle, the bracelet fell, bouncing with a clatter off the edge of the table. Landing with a clank on the floor, it then rolled a couple feet toward them on its edge before tipping over to rattle against the flagstones.

Lord Solmurrian bent down to pick up the bracelet without loosening his grip on Teine in the slightest. "All finished?" he asked Hamoni, holding it up to peer through.

"Yes, sir," Hamoni agreed, wisely averting her eyes and backing away.

"She's done with her part," Madric added. "She does the pre-enchantment preparation, but I need to finish the enchantments myself. It won't be ready for a few hours yet. You'd probably be best heading home."

Lord Solmurrian's expression darkened further. He set the bracelet down very carefully on the worktable next to Holly. Teine could feel the man's fury compressing the skin of his wrist, where the Aoife's grasp was like an iron band. Madric had forgotten his own cardinal rule of dealing with his brother: "Always let him think it's his idea." Instead of immediately capitulating to Madric's suggestion, the Aoife lord looked around the room one more time, carefully reading all their faces. Then, his grip on Teine's wrist shifted suddenly, and a savage jerk forced Teine to look at him, eye to eye.

"*They* can lie to me, but I bet you probably can't," he growled, his gaze piercing and his breath smelling like stale wine. Teine did his best to meet the master's gaze and divine what was expected of him. The

Aoife's eyes were glazed like those of a madman, and Teine was now absolutely certain the man was suffering from some form of insanity. "Why did you and Marne follow me up here? It didn't have anything to do with a couple of damn books, did it?"

Chapter 10: Heart of Stone

"N-no, sir." Teine stammered. "I came up to ask you if Marne could have his Holidocrith back." Even if there had been a point to lying, Master Solmurrian was correct in one thing: Teine wasn't inclined to do it. His few minor experiments with dishonesty had never worked out well. The notion that honesty is always best had been planted solidly in his brain from earliest childhood, then reinforced repeatedly through experience.

The Aoife lord must have been at least partly satisfied with that because his grip on Teine's wrist immediately slackened. "You came to ask me?"

"Yes, sir." Teine nodded, flexing and rubbing his wrist to restore feeling. He didn't understand the master's behavior. Neither he nor Marne had been up to anything more nefarious than retrieving a toy. It was one big misunderstanding, and the torrent of words that flew from his lips was a desperate attempt to convince the lord. "When I got up here I saw the door was mostly closed so I thought maybe we shouldn't interrupt you, and then Hamoni was doing the..." He shrugged and waved his hand nervously in her direction. "Whatever she was doing. I didn't know if I should just knock or come back later, and then you saw us and it was too late to leave, and..."

"See?" Madric soothed. "It's nothing at all. No need to get up in arms."

"Hmmm," Master Solmurrian's brows were still furrowed in doubt, and his expression stormy. "So," he turned once again to Teine. "What about these books? Did you really come to this room to skulk in the corners, for *books*? A straight up yes or no will do."

"No, sir," Teine reluctantly replied. "I came to see if Marne could have his toy back. But I have borrowed a book and expect to borrow yet another before we leave. Madric has some reading he wants me to do and..."

A ringing, stinging slap to the face cut him off mid-sentence. Teine yelped in surprise and pain, a sound echoed by Marne. Tasting the copper tang of his own blood where he'd bitten his tongue, Teine was stunned into silence.

"Did I or did I not just say a simple yes or no will do?" Master Solmurrian snarled. He then pointed toward one of Madric's stools. "Now sit down, and for once in your ill-earned life, be silent!"

Before Teine could even sit down, Marne had somehow leapt between them, holding his arms wide as if he could shield the much-larger Human boy from any further abuse. "Father, I..."

"Liars." A poisonous glare from the lord silenced Marne as quickly as the blow that had just silenced Teine. "My dear brother. My own son," Lord Solmurrian spat, sweeping his arm from one to the other accusingly. "So full of venom and lies, and the only one who can tell me the truth is Human."

Madric's eyes narrowed, his usually amicable expression giving way to a baleful scowl. Teine prayed silently to both Alemis and Vuaren that Madric would just hold his tongue, give the lord whatever it was that he wanted, and just let it go. A feeling of foreboding clenched his chest so tightly he could barely breathe. Despite his father's tirade, Marne had not budged, though Teine could see him shaking.

"If you want to discuss venom," Madric quipped, his tone pure acid laced with comic irony, "I can bring over a mirror if you need a visual aid. Nobody would be forced to bend the truth at all if you weren't so ridiculous and unreasonable."

"So you admit it?" his brother countered, looking as pleased as if he'd just won an epic court case.

"Proudly," Madric snapped. "You're being a fool and letting your paranoid, foolish insecurities cause you to mistreat your son, the one person in this world who loves you without reservation. This entire conversation is ridiculous! Must we keep dancing this dance every time you come home?"

"Rubbish." Lord Solmurrian cut him off with a rude snap and a wave, knocking Marne's bracelet to the floor. Turning from his brother, he swooped over to tower above Marne. "Why do you always side against me?"

"Father, I..." Marne began, his alien face a tragic mask of hurt defiance. But this time it was Madric who interrupted him.

"Maybe if you weren't absolutely swiving insane?" Madric growled, under his breath.

Master Solmurrian favored his brother with a withering glance, then reached out and grabbed Marne's arm. "Why did you lie to me?" he hissed. "Even if Madric gave you the fib about coming up here for books, you didn't have to parrot it."

Marne raised his chin, rebellion in full swing. "What does it matter? You never believe what I say or care what I think anyway."

Jaw muscles clenched, the Aoife lord stood perfectly still, reflecting both contemplation and fury. Teine's stomach did a lively jitterbug. After what seemed an eternity, Lord Solmurrian finally let go of Marne's slender arm. "In this wretched world of ours, we Aoife are the only people who never engage in any kind of violence against each other."

His voice lowered to a conversational tone, as if he was delivering a lesson. "Duels have been outlawed for centuries and we don't even indulge in the barbaric practice of spanking our children, no matter how richly they might deserve it."

Teine felt a momentary wash of relief for his young companion, until the master changed his focus and locked his malevolent stare directly on him.

"Teine, between you, my brother, and my son, you're the only one who has done right by their honor and station today," Master Solmurrian told him. He grimaced, a chilling approximation of what would be a warm smile on anyone else's face. "I'm actually very proud of you." The Aoife lord began unbuckling his decorative overbelt from atop his velvet tunic. "It's a shame that you will be receiving Marne's punishment in his stead."

"What?" Teine exclaimed, his voice cracking.

"Father, *no!* That's not fair!" Marne howled.

"You've got to be kidding," Madric interjected. "So, the boy does something praiseworthy—something you approve of—and you reward him with a beating? Oh, *that's* the way to build loyalty and encourage good…"

"Enough!" The belt coiled, supple and serpent-like, in Master Solmurrian's practiced hands. Bending down, the lord retrieved Marne's golden bracelet from the floor, tossed it onto the table, and then pointed to Teine. "Off with that shirt!" To Madric, he added, "The standard penalty for lying to me is ten stripes. Teine is only going to get five, for his good behavior. Now, off with that shirt!" he roared.

Teine had been frozen in place, numb with surprise and sick with fear and indignation. Once he had the order, though, he scrambled to do as he was commanded.

"Father, this isn't fair," Marne appealed, again placing his slight frame squarely between Master Solmurrian and Teine. The boy's voice was soft, non-confrontational, and almost soothing as he placed a hand over the coiled belt, looking up at his father with pleading eyes. "It was my error. I should be the one punished."

Even though Teine remained hopeful, off came his overtunic, which he laid on the table. His undershirt needed to be unlaced before he removed it, and he picked clumsily at the knot while the drama played out right in front of him.

"Son," Lord Solmurrian dropped to a crouch, to be on eye level with Marne. His voice was surprisingly gentle. "You *are* the one being punished, and you know it. I could devise nothing worse."

Marne's eyes widened as he realized his father was right. The boy shook his head, eyes suddenly brimming with tears.

"This is a hard lesson, I know," his father told him. "But it's one you need to learn—the sooner, the better. Your actions can jeopardize the safety of the Humans in your care, just as the actions of your Humans reflect on your personal honor and the honor of your house. For what it's worth, I'm very impressed with Teine. I think you made an excellent choice. Few Human boys his age would have acted as nobly as he did. I'll make it quick, and then it will be forgotten, but the lesson will remain."

Hypocrite, Teine thought, still fussing with the fastenings on his tunic. The mock-compassion in Lord Solmurrian's voice made Teine physically nauseous.

"Hurry up, now," Master Solmurrian urged. "Let's get this over with."

Now that Teine's beating was unavoidable and all pleas and negotiations on his behalf had failed, Marne keened an eerie cry of sorrow and shame, burying his face in his hands. Unmoved, the master nudged the boy aside. As swiftly as a barn swallow, Hamoni darted in and grabbed Marne up, wrapping him in her arms and carrying him out of the way.

With a resigned sigh, Teine abandoned the lacing and just pulled his undershirt off over his head. The lord nodded his approval. Master Solmurrian had gone from furious to composed in about four seconds; it was disconcerting. Detached and professional, he kicked the instep of one of Teine's feet to encourage him to move it. "Spread your legs about shoulder wide," he instructed. "And remember not to lock your knees. If you do, you may faint."

"Yes, sir," Teine replied, his voice nothing but a ragged whisper. His mouth had gone so dry he wasn't sure if he'd even be heard over Marne's wails. One perverse corner of his mind wondered what it was that Lord Solmurrian wanted. Did he want to be shown that his blows counted? Did he prefer his subjects suffer in silence? His overwhelming sense of personal failure warred with his righteous indignation, and left his thoughts a jumbled mess.

The five lashes were both more and less painful than Teine had anticipated, and were literally over before he knew it.

"Bring them home when you're done with them," the lord told Madric when he was done delivering the blows to Teine's unprotected back. To Marne he added, "I have business at the shipyard, but I may see you when you return to Solmurry."

Marne fought his way out of Hamoni's grasp with a truly vicious and un-Aoife-like growl. Tears streaming down his alien face, the boy whirled to face down his father. "I don't care if I ever see you again! I *hate* you!" Marne's howls of anguish covered the electric surge of Hamoni's enchantment device as it fired up on its own and sparked violently. When Marne fled the room, slamming the door behind him, the magical machine continued to crackle vividly for several seconds before burning out.

Master Solmurrian sighed, his shoulders drooping and the bloodied belt laying limp in his hands. "Just like Father used to say," he grumbled. "If they don't hate you..."

"...you're not doing it right." Madric finished.

Lord Solmurrian ignored his brother and turned on his heel to head for the door. "See to that," he told Hamoni on his way out, jerking his thumb at Teine. "He'll be no good for Display if he's marked up." Hamoni nodded, her eyes wide and frightened. She skittered out the door ahead of him, and the lord pulled the door shut behind him, leaving Teine and Madric alone to stare at each other.

"Are you alright?" Madric asked, rushing over as soon as the door was closed. The magician's brow furrowed with worry and he was nearly ashen. "I'm sorry, truly I am. He was just set to explode today, and I'm afraid everything I said only made him worse."

Teine, touched and embarrassed by the Aoife's heartfelt apology, tried to shrug it off. "It's all right, Madric." The shrug worked, but he winced. "Ow. Is he always like that?"

"He's not usually that bad, unless I egg him on," Madric admitted. He shook his head disapprovingly as Teine twisted around to get a look at his injuries. "Don't do that. It will just make you bleed. Try to stay still until Hamoni gets back with the dressings."

Teine sighed, leaning up against the table and trying to tune out the pain stinging his back. His position gave him an excellent view of the disemboweled toy Holidocrith that was the innocent cause of the incident. He reached out with one finger to stroke Holly's worn suede and whispered, "Poor Marne." The lashes had hurt. But it didn't hurt as much as the injustice of the situation. How could Master Solmurrian not understand the indelible damage he was doing to his own son?

"Indeed." Madric crossed over to stand next to Teine, and picked up the small, heart-shaped stone he'd extracted from the toy's chest. He flipped it over in his fingers, turning it this way and that. "He forgot his damn stone."

"What's it do?" Teine asked, eyeing the rock and hoping the explanation would distract him from his pain. Aside from its natural heart shape and some symbols scratched on it, Teine thought the stone didn't look like anything out of the ordinary. But things aren't always what they seem, especially when magic is involved.

"It's a family heirloom—one of our oldest, in fact," Madric replied. "Sew it into a stuffed animal and it imbues the toy with a few minor protection spells and makes it traceable. It's been in the family for a long time, but I only realized it was enchanted after I was released from the Monastery."

"Neat," Teine marveled. He was feeling a little blurry around the edges as exhaustion and pain caught up with him.

"Also," Madric continued. "Items that are treasured personal possessions develop their own aura after a time, almost like a primitive form of identity magic. A stone heart like this absorbs and retains the aura of the original item and can transfer it to a replacement." Madric examined the stone for a moment before pocketing it, a somber expression on his face. "Once we realized Marne wasn't aging normally we began looking for ways to make him more comfortable and give him some constants he could count on."

"We?"

"Not so much his father, if that's what you're thinking," Madric clarified. "Marne's servants and myself, of course, have handled the bulk of his care over the years. But my brother did come up with the idea to buy multiple copies of the same toy and to dispense them as needed. We've got another Holly or two stashed in the vault at the Demesne."

Teine nodded. *Good. Marne was right about there being multiple copies of his favorite toy. He'll have another Holly to comfort him.* "Makes sense," he agreed.

"It would be hard to be a child forever, with everything always changing around you." Leaning heavily on the table, he fidgeted. His back felt like the skin had been completely flayed from it. When he'd heard how painful a strapping could be, he'd never really taken it seriously. It almost never happened. He was very sorry to have first-hand experience now to change his mind.

Madric pushed one of the rolling chairs at him. "Better sit down. You're looking kind of green. Here, have a drink." Teine sat down, taking the flask the Aoife magician pushed into his hands. "Not too much, though. Drinking alcohol makes you bleed more."

Teine sputtered through three more or less strong pulls from the flask, the burning in his eyes and throat distracting him from the sting of his wounds. By the time Hamoni got back, his back still hurt but he felt pleasantly numb from the neck up. She unslung a leather satchel from her shoulder and prepared to dress his injuries without comment.

"How's Marne?" Madric asked.

"He went to the basement, I guess," Hamoni sighed. "At least he left before he could ruin any more equipment. I don't know if I'll be able to fix that enchantment feeder or not." With a steady hand, she spread a soothing paste across the first of Teine's stripes. It smelled strongly of tar and stung a bit, but Teine didn't mind her gentle touch and the ointment provided relief.

"You know, Madric," Hamoni continued, shaking her head reproachfully at the magician. "You really did it this time. He's been bad before, but I think this time takes the cake." Her lips pursed in distaste from the memory of Master Solmurrian's temper. "What a bastard!"

Teine found himself nodding at her assessment as he took another pull on the flask. He was worried that Hamoni would be in trouble for insulting one of the nobles outright, but instead Madric just shook his head. "Told you," he snorted. "He's a fool. Worse yet, he *knows* he's a fool. His pride makes him one dangerous little tyrant-in-a-teapot to anyone he has power over."

"Can you do anything about him?" Hamoni pressed. "I mean, seriously, Madric. That man shouldn't have a pet goldfish, much less a child! Marne would be so much better off here with us."

"Here? Where he'd be exposed to the ever-present threat of government scrutiny? Inspectors and Inquisitors coming and going as they please?" Madric scowled, as if he'd thought of this all before and always come to the same unsatisfactory conclusion. He took the flask from Teine and had a swig before capping it and tossing it into his desk. "No. I hate it, but he's better off at Solmurry proper. Fortunately, my brother spends so much time at Court with the Doyen Prince, the Prior, and their flunkies that he's somewhat limited in the damage he can do to both his son and his holdings."

Hamoni touched Teine's back gently, running a finger down his new bandages. "How is that? Better?"

Between the strapping and the pulls off Madric's flask, Teine felt like his head was stuffed with cotton. "Just fine," he told her, then realized he was half undressed in front of the Aoife girl. He grinned stupidly at her and reached for his shirt.

Madric punched him playfully in the arm. "Damn. For such a big kid, you're a real lightweight. Remember that if you take up drinking when you get older."

"Right."

The Aoife magician gave Teine an appraising eye. "You know, Teine, you did a very good thing back there."

"You aren't angry?"

"No," Madric assured. "That was a no-win scenario for all of us. He was in a foul mood from the moment he arrived and was looking for someone to take it out on. I wonder what got him going?"

"Who knows?" Hamoni waved the question away and rose gracefully to her feet. "I think I'll go find Marne and begin the usual damage control."

Teine stood unsteadily and grabbed the table for support. "I should..."

Hamoni waved him off. "No, not yet. I know him, and I think he's probably going to feel too guilty to see you just yet. I'll tell him you asked and see if I can get him calmed down."

"Heads up," Madric called out. Hamoni turned just in time to catch the bracelet the magician tossed at her. "Maybe the sizing ability on this will cheer him up." Hamoni nodded, then left.

"What now?" Teine asked, suppressing a sudden yawn.

"For you? Nothing." Madric assessed him with a single glance. "Bunk in the Blue Room for tonight. Softest bed in the house, and you'll need it. You're off duty until tomorrow morning."

Teine felt relieved, but couldn't stop himself asking, "What about Marne?"

"We'll tell him you asked about him. He needs time to calm down. Everything will look brighter in the morning."

Teine nodded his agreement. A minute later he was slumping down the stairs, replaying the day's events in his mind. Despite Madric's reassurance, he still felt like a fool. If only he hadn't been so surprised to see Hamoni working with Marne's bracelet, he might have been more graceful at deflecting Lord Solmurrian's paranoia. His thoughts tumbled for a moment, like the bracelet caught in the arc of magical electricity, when a sudden realization hit him. Marne's bracelet. Hamoni hadn't been *preparing* the item for Madric to enchant. She'd been the one doing the enchanting!

Chapter 11: Lay of the Land

April 12, 3131

The next morning passed uneventfully. No one really felt like talking, and a generally somber mood hung over all the inhabitants of Madric's Tower. The morning routine proceeded and preparations were made for Marne and Teine's departure.

Early afternoon found the boys and Madric riding along the road back to Solmurry in the magician's red carriage. Madric's matched set of greys trotted gracefully in step on a loose rein, while seabirds called and rode the thermals overhead.

"Beautiful day," Madric remarked. He was dressed in casual clothes and had skipped the waistcoat completely, wearing the collar of his shirt unbuttoned at the neck under his tailored vest. His battered bowler hat was once again perched jauntily on his head, and he'd propped one boot on the front rail of the carriage. If it weren't for the expensive carriage and horses, Madric could have been mistaken for a small holder or freeman.

"Yes, sir." Teine replied, mostly out of habit.

"Hmm," Marne muttered, the very picture of non-committal inattention. He slouched in the front seat next to his uncle, gazing out over the landscape.

Teine was grateful to have the entire back seat to himself. In addition to plenty of legroom, the position offered the best view—of everything. From his vantage point, he could watch both Solmurrians and the landscape. He found himself sneaking looks at his young master and hoping he wasn't being too obvious about it. Marne clutched a bag of his personal possessions to his chest with both arms. Teine couldn't tell whether the boy wanted to protect his bag or hide behind it.

In the bright light of day, the illusion spell on Marne's bracelet was as flawless as it had been in the dimly-lit rooms of the Solmurry Demesne. Teine was utterly amazed at the complexity and *completeness* of the illusion, and how the bracelet now fit around Marne's slender wrist as tightly as a prison shackle. Marne was now, in every way, indistinguishable from a normal Aoife child of about eighty years. The disguise turned Marne into a blandly good-looking boy, but after two days of seeing his real face, Teine had gotten accustomed to the unusual angles of his cheekbones and his odd alien eyes. As an Aoife, Marne now seemed somehow lacking.

More unsettling than his changed appearance, though, was his distance. Since the traumatic event the day before, Marne had barely spoken three words to anyone. Teine knew children in general could be moody, but Marne's attitude seemed to default back to "aloof" unless someone was making an active effort to engage him. Teine didn't know whether to feel annoyed, hurt, or concerned. The part of him that was irritated insisted that Marne should be the one to say something. After all, Teine was the one who'd taken the beating. But the sympathetic part of him realized that Marne was struggling with his own guilt at Teine being punished in his stead.

Whatever the reason, Teine thought Marne's behavior was making the trip mighty uncomfortable. Even Madric's cheerful banter, amusing anecdotes, and bag of saltwater taffy didn't do anything to restore the peaceful coexistence the two boys had enjoyed prior to the incident.

To top it all off, after only a few miles, Teine had to admit he was bored. While the landscape was attractive, the carriage rattled too much to draw or write, and trying to read would have even been problematic. Unused to having idle hands and an idle brain, Teine found himself mentally rehashing his experiences over the last few days. Although the vast majority of time he'd spent on this trip had been satisfactory and even enjoyable, Teine was filled with nagging uncertainty as to what kind of life he'd be leading in the future. He'd always worked so hard to make good choices for himself, and now none of those choices seemed to matter in the slightest.

Leis had been right. Teine's new life was far more interesting and adventurous than he would have ever chosen—and more complicated! He was looking forward to seeing his sister again and telling her all about what he had learned. Her insights on the situation were guaranteed to be helpful, as she most likely knew Marne much better than he did.

He sighed, restlessly shifting in the back seat so that he was sitting sideways, with his side leaning against the back of the seat and his long legs stretched over the bench. His mind wandered to his cohort mates. He was surprised how badly he missed his friends from Mastiff Cohort, especially Marcus and Seymour. It was fairly certain he wouldn't be able to see them regularly now that his life in the barracks was over. And he'd probably be taking many of his meals away from the camaraderie of the Commons, as well.

Even if I could see them, what could we talk about? Teine knew how crucial it was to keep the secrets entrusted to him. He could easily thrill the whole gang—especially Seymour—with his descriptions of Hamoni and how she'd gotten in trouble for flirting with him. He could dish on the illiterate slobs that ran Madric's stables, or keep his friends spellbound describing the breakneck carriage ride through the storm.

But Teine knew that any of these topics, while safe, were merely superficial. Could he still keep his closest friends if he had to keep so much of his life a secret? He'd love to tell Marcus what Marne really looked like under that finely crafted illusion. But he'd probably have to settle for picking the other boy's brain on how to deal with girls instead. Would he confess he'd gotten the first, and hopefully only, beating of his life?

"Hey, Teine," Madric cheerfully called out over his shoulder. "Look to the left."

Teine shifted in the carriage, glad to have a distraction from his dark thoughts. When he twisted in his seat to see what Madric was talking about, his jaw practically fell into his lap. The carriage was traveling down a high, narrow road, with an absolutely amazing view of the ocean. Everything seemed as though it had been washed clean by the storm. All the colors were brighter and the salty tang of the sea was fresh as the breeze stirred his close-cropped curls. There were even a few ships on the horizon, their white sails standing out like seagulls against the turquoise sky. Teine felt such a strong desire to paint the scene that it practically made him weak in the knees.

"Looks like a warship," Marne commented, pointing to one of the vessels closer to the coast. Teine turned his head to catch a better look at the ship, having only seen warships in pictures before. His fingers itched for the sketching supplies that were packed safely away in his bag.

Madric nodded. "That's floating guns and trouble, all right. They really have stepped up both land and sea patrols since those outlanders made it to shore. I hear we've got three more ships and fifty Rangers for our district alone."

"Are they going to make you ride along again?" Marne asked.

"Possibly," Madric replied. "But I doubt it. It makes more sense to have me up in the tower, working on artificing, rather than dragging me along on some boat or patrolling with the Rangers."

Three days ago, Teine wouldn't have understood. However, he'd now seen more magic than he ever knew existed! Madric's gift—even when it was performed by Hamoni—was very rare and valuable, and that would make him a high-demand strategic resource.

"Dangerous," Marne grumbled. Teine could see Marne's new Aoife face in profile, and he marveled once again at the enchantment as the boy frowned. "I hope you don't have to go." Teine felt a pang of sympathy. Marne's worry for his uncle was the only emotion he'd shown the whole day, and it must have been a powerful one to break through Marne's forced stoicism.

"Could Hamoni go in his place?" Teine asked, hoping the suggestion would soothe the boy. "I mean, if they need someone that bad?"

Madric glanced over at Teine, an expression of abject shock on his face. "Oh no!" he chortled in mock glee. "No women in the military, not even the common-born women. Besides, Hamoni wouldn't do them any good. They'd need a *magician* to replace me."

"But, didn't Hamoni do the enchantments on Marne's brac...?" Teine began, thinking back to their work in the lab the day before.

"Hamoni has no magics," Madric insisted. "She helps me with preparation sometimes, but anyone can do that, with the proper training. She has no magic at all. Understand?"

Teine nodded. Madric's forceful denial of what Teine had seen with his own eyes painted a pretty clear picture. Madric was protecting the girl. *But wasn't he also taking credit for her work?*

As if sensing the turn Teine's thoughts had taken, Madric pulled the carriage to a full stop, set the parking brake and stood up. Teine was certain he was going to get a dressing down, but Madric merely pulled out a piece of candy, unwrapped it, and popped it in his mouth. "Ready for a geography lesson, Teine?" he asked, chewing.

Teine straightened up in his seat. "Yes, sir."

"Bah! No 'sir.'" the magician reminded him, waving his buggy whip in a mock-threatening manner. "Madric. Call me Madric."

Teine realized that Marne was glancing, wide-eyed and wary, back and forth between Teine and the whip, as if he was worried Teine would be hit again. Or as if he was worried that Teine was worried. Teine grinned at Madric, hoping to put the boy at ease.

"It's a hard habit to break," Teine confessed. "They really beat the 'sirs' into you at an early age. Not *literally*, of course," he added, for Marne's benefit. "It's more of a browbeating."

Madric chuckled and waved him off. Then he pointed out to sea, where a peninsula jutted out from the mainland. "What's that?" he asked Teine.

"Emmett Peninsula. That's Hilliard land," Teine replied automatically. "They're our closest neighbors, with their Demesne proper less than twelve miles from the Solmurry closehold. The township of Emmett sits on Empyrean land, between us."

"Good," Madric nodded his approval. "What do they do at Hilliard? Besides irritate my brother at every opportunity?"

Marne giggled at the joke, and Teine supplied the answer. "Hilliard is the third-largest cotton producer in the Empyrean," he recited. "They produce more than raw cotton, though. Finished fabric yields an even better profit margin. They're number two in the production of finished cotton cloth."

"Good," Madric grinned. "As far as exports go, one could say they produce some of the finest-looking Aoife women in the Empyrean, as well," he chuckled. "But you didn't hear that from me." Madric winked playfully at Marne, then sat back down in his seat. With a practiced hand, the magician took the brake off and urged his team forward. "Are you up for a trick question?"

"I feel lucky," Teine countered, glad that they all seemed to be feeling less tense. "Bring it on!"

"All right, then, professor." Glancing at Teine out of the corner of his eye, Madric settled his bowler firmly on his head at a rakish tilt, as if he were a gentleman going courting. "What percentage of our total cotton and cloth consumption does Solmurry currently purchase from Hilliard?"

Teine blinked. He was sure they'd have covered the topic under local economics or some of the other classes he'd taken, but now that he was on the spot he was drawing a complete blank. "All?" he guessed, making the choice that made the best economic sense.

"None," Marne supplied.

"None?" Teine was surprised. "That can't be right. If you have such an obvious resource so close, it makes nothing but sense to take advantage of it."

"Lord Hilliard went to school with us Solmurrian lads," Madric interrupted. "I'm sorry to say that Marne's right. Due to a foolish schoolboy feud, my brother refuses to do any business with Hilliard, no matter how much logical sense it makes."

"Ugh," Teine groaned. He, like everyone else in the world, had heard of the feud between Master Solmurrian and the Hilliard clan. "It's that bad, huh?"

"Indeed. And expensive, too."

They passed the next few miles in relative silence, each lost in his own thoughts. The time passed quickly and soon they were driving under the arched limestone trellis where espaliered ornamental cherry trees marked the Solmurry main road. With the downpour of rain they'd received and the mild weather since the storm, the trees were bending under the weight of their fragrant blossoms.

Teine was surprised by the strong emotion he felt when they passed under the arch. He was home. The Solmurry estate sign, carved in stone and decorated with flowers, was both familiar and comforting. It was a part of his heritage, something strong and solid he could take pride in. No matter what direction his life took, he would *always* be Teine of Solmurry. That name was better than hard currency, in some places.

A few minutes later they turned right at the privet hedges and bell house and began clattering up the brick lane. The servant on watch began ringing the bells as soon as she recognized the carriage. As Solmurry had so many different kinds of visitors, they had an excellent system for identifying which ones required special treatment upon their arrival. Madric was always announced with a ring from the high bell, then a ring from the low bell.

The magician tipped his hat to the buxom red-headed Human girl watching the post as he went past, then tossed her a handful of saltwater taffy. She squealed with delight and called out her thanks as they pulled away. Teine was certain she was one of Leis' Cohort, but he couldn't remember her name. When he turned around for a better look to see if he knew her, she pulled the neckline of her blouse down to expose her bare breasts to him for a second, before blowing him kisses and waving goodbye.

"I love my job," Teine whispered under his breath.

Ahead of them, almost as if summoned by the bell, a tattered form came streaking out of the fields where a mixed herd of goats and sheep grazed. Barefoot and swift, the shepherdess reached the road just a few seconds before them and stood in their path, eyes downcast.

"Oh, not again!" Madric groaned, pulling his team to a halt. "Get out of the way, you crazy bat!"

Teine sat up taller in the seat to get a better view of the goings-on. The shepherdess was a Human woman, perhaps in her twenties. She might have been very attractive, except for her unkempt wildness and blank unfocused expression. Teine thought he caught a glimpse of a green diamond on the back of her left hand and wondered if she might be simple.

"Oh, it's Miska!" Marne cheered, patting the side of the carriage like one might call a dog. "Hi, Miska! Come on over and see me!"

"You only encourage her when you do that," Madric lectured. "It'd be better for her to put a couple of stripes across her legs. I know you mean well, but she's going to get run down sometime if she keeps this up."

With a wide and vacant grin, Miska bounded over to Marne's side of the carriage, petting and stroking the boy's hands in an embarrassing display of servile affection. "Aww…" Marne murmured. "Don't be so mean! She just likes the attention. She used to love it when she was little and I read stories in the nursery. Are we out of taffy? Do you have any left?"

Madric grumbled, but pulled his rucksack into his lap and began digging through it for more candy. For the second time that day, Teine's jaw dropped in astonishment as he saw the woman and Marne deftly exchange and tuck away folded up squares of paper. Then, while Madric was still occupied, Miska's demeanor completely changed. The simpleton facade fell away as she caught his eye, looked him frankly up and down, and then gave him a wink that was half mischievous, half seductive. It left him surprised, both embarrassed and aroused. But by the time Madric turned back, she was firmly back in character as the simple shepherdess.

"Here," Madric shoved a few pieces of stray candy into Marne's hands. "I know she's probably lonely out here, but she really shouldn't be encouraged to mob carriages."

Marne passed the sweets along, and Miska fell on them, ripping off wrappers and shoving them into her mouth, licking and smacking noisily. "Oh, all right," Marne acquiesced, pushing her gently away. "Bye, Miska! See you later!"

She appeared not to notice as the carriage pulled away, and Teine had to force himself not to look over his shoulder to see which Miska would be looking back at him.

Chapter 12: Homecoming

Madric's carriage crested the top of the last hill before the long, gradual slope wound down into Solmurry's valley. Neat hedgerows broke up parcels of land, and animals and people looked like little toys on an expanse of patchwork carpet, verdant in its spring splendor. Teine could still smell the cherry blossoms.

A noisy, mixed lot of hunting, herding, and varmint dogs, led by Stinky, burst out of one of the ditches intersecting their path. Marne whooped with delight, yelling greetings to his favorites, though the canine din mostly drowned out his words. Even with his permanent arthritic gimp, Stinky the Wolfhound outpaced the rest of his fellows by virtue of his long legs, without looking like he was even trying. His grizzled face wrinkled with that peculiar doggy grin as he panted alongside the carriage, leaping to lick Marne's outstretched hand.

Teine hung over the edge, watching the throng of dogs with amusement. He didn't have to be a dog expert to see that most of the dogs weren't just chasing a carriage; they were there for Marne. Now that he thought about it, he'd frequently seen Marne out and about with a pack of canines following him. Teine wondered what that would be like. From as far back as he could remember, he'd always longed to have a dog of his own. A great big one, a powerful swift breed, perhaps a mastiff or a wolfhound like Stinky. It'd be nice to have someone who was always glad to see him, who followed him around and belonged to him.

It was then that he realized that *he* was, for all intents and purposes, a dog. Marne's dog.

His good mood evaporated and he slumped back in his seat, trying not to dwell on that thought.

As they approached the Demesne, they had to yield the road in the last hundred yards. Madric deftly reined in his team and guided them off the bricked road and onto the neatly manicured shoulder to make room for a massive horse-drawn contraption coming the other way.

"What's that?" Teine asked. "It sure looks fancy."

"That's the lorry," Madric answered with a rueful chuckle. "And it'd better be fancy, for what they charge. Only the most expensive horses ever get to ride on it. The cheap ones aren't worth the trip." Seeing Marne's reproachful glance, Madric added, "I'll bet they just dropped off Willis."

The squarely-built horse box was a conveyance drawn by a team of six powerful white draft horses. With legs like marble pillars, each weighed in at about twice what either of Madric's greys would. Hooves the size of dinner plates, clad in iron, hammered down on the brick road, creating such a racket that Madric's greys flinched and twitched as they approached. Looming behind the draft team, the conveyance towered, with two Aoife drivers and a whole handful of sturdy Human footmen. A series of scaffolding, metal poles, and canvas netting was secured tidily to the top of the rig. Teine couldn't stop staring as the crowd of Solmurry dogs parted and the lorry rattled past.

"We need to go right to the main stable," Marne insisted, as soon as the hoof beats had passed far enough for him to be heard.

By the time Madric's red carriage and noisy canine escorts had made the last hundred yards to Solmurry's closehold, Teine noticed an official Church stagecoach parked under the carriage stand at the main house. The elaborate rig—fancier than Madric's, even—was emblazoned with

Prior Vihah's personal heraldry. The four-horse team of powerful bays and their carriage were slowly circling the drive. Lathered up and still breathing hard, the tired horses were being cooled off gradually at a walk before they were offered water or feed.

"Looks like the Prior is here," Madric observed. "And he rushed." The Aoife practically had to shout to be heard over all the yapping. "Probably to pray for Willis's healing, I'd wager. Sounds like she needs all the help she can get."

"I hope he can help," Marne agreed. "Willis is one of my favorite people, even if she's not a two-legged one." His voice sounded a little shaky, and Teine could see his pale hands gripping the rail.

Madric reined in his team and turned them into the driveway roundabout, navigating his rig around the Prior's conveyance.

All the appropriate household staff was assembled and waiting to see the Solmurrians home. There looked to be at least fourteen Humans in the press, and Teine was relieved to see Leis there, front and center, like the Head Nanny should be. Teine admired her tidy grey pinstriped uniform and white head kerchief signifying her new status. She looked so young and trim next to her more matronly counterparts. As Teine scanned the rest of the faces, he realized they were mostly strangers. Once again, he was impressed with the vast amount of people it took to run a Demesne like Solmurry, and how little he actually knew about how it all worked.

"No!" Marne yelled, stamping his foot as Madric reined his team in, and guided them toward the Demesne to park. "To the stable!" The magician reached over and ruffled Marne's hair, turning his team away from the pull-in. The dogs fanned out behind them, like the tail of a very noisy comet.

"Well, you heard the boy!" Madric called to the assembly, waving them along to follow as if he were a general mustering his troops. "To the stable!"

Teine looked back over his shoulder to watch the entire mass of people abandon their posts at the carriage stand. He was a little bit awed to see how many people had to change their plans to suit the whim of one child. Even if Marne didn't seem to be spoiled, it was still a lot to take in.

While Teine was watching the household staff follow, Leis caught his eye and snuck a quick, silly finger-wiggle of a wave at him. Proper uniform or not, she was still Leis.

And, as Madric was still Madric, he didn't bother waiting for the servants to catch up or the grooms to join them before disembarking the carriage. He simply drove up, set the parking brake, and jumped down into the throng of excited dogs. His team of greys, although high-strung, had the advantage of having enough exercise and enough experience with the Solmurry dog population to be in no hurry to rush off. Solmurry's stables meant a good rubdown, a bit of leisure, and as much good, leafy hay as they could eat. The pair, unimpressed with canine foolery, stood patient except for an occasional head toss.

Both of Master Solmurrian's personal manservants were the first ones to reach the stable and greet Madric. The two mature Human men were absolutely resplendent in their scarlet and gold Solmurrian livery. Teine inspected them closely. Theirs was a position of privilege, and they were the closest thing he'd have to peers in the household. Their hair was worn longer than the common servants were allowed, and tied back with a velvet ribbon in the style that was popular with the Aoife noblemen. Just as Teine was wondering if he'd get a uniform like theirs in time, Madric clapped both of them on the back, shook their hands and greeted them by name.

"Andreas! Lesmar! By Pete, it's been forever since I've seen you lads!"

'Lads' they were not. Teine couldn't help but grin as Lesmar of Solairn—his own sire—caught his eye and winked. Teine hoped his red flush of embarrassment was hidden under what was left of his sunburn. He couldn't believe he had almost failed to recognize his own sire because he'd been too busy looking at clothes!

Square-jawed, proportionate, and handsome, Lesmar was aged but exuded an aura of vibrant health that put many a younger man to shame. He'd already been in the service of Master Solmurrian for a full thirty years and had over a hundred offspring on the ground by the time he'd sired Teine. Even so, his full head of wiry auburn hair and proud bearing defied attempts to guess his actual age. Whenever Teine had spent time with him, he'd carried away an impression of Lesmar's unique blend of dignity and enthusiasm for life. His sire was good company and he hoped they'd get to speak when it was convenient.

"I bet you're proud of our boy, here," Madric continued. "Good head on his shoulders, problem-solving skills, and doesn't miss a trick, does he? Marne made a good pick."

"I always expected the best for him, sir," Lesmar rumbled, returning Teine's grin. His chest puffed out so much that Teine wondered if he might lose a button.

"I did my research," Marne added, readying his bag, canteen, and other things to disembark the carriage. "I thought he'd be the best fit."

It was then Teine realized they were talking about *him*. He'd spent a lifetime being proud Lesmar was his sire, but this was the first time he'd ever heard Lesmar praise him—and to an Aoife, no less! It was a heady feeling. Teine was mentally basking in the praises of his sire when the rest of the staff caught up one and two at a time.

Marne nodded pleasantly to Lesmar, who'd taken it upon himself to hold the carriage door open. Clambering down into the mess of dogs, he dodged an onslaught of sloppy dog kisses while the two-legged committee mostly ignored him. Without a word to anyone, Marne held his arms out to the dogs, and as if by magic, Stinky was there. The boy hugged his grizzled old favorite around the neck, his eyes squeezed tight. Teine thought he saw moisture there, but perhaps he was the only one to notice. Then Leis arrived and crouched to embrace both the boy and his hound.

"You still in there? What's keeping you?" Phoebe's voice grated on Teine's ears and he immediately winced, remembering their first meeting. She and Leis had walked over together, and Phoebe was standing on tip-toe to see over the edge of the carriage.

His irritation ended there. Phoebe, still heavily pregnant and sweating profusely, stood with both hands on her mid back and her belly out ahead. Her ankles were nearly the size of her calves. Her hair had partially pulled free of its confining bun, framing her clammy face with unruly wisps. The dark circles under her eyes belied the rest of her otherwise youthful appearance. Teine found himself immediately sympathetic. Now that he'd had more exposure to Master Solmurrian, he could completely understand why his mere presence under the same roof could cause any housemaid a few sleepless nights. He expected that Phoebe would feel much better once His Lordship was tucked away in a carriage and headed back to Court again. He knew *he* would.

"What's your hurry?" Teine bundled his satchel over his shoulder. "Did you miss me?" There was something tragic about Phoebe's situation that left him unsettled and desperate to move. Rather than wait for the Aoife to clear the way, he vaulted over the side of the carriage and landed in front of the pregnant woman with what he hoped was a comic flourish. "Ta da!"

He was rewarded by her wan smile. "You're a goof. You and Marne are going to get along just fine."

Marne turned to glance at them for the barest of instants before looking away. He still refused to meet Teine's gaze, and Teine still wasn't certain exactly how he felt about taking the beating in his place. Suddenly it was all a blur, his father's praise, the lash welts stinging on his back, Marne's avoidance—too many uncomfortable feelings, all at the same time.

Teine was relieved when Madric broke the awkward silence, snapping his fingers to get the attention of one the grooms tending to his team. "Is Willis in there?" he asked, hooking his thumb toward the stable.

"Yes, sir. She's laid up in first broodmare stall, to the left."

Madric crouched to look his nephew in the eye. "Marne, are you sure you want to visit her? She only just arrived." He looked around, helplessly, for advocates. Teine was surprised when Lesmar spoke up.

"Young Master, her wounds are grave," Lesmar rumbled. Then, the big man crouched down to look Marne in the eye. "She may not make it."

"All the more reason," Marne told him, peering out from around Leis' waist. "She is my friend."

"She has a lot of friends," Clinician Nocdoramus quipped, stepping out of the barn into the light. "And that damn horse hauler from town isn't one of them. Honestly! Just because you own a medical EVAC vehicle does *not* make you a veterinarian!"

Teine blinked in shock. The clinician usually had the calm, confident air of professionalism. But today, her usually tidy smock was splattered with red stains, some of which were darkening to the rusty shade of dried blood, and her eyes were a little puffy. Teine was certain the good doctor had been crying, or trying very hard not to.

"Prior Vihah got here just in the barest nick of time, and I do mean the barest." Nocdoramus smiled down at her gore-covered rubber gloves, then peeled them off with an expression of triumph. "I don't care *how* we save them, as long as we save them!" Madric gave her a sharp look, and she shrugged. "It's no secret. I'm not fond of the man, or his methods."

"Woah, settle down there now!" the magician laughed. "Come on, Doc. How long have you been on your feet today? Have you even had lunch yet?"

The clinician looked for the sun's position, shielding her eyes with one hand and grabbing her back with the other one. Her stiff, hunched position reminded Teine of poor pregnant Phoebe. "Lunch?" she murmured. "I'd settle for breakfast."

With that, Madric gently gathered her arm in his and patted her hand. "My dear, it's midafternoon. Let's get you a mug of cider and some good stew before you get in trouble with the Theocracy."

Nocdoramus allowed herself to be steered away, but not before she caught Lesmar by the sleeve. "Lesmar, will you please make sure those grooms have it right? Willis is *never* to be left without at least two grooms. Big, strong ones who can turn her over, I mean. Make sure they know to change over the bag before..."

"Did you write it all down, Doc?" Madric asked.

The clinician nodded. "Yes, it's all there on the table with the gifts. Shifts, spare fluid bags, and everything. Just..."

Madric nudged her along gently. "Lesmar will review it all and assign personnel if he needs to. Come on. Time to take care of yourself before you head back to town."

"No, I'm staying here. There's a cot..." Madric opened his mouth again to interrupt her, but she swatted him with her surgical gloves. "And I *am* staying at least a day or two with her. I won't hear otherwise. However, I will take that bowl of soup. And a bottle of hard cider."

Inside the stable, a knot of onlookers seemed to have broken up and were leaving the building. In the confusion, Teine glanced around for Marne and realized he was gone. "I think Marne went in already," Leis told him.

"He did." Solmurry's resident barber, a half-breed nicknamed "Snippy," pushed between the siblings on his way out the door, rudely shouldering into Lesmar as he went. "Poor little son is in there crying his eyes out."

A protest was forming on Teine's lips, but died unuttered when he recognized the speaker. Oddly enough, at that same moment, Snippy turned back around and paused to give Teine a critical once-over. "Don't miss your appointment, boy. Better look sharp if you want to travel in such exalted circles." Then, shoving his hands into the pockets of his barber's smock, Snippy walked away, whistling a jaunty tune.

"What a jackanape," Leis whispered. Of course she'd whisper. Behind every half-breed is a story, and Snippy's story was simple. Even though his mother had been Human, Snippy was half-brother to both Lord Solmurrian and Madric.

"Aww, he's not bad." Teine liked Snippy. The barber had never been anything but nice, in his own gruff way, to Teine and his Cohort. But he did have a reputation for throwing his status around with some of the adult Human men.

Lesmar barely shrugged, as if the exchange was beneath him. "Better go to the young master," he said. Teine agreed. He could hear Marne's wracking sobs from where they stood.

Chapter 13: A World of Pain

Teine pushed his way into the large broodmare stall where Willis lay. The sheer number of people in attendance was a bit of a surprise.

Willis had been a fixture in Solmurry since the last war. Having carried the Old Master into battle long before Marne's father was even born, Willis had notoriety. Even the Doyen Prince knew her name, as Emperor Vondahasha had awarded the Holidocrith a title and medal of valor.

Now Willis the True was just simply Willis, and had aged her way out of active soldiering decades ago. Old war wounds had rendered her telepathically mute and unable to communicate through projection, as her kind was wont to do. Because of her disability, she'd been given a post to guard out in the pasturelands, where she would rarely need to express much of anything. But here, in the closehold, her notoriety still held sway. She was Solmurry's own, a hero in her own right. Now that she lay beaten and bloodied by unknown assailants, her people rallied around.

Human and Aoife alike clogged the barn aisle way, loitered in the doorway, and lined the perimeter of the stall, three and four deep in some places. Their gifts, mainly flowers and edibles, overflowed a table set aside. Their soft-spoken conversations did nothing to drown out Marne's gut-wrenching sobs. Mentally, Teine kicked himself for letting Marne slip past him. The last few days had taught him that despite all his years, Marne was still just a child. No child should have to face such a scene.

In the center of the stall, Marne huddled over the Holidocrith's still and bandaged form. Teine winced, grateful he'd been somewhat prepared for the sight. Willis was the most damaged creature he'd ever seen that was still breathing. Even though Clinician Nocdoramus had only just left, deep maroon stains were already spreading across Willis' fresh bandages. And oh, the bandages! They covered most of the Holidocrith's leathery body. If it weren't for the regular rise and fall of her flank, Teine would have doubted that any creature could live through such grave injuries.

He wormed his way through the throng to crouch at Marne's side, the bite of antiseptic odors warring with the sweet scent of straw bedding and flowers. "Hey there," he whispered, placing a hand on the boy's back. "She's going to be all right."

Unable to stop weeping, Marne simply pointed at Willis' head. The bandage over her empty eye socket was already soaked clear through. Worse yet, the area was misshapen, as if the blow that had taken her eye had also caved in her skull. Teine found himself fighting an unexpected wave of dizziness and wishing he hadn't looked so close. No wonder Marne was distraught.

Resigned, but uncertain of what he should do or say, Teine folded himself into the straw and sat cross-legged next to the boy and his wounded friend. He glanced up at the adults, hoping for some guidance or approval. Either would do.

"Who would do such a thing?"

"I heard it was a peasant uprising."

"I heard it was shipwrecked brigands."

"Are we safe? Should there be more guards? Should we close the Demesne gates?"

Nobody was volunteering anything useful, so Teine found himself staring helplessly at Willis. Although he'd only met her once, he couldn't help but feel like she was a friend. To think, he'd lived his whole life unaware that she and others like her silently patrolled the wild lands, protecting the Demesne from threats. It made his throat constrict and his eyes fill to realize that she'd almost died protecting a bunch of people who didn't even know she existed, much less knew her name. Live or die, he was profoundly grateful he'd gotten to meet her. He could only hope he'd have the opportunity to tell her that someday.

He'd always been curious about Holidocrith and their unique anatomy, and the part of his brain that was always clamoring for more knowledge was screaming at him to pay attention. Teine had always thought Holidocrith had some horse-like and some dog-like properties and were covered with a dragon-like skin. But the more he saw of them, the more intriguing and complex he found their anatomy. At the moment, he was graced with a fantastic view of the underside of Willis's front paws, and they were nothing like a dog *or* a horse. He longed to pick one up and manipulate it, so he could examine the delicate but strong system of bone, flesh, sinew, and claw that allowed Holidocrith to run as fast as a coursing hound, carry a rider, and still command a somewhat functional ability to grasp and manipulate objects. All that, and retractable claws, too! Teine could do nothing but marvel at their versatility.

Marne was still crying, his small hands stroking Willis' neck, his features contorted by grief. Feeling the hot prickle of tears behind his own eyelids, Teine threw himself back into his own thoughts to avoid having to deal with the raw emotion in the room. Curiosity overrode decorum, and he reached for one of the Holidocrith's paws with both hands.

The instant his fingers brushed the pad of her foot and her fetlock, Teine was overcome by a dizzying rush of sensation. Suddenly, he *was* a Holidocrith! Air pouring in and out of his nostrils, he could scent the prey on both nose and tongue as he raced at full gallop in pursuit. Sinewy and powerful, his thickly padded feet drummed out a staccato pattern on the dirt while his muscular tail and elegant neck counterbalanced each other and aided his graceful, high-speed direction changes. He was power. He was speed. He was—suddenly overwhelmed with a wash of rage and sense of betrayal! He blinked quickly, shaking off the feeling. What in the world?

"Look, she's dreaming," Marne sniffled. Willis' legs, tail, and ears were all twitching. She looked for all the world like a sleeping hound dog. "Must be chasing something."

Or fighting something, Teine thought.

"That's a good sign," one of the medics proclaimed. "She's using both sides of her body. This means if she has damage to her brain, it probably isn't serious."

Teine released Willis' paw, shaking away the odd sensation of speed, and breathed a sigh of relief. He felt somewhat guilty, as if he'd inadvertently witnessed something deeply personal and private. "Must be," he agreed, then lapsed into silence. At least Marne wasn't crying anymore.

After a few moments, he looked back over his shoulder at the adults. "So, what happens next?"

"We watch, in rotating shifts," replied a familiar voice. Teine craned his neck to see who spoke, and was rewarded by Marcus beaming at him. "I've volunteered for a few. We're supposed to alert the Clinician if anything changes."

Teine only nodded, amused at how relieved he felt. Marcus was just like him, with no special skills or training, but Teine knew Marcus was solid. Trustworthy. Responsible. Absolutely nothing was going to happen to Willis on Marcus's watch.

"I wish she'd wake up," Marne sighed. "Then she could tell me what happened. I want to know who attacked her, so they aren't out there, running around loose."

The crowd murmured their agreement, and Teine rose to his feet to stretch for a minute. He just couldn't sit still any longer. The close quarters and stifling concern of the onlookers was wearing on him. It was time to *do* something.

He was surprised to find Marne following his lead. The boy looked up at him, straw on his clothes and tear-stained face, then slipped his hand into Teine's. It was Marne's first real interaction with him since Teine had been punished in his stead.

"I want to go home now," Marne told him, then pulled them toward the door.

And, at that, the crowd parted to let them through.

Chapter 14: Settling In

Teine was surprised to see both Leis and Phoebe still waiting for them outside the stable. He wasn't surprised to see Stinky the Wolfhound, who lay grinning and panting in the shade nearby. Marne turned Teine's hand loose the instant he saw Leis, and ran over to exchange embraces. Teine smiled as he caught up. Although the master didn't seem interested in his son, Marne wasn't short on people who genuinely cared for him. It was clear that Leis was doing a good job taking over for their Amagi. And Madric seemed to have stepped up and filled the void left by Marne's father. It wasn't a stretch to see how Marne was better off for Madric's attention.

The next thing he knew, Marne was dodging another onslaught of sloppy wolfhound kisses, wiping away his tears. "Stop, Stinky!" the boy giggled. "Now I'm covered in dog slobber!"

"So, how was your trip?" Leis asked, hoisting Marne up to carry him on her sturdy hip as if he were just any child from the nursery.

"Madric fixed my bracelet. See?" he showed her, holding his arm out and shaking it.

Leis took hold of the bracelet and tried to slide it up and down on his arm, then nodded her approval. "I'm sure that'll be more comfortable. Speaking of comfort, I have a surprise for you, too. You received a late birthday present. I bet you can't guess."

"The soap? Oh, please let it be the soap!"

Leis made a mock grimace of annoyance. "Ugh, you always win at guessing. Yes, you got your soap. And a good thing, too. You were almost out. We sure don't want you to be one solid rash from head to toe." Ignoring Teine as completely as if he had ceased to exist, she turned and began to carry her charge indoors.

"Oh, yes. I do prefer rash-free personal hyge- Leis, wait!" Marne exclaimed, pointing over his shoulder. "Teine?" he asked the girl, the main gist of the question unspoken.

"Phoebe can show him around." Teine bristled a bit at the dismissive wave his sister made in his direction.

"Teine," Marne leaned over to look at him and Leis turned her torso to accommodate. "You're free for the remainder of the day. Get settled into your new quarters here in the Demesne. Phoebe can show you around."

"A pleasure, sir," Phoebe interjected, stepping into the conversation.

"And, Teine? You'll begin training tomorrow morning, early," Marne added. He smiled the polite smile Aoife used when delivering orders to Humans. Teine thought it didn't look right on his face, but he couldn't tell if it was the illusion, or something else. "You don't have a curfew as long as Father isn't here, but it could be an early morning. Getting a good night's sleep might be helpful."

Teine bowed perfectly, the correct gesture for the first official order Marne had given him. "Yes, Marne. Have a nice afternoon."

Marne nodded again, all pleasant and phony, then turned his attention back to Leis. He chattered amiably at her while she carried him inside and out of earshot.

Teine couldn't help but feel—dismissed. It seemed odd, somehow, but Teine didn't have the energy to consider it in depth. The day's events had left him feeling drained and off balance.

"Your friend Marcus brought your belongings," Phoebe offered. The ice in her demeanor melted the instant they were alone. She gave him a wicked grin. "He's easy on the eyes, that one. Is he an IM? I didn't see a diamond."

Teine chuckled despite himself. Marcus would be embarrassed and delighted to hear that one of the attractive older women in the kitchen was asking about him. The girl Marcus had been sweet on had a cute, upturned nose like Phoebe's and a similar shade of hair.

"Indeed. We're from the same Cohort. He still needs to go through First Rites, like me, but he'll have at least a limited roster by next spring, I'm sure."

Phoebe's grin widened, and she rubbed her hands together with glee. "That's good news. I like breaking in the young ones." She elbowed Teine playfully, and he felt himself flush to the very soles of his feet as he eyed her obviously pregnant belly.

He was relieved when Phoebe returned the conversation to business. As it turned out, she told him, Master Solmurrian had gone to his nearest shipyard, a couple days' journey from the Demesne. He wasn't expected back for the better part of a week, even if it were a rushed trip. Although Prior Vihah was laying over to get a rest and fresh horses, he was expected to be gone as soon as they were hitched and ready to go. The girls from the kitchen were packing him a hamper for lunch on the road in hopes it would speed his departure. Of course Madric was going to be around, somewhere, but his presence never disturbed the natural flow of Solmurry's workings. Needless to say, nearly everyone Teine met as Phoebe took him around the Demesne was in a far better mood than the last time he had visited the big house.

Although Teine had grown up practically in the shadow of the massive stone Demesne, he'd never begun to dream of how many people it took to properly care for such a large dwelling. His head was spinning after meeting just the kitchen and linen staff, much less the maids, butlers, gardeners, footmen, window-washers, and all the other people who were cogs in the grand machine that was Solmurry. It was complicated, but he welcomed the opportunity to expand his knowledge on that front. It'd probably come in handy later.

Phoebe was a surprisingly good guide, chatting about the local gossip and dishing out good-natured teasing. Every so often she paused to rest, placing both her hands on her hips and leaning back to relieve the pressure of the growing baby on her back. It turned out that Teine's Amagi had trained Phoebe when the girl was new to the Demesne. "I'm sorry I was so hard on you when we first met," she confessed. "It's actually an honor to be the one showing you around."

By the time Phoebe had walked Teine through the sections of the house he'd be using regularly and introduced him to all the staff, he wished he'd both taken notes and drawn himself a map. He'd also completely forgiven her for slapping him the first time they met. Now he found he quite enjoyed her company. When he looked at her he could see the kind-hearted woman, rather than the stressed harridan of his first encounter.

And here is where you'll be living," Phoebe stated grandly, throwing open the double doors to Marne's third-floor playroom and quarters. Teine was still a bit overwhelmed by the lavish furnishings he'd seen throughout the Demesne, but furnishings were easy to overlook here. The picture window dominated the entire room, stretching from floor to fourteen-foot ceiling across the entirety of one wall. Glass doors opened out to a section of the deep stone balcony where colorful caged birds and feather-dragons lounged and frolicked.

Turning back toward the room, a modest student's harpsichord caught Teine's eye. He was eager to run his fingers over the keys. His Amagorra played and he'd always longed to take lessons himself. He wondered if this was the instrument she'd learned on. The thought was exciting, but there was still so much to see!

Turning from the harpsichord, Teine was thrilled to find vast bookcases overflowing with a variety of tomes and fascinating models—everything from ancient suits of armor to tiny, detailed replicas of modern postal carriages. A model section of the Capital City railcar system was built into a large, multi-tiered table. The setup was laid out and ready to play with, complete with buildings, carriages, toy Holidocrith, Humans, horses, and Aoife—all to scale and dressed in costumes from antiquity. Although Teine was old enough to have outgrown most of his desire to play with toys, his fingers itched to examine and move the little models around and become the conductor of the miniature railroad.

In another corner by the windows were tables filled with art supplies and several easels holding drying paintings. A roughly twenty-five-year-old suit of fabal armor that Teine recognized as having belonged to a famous retired player hung in a glass-fronted shadowbox. Several last-century model aircraft hung from the wooden ceiling beams, the largest at least as wide across as Teine was tall.

"Pinch me," Teine whispered. "I think I've died and gone on to the afterlife..." He blinked. All the toys were still there. "...and I must have been a *very* good boy."

"I know. The first time I came in here, I stood with my mouth all agape just like you." Phoebe smiled at the memory. "Isn't it grand? Like a museum filled with everything you'd ever want to see."

Teine couldn't help but giggle like a schoolboy on a snow day morning. Everything was so enticing that he didn't know where to start. The fact that it all looked *used* was even more exciting. This was no stuffy museum. Someone with small hands had been potting plants on the terrace and had left a muddy hand-print on the inside of the vast bank of windows. Projects sat in various stages of completion. Teine was delighted to know that his very own master played with all these wonderful things. And he had an unquestioning confidence that Marne wouldn't deny him the use of anything.

As Teine stood contemplating his incredible good fortune, Leis slipped out of one of the side rooms and softly shut the door like a pinstriped grey ghost. She and Phoebe exchanged a glance. Phoebe nodded politely, then left without comment.

"Have you figured it out yet?" Leis whispered, looking up at him.

His sister's gaze was so intent that he could swear she was trying to look right into his brain. She'd always been an intelligent, thoughtful girl, but Teine had never seen her look so serious. "Figured out what?"

Before she could answer, the other door leading off the playroom opened to reveal the siblings' maternal grandmother. Their Amagorra was dressed in a similar manner to Leis, except her grey dress suit had no striping. Her rose-gold white-streaked hair was tucked into a bun and covered with a white head kerchief, and her wrinkled face had a very matter-of-fact expression. No one except Volsney the record keeper knew her exact age. But she had three daughters still at Solmurry, and at present a total of fifty-eight grandchildren and countless great grandchildren. Amagorra, indeed.

Teine found himself grinning as he sometimes did when he was nervous. He knew Amagorra well, even though he was not as close to her as his female siblings and cousins were. Normally, he'd stride right over, bend down, and give her sturdy old bones an affectionate squeeze. But something in her demeanor froze him in his tracks.

"Have you figured out why Marne chose you?" Amagorra asked, taking over the line of questioning from Leis. She approached Teine, stopping close enough to touch. Her vivid golden eyes were the same shade as Teine's own.

"Uh..." Teine hesitated, unsure of what to say. He'd been so overwhelmed by the circumstances of the last few days that he hadn't given the matter much thought. Now that someone asked him directly, the question made him instantly uncomfortable. It hadn't mattered to him why Marne had chosen him. The important thing to him was that he'd had his own plans and expectations on how his life was going to go and what he'd wanted to do. He hadn't explored any reasoning beyond his own initial resentments. But, clearly, Amagorra expected him to say something. "...for my pedigree, uh, and maybe..."

"Nonsense!" Amagorra cut him off. "There are fourteen other boys in the right age range with similar breeding. Look around the room here. You should have plenty of hints."

Teine bit his lip and dropped his gaze, feeling like a fool. Taking a bare instant to collect his thoughts, he took Amagorra's suggestion and began studying his surroundings. Looking around the room, he was excited yet again at the marvelous diversity of literature, art, and projects he could entertain himself with, and...

Suddenly, realization dawned. It was as if he'd been in complete darkness and was now illuminated in one of those spotlights they used in the theater. Of the fourteen other boys that Marne could have chosen to show in Display, Teine himself was unique.

"I think he's starting to figure it out," Leis whispered. She was beginning to smile, though she seemed to be doing her best to conceal it.

"Shh."

"I think I understand now," Teine replied, looking up at the model aircraft hanging from the ceiling. "It's not just the pedigree. Like you said, there are a lot of us. It's not my grades. Most from our line are good students and stay out of trouble. It also can't be that Marne actually cares if I win at Display, because if he'd cared about that he would have chosen Marcus. He's a lot bigger and more muscular than me."

"Good," Amagorra nodded. Her expression was no longer stern and her eyes sparkled with merriment. Or was it pride? "Go on," she urged.

"It's my mind," Teine offered, then immediately added "Er... or my art?"

Amagorra and Leis looked at each other, then both giggled. "Close enough," Amagorra agreed, hugging Teine around the waist. Teine returned the embrace, his chin resting on the white head kerchief covering her carefully coiffed locks. She smelled like old lady and lilacs. He loved her as much as he loved Leis and their Amagi. The family bond was something Aoife believed that most Humans lacked, but if that were true, Teine knew he and his kin were an exception. If they loved their kin, then perhaps *all* Humans did. Could the Aoife be wrong?

"Honey, I'm home!" he laughed, throwing his arms wide. On a silly impulse, he grabbed up Leis and whirled her around and around, delighting in his revelation and their shared good fortune.

Suddenly, the door Leis had come out of banged open. Marne stood in the doorway, his hair rumpled and a sleepy, irritated expression on his face. He had a stuffed bear a lot like Teine's old one tucked under his arm, and was wearing a set of richly embroidered but overly large silk pajamas. "Will you peahens stop cackling out here?" he scolded, waving a finger at the women. "I'm trying to take a nap!"

Amagorra came over and kissed him on the cheek. "Don't be cross with us, little Master Grumpy Pants. We're just breaking in your manservant."

Marne's annoyed expression faded, though he did squint one eye and act as though he were rejecting the kiss. "Oh well, if you're heckling Teine..." he told them, hitching up the waist of his pajamas. "...by all means, continue. Just do it *quietly!*" With that, he extracted himself deftly from the old woman's grasp, returned her peck on the cheek and retreated to his room. "G'night, Leis, Teine, Silvia."

Teine nodded his head, replying before Marne shut the door, "Good night, kiddo."

Amagorra waited a couple seconds after the door shut, affection for the strange boy as plain on her face as when she looked at her own flesh and blood. Then, she turned back to the siblings. When she spoke again, she whispered, "Congratulations are in order, Teine. But there are some things you really need to know."

Chapter 15: The Sin of Drome

Amagorra gestured to the glass doors opening to the balcony. "Let's talk out here. It's unlikely we'll be overheard." Following her lead, Teine stepped over to the massive wall of windows, then opened the door for Leis and Amagorra. Nameless anxiety warred with painful curiosity, a sensation that was becoming uncomfortably familiar for him since becoming Marne's personal manservant.

The balcony was elegant, yet comfortable, surrounded on three sides by a tall screen of thick, heavy embroidered drapes made of sturdy outdoor fabric. It was a beautiful spring day, so all the drapes were wide open until Amagorra pulled them most of the way shut.

Both Teine and Leis settled into comfortable, padded, willow-made furniture. Teine wanted to relax, but he couldn't help but lean forward, as if by doing so he could meet any incoming information halfway and thus get it sooner. Amagorra held the keys to his firm grip on reality, he was certain. However, Amagorra wasn't in a hurry, and she didn't move directly to seat herself. Instead, she went to a cabinet tucked behind the settee and began winding some kind of mechanism. Leis caught Teine's eye, and hid her smile at his overeager expression.

When Amagorra closed the cabinet, the box began to plunk out a delicate, soothing tune. Immediately, the caged songbirds and feather dragons perked up and added their voices to the chorus. Teine couldn't quite place the sound—it was an instrument he'd never heard before—

but it sounded like an overgrown music box. He was trying to puzzle out the melody when Amagorra finally spoke.

"I take it you've seen him?"

Teine nodded, knowing exactly what she meant. He was not surprised by her direct approach. Once she got down to business, she wasn't known for dancing around any issues or wasting time.

"Without his bracelet, I mean?" she clarified.

"Yes, ma'am," Teine responded. He opened his mouth to elaborate, but a sudden stroke of insight silenced him. It wasn't his place. His opinions on what he'd seen were largely irrelevant to the big picture, and the situation simply was what it was. No amount of editorializing on his part would effect any change or add anything helpful. *Besides*, he thought, *considering our relative lack of privacy, the less said, the less overheard.*

Amagorra noted his self-control and nodded her approval. "Good boy." A light breeze stirred their hair, caused the birds and feather dragons to flitter about in their cages and the wind chimes on the balcony to tinkle in melodious discord with the mammoth music box.

Teine wondered if this speaking area had been set up to make it more difficult for unwanted eavesdroppers to listen. After all, they were three stories up, and the heavy drapes were effective at muffling sound, as was the music box at disguising it. Perhaps the caged pets and the wind chimes also had been deliberately placed to play their parts. It made sense. But he was still eager to get to the information.

"So," he ventured, speaking just loudly enough to be heard by his companions. "What is it that I need to know?"

Amagorra sighed, suddenly looking very tired. Her wrinkled skin had a parchment-like thinness around her eyes that Teine had never noticed before. "It's time I pass the torch, at least on some things. I won't be around forever, and it's going to be up to you and Leis to carry on."

The words struck Teine like a physical blow. *Was she ill? Dying?*

"Don't talk like that, Amagorra!" Leis' eyes were wide with alarm. "You're doing very well! Clinician Nocdoramus said just yest..."

"Clinician Nocdoramus is a complete and utter genius," Amagorra stated flatly. "But even she won't be able to keep me alive forever." Their grandmother turned to Teine, and nodded sagely. "I had the scarleteen fever when I was a child, caught it from a bad batch of vaccine. Our lovely little Clinician—fresh out of medical school then—pulled me through when no one expected me to survive." The old woman sighed, a content and reflective expression on her weathered features. "I've had a long, full life, and I've been living every moment of it with the knowledge I was very lucky."

Teine watched a brief dreamy expression play over her features, understanding now why Clinician Nocdoramus never failed to inquire about Amagorra. He had no idea they had such a long and close history.

"The fever damaged my heart, but other than that, I'm healthy as a Holidocrith. Since my weakness wasn't hereditary, I was still useful for my bloodlines, but I wasn't able to hold up to the rigors of many of the women's jobs. They couldn't sell me or put me to work, and every pregnancy would be a risk, so Marne asked if I could live in the house and keep him company. Master Solmurrian initially said no, but Marne eventually wore him down."

"That sounds like Marne," Teine agreed. "He seems like a stubborn little fellow."

Amagorra shook her head. "Not stubborn. Stubborn implies obstinacy and a lack of reason. Marne's..."

"Willful," Leis interjected.

Amagorra nodded. "Oh yes. Willful is an apt description. And occasionally too insightful for his own good. But not stubborn."

"He's really very sweet. He'll do just about anything you ask with a smile if you only ask nicely," Leis added, an almost maternal expression lighting up her face. "So, how old were you, Amagorra?"

"When I came to live in the Demesne, or when I became head nanny?"

"Both," Teine spoke at the same time as his sister.

"You two are as alike as peanuts in a pod. You both love your stories," Amagorra chuckled. "I was eight when I got the fever, and just at the point where my Cohort would have been expected to go to work part time in the dairy, vegetable gardens, kitchen, or laundry. My schooling was put on hold while I was ill, but I caught up quickly once I moved into the Demesne with Marne. I became head nanny only a year later."

Leis blinked in surprise, "A nine-year-old nanny?"

Amagorra shrugged, "Closer to ten, but no one wanted the job after the last one died of fright."

Somehow, Teine wasn't surprised. "He didn't have his bracelet back then, did he?" Marne, lurking in the shadows without his illusion, was undeniably the most frightening thing Teine had ever seen in his whole life.

"Oh no! Madric couldn't make anything that worked until just a few years ago."

Teine chuckled inwardly, suspecting that Madric's "success" at enchantment hadn't happened until Hamoni came to work for him.

"So, when you saw him, how did you take it?" Leis asked Teine. "Were you scared?"

Pulling his thoughts away from Hamoni's beautiful face and how she'd looked at him, Teine forced himself to mentally rejoin the conversation. "I dropped a candle," he admitted, with a shrug. "Gave me quite a fright. But not too bad."

"I was at least a little prepared." Leis patted his arm gently, as if to console him. "And I still was pretty startled, even though Amagi told me he had an odd look about him."

"It would have been even more of a shock if you two hadn't spent all that time constantly stretching your imaginations, trying to outdo each other with your wild story writing," Amagorra chuckled. "Chips off the old block. And you're both avid readers. Like me, you're a lot more inclined to view the strange or unusual as wonderful and exciting, rather than terrifying." The old woman reached out into one of the cages to tickle a cheeping feather dragon under the chin.

"It seems that's a useful trait in this line of work," Teine sighed.

Amagorra nodded. "Before I'd gotten ill, we children all heard tales of the head nanny, fleeing the room, screaming about strange things. She was a fool, and because of that there was an awful lot of gossip going around about the young master back then. Almost all the Human children were terrified of him, even though we rarely saw him. Utterly ridiculous," she snorted with disdain.

"Were you scared, Amagorra?" Leis ventured.

"The first time I laid eyes on him I had a burning fever and was delirious, but I was also lucky enough to have been the age where I could see Marne as just another child." Amagorra's eyes softened at the memory. "He was there, holding my hand as I got better. I could see that he was different, but nothing to be afraid of."

"So, then you got to live in the main house?"

"After I got out of the infirmary, I went back to my Cohort for a time, but Marne missed me and I missed him. We'd both sneak away and play together." Mischief danced in the old woman's eyes, along with remembered defiance. "None of the other girls in my Cohort wanted anything to do with me anymore. They said I was spooky and tainted. I even got into a few scuffles over it all. Finally, Marne got his way, and I got to come stay. Then we were together all the time. He taught me to ride a horse—astride, even!—and we used to race through the forest we share with the Hilliards."

Leis gasped and Teine chuckled at her response. Likely she was both jealous and scandalized. She was absolutely crazy about horses but she'd never had the opportunity to ride one, side saddle or astride. He'd have liked to tease her, but Amagorra didn't give him the pause he needed to heckle his sister properly.

"We played with Niri, the youngest Hilliard daughter, all the time. She and Marne are good friends to this day." Amagorra's smile was almost child-like. "We played fantastic games of pretend that could stretch for days. Marne always told the best stories. And not from any book, either! I learned to play harpsichord..."

It was Teine's turn to feel jealous. "Lucky," he muttered.

"And now the both of you are lucky, too!" his grandmother enthused. "Far luckier than you realize, Teine. I hope someday to be able to explain the sheer depth and breadth of your good fortune, but for now your primary job is to grow into a sound adult. Learn everything you can. Take good care of Marne, and..." The old woman caught herself, then smiled. Suddenly, her eyes were bright with unfallen tears, but instead of sad she looked both pleased and happy. "Don't mind me." she huffed, dabbing at her eyes with the sleeve of her dress. "We old people tend to ramble and indulge our sentimentality." She sighed before she continued.

"You're inheriting quite a legacy. But you're going to need a few explanations and instructions before you get settled in. Oh, and you'll love your bedroom," she added, giving Teine a look as pleased as a cat bringing its master a mouse. "It used to be mine."

"Whose did mine used to be?" Leis asked.

"Mine, as well," Amagorra told her. "I've lived in both, in turn. But I like the one Teine's in better. It's got the view to the front, its own forward balcony next to this one, and I chose the wallpaper myself." Leis made a face at Teine, and he chuckled under his breath as Amagorra continued. "Both of the rooms off Marne's bedroom were used for either nannies or companions for as long as he's been alive. This whole suite used to be his mother's. When a room sits empty for a long time, Marne uses it for models or as a dressing room or private dining room."

Teine shifted in his chair, trying not to feel frustrated despite his overall enthusiasm. Although he was enjoying the conversation and gleaning useful tidbits of information and history, the one question that was burning in his mind had yet to be answered. "So..." he ventured, hoping he could test the water a little. "Are there any special instructions for taking care of Marne? How do we best keep a secret like this?"

Amagorra made a clucking noise, and her voice lowered to a whisper as she leaned in to fix Teine with a very serious stare. "You're right to ask those questions, young man, but the fact is there are no hard and fast answers here. He didn't come with a manual. I can't just give you a list of rules that will keep him safe. You're simply going to have to watch yourself and learn fast from here on out. Master Solmurrian travels in some dangerous circles with people who wouldn't think twice about cutting your throat for fun—or worse, bundling Marne off to one of the Monasteries faster than you can say "only 'Drome survivor.'"

Leis nodded, and Teine noticed the two women were looking at each other as if they shared knowledge that Teine himself wasn't privy to. Realizing he'd missed something important while focusing on the possibility of getting his throat cut, he thought he'd better speak up. "Excuse me," he asked, frowning. "Do you mind explaining?"

"Not at all," Amagorra answered, her expression agreeable. "This is important, and likely not something you'd have ever caught wind of, being a boy."

"Knowledge of how the universe works is the trade-off for not being able to piss standing up," Leis added, shooting him a mock-smug grin.

Making a wry face at his sister, Teine muttered "You think you're so funny. I'm trying to be serious, here."

"Have you ever heard of 'The Drome?'" Amagorra asked. "It might have been called "The Sin" or "The Sin of Drome?'"

Teine thought hard, but he couldn't recall ever hearing the phrase. "Nope."

"Or the archaic version, 'Syndrome?'" his grandmother pressed.

"Doesn't ring a bell at all." Teine shrugged.

"Sit up, young man," Amagorra scolded. "You look like a slack-jawed layabout when you slouch and twitch like that. There are times when having your intelligence underestimated is useful, but *now* isn't one of those times."

"Yes, ma'am. Sorry, ma'am," he replied meekly. The apology and honorific were completely and totally automatic, but no less heartfelt.

Amagorra continued her explanation, "It doesn't matter what it's called, but 'Drome, the Sin, the Sin of Drome, and Syndrome are all the same thing: a specific set of birth defects that plague Aoife children. It's slightly more common in the nobles, but still rather common within Aoife in general. Also," she added, lowering her voice even more. "It's always been fatal. The last report I heard is that Syndrome affects one out of every ten Aoife live births and over eighty percent of Aoife miscarriages."

Leis gasped. "That many? I had no idea!"

Amagorra's lips were pressed together in a thin line of frustration. "Even though it's very commonplace, it's just not something that's spoken of in polite society. Rather like half-breeds." She paused thoughtfully, then continued, "Oh, before I forget. About the half-breeds: Syndrome never affects them at all. Apparently any Human blood is enough to keep it at bay."

The old woman beckoned the two siblings to move in closer so she could explain in more detail with less risk of being overheard. "As the common perception is that it's caused by something the mother has done—that's why it's called a sin—it's usually kept very quiet. The superstitions are fuzzy on exactly what causes it. Some swear it has to do with the cycle of the moon when the baby was conceived, some say it's from drinking alcohol while pregnant. Some say it's from having intercourse while pregnant. There are theories that are even more scandalous, but the bottom line is that none of the Aoife know, and their science has failed them in getting any answers or keeping any of these poor infants alive more than a week or two."

"Until Marne," Leis added.

"Yes, until Marne."

Teine blinked, then blurted out several questions before he could restrain himself. "So it's always fatal, but he's alive? How can that be? What makes him so different that he's survived and the others don't? Was it something Clinician Nocdoramus did?"

Amagorra shook her head. "No, Marne was already alive and holding his own before our Clinician even declared a major in school. Syndrome is why pregnant Aoife women rarely leave their homes, and more or less disappear from society once they marry. They don't want to give anyone anything to gossip about or speculate on. Once they are with child, no one knows whether they'll have a live, healthy birth or not until the baby's born. Some families will even go as far as to abandon a baby born with Syndrome in the forest, or drown it so it won't have to die slowly, gasping for breath and turning blue."

An image of Master Solmurrian holding his infant son under water leapt to Teine's mind, and he had to struggle to force it away.

"Some villages still blame the mother for the child's defects," Amagorra added. "It's very tragic. That's why the nobles hide their pregnant women from unkind scrutiny until they know the baby is alive and well."

Teine turned to his sister in alarm. He had no idea how he'd lived his entire life and not known that Aoife babies were dying all around him. "Did you know about all this?"

Leis nodded, her expression grim. "We cover it in Women's Studies. It's in the part about the physical differences between Human and Aoife women. We all have to know the basics, in case we end up attending a birth."

His thoughts turned inward on themselves as Teine sat on the willow furniture, considering the strange knowledge his kinswomen shared. Aside from the issue of all the dead Aoife infants, he'd never imagined that there were things that women studied that men didn't. "And science has done nothing to improve the situation or prolong the lives of any of these infants?" he asked in amazement.

"Science has utterly failed them on this matter," Amagorra replied, her expression grave. "None of the Aoife have even come up with a good theory."

"Perhaps magic will have the answer. Or, perhaps there are other children like Marne, hidden away in their own homes."

"Perhaps, Teine," Amagorra nodded, thoughtfully. "But I doubt it. Magics wax and wane, but this has been going on as long as there have been Aoife. When I was young, I did a lot of extra research on the subject, but to get any real answers at all I had to turn to other Humans."

Leis squirmed excitedly in her seat, moving even closer to her grandmother in her enthusiasm. "I haven't heard this part yet."

"Humans?" Teine repeated, trying not to sound like a dullard. "What would we know about Aoife medical problems, beyond what they've chosen to teach us? Do you know how hard it is for a Human to get permission to take any med-tech training beyond basic first aid?"

"Human oral tradition and good old-fashioned storytelling has had far more insight to offer than any of the Aoife sciences," Amagorra insisted. "That's why I was so proud of you when you took up writing together. There are many storytellers in our line. It's a grand tradition. Some say it goes along with the red hair." She patted each of them on the shoulder, in turn, looking very pleased. "But, before I go any further, I need you to both make a solemn oath."

Chapter 16: The Story Tellers

"Amagorra, what kind of oath do you need us to take?" Teine asked, wondering why his grandmother felt the need to dramatize. "And why would you even think an oath would be necessary? I don't mean to be disrespectful, but looking after Marne's best interests is very much in *our* best interests." Teine didn't want to draw disapproval, but he wanted to be understood "Marne owns me. It's not like our loyalty is in question; it's just the way things are."

The old woman sighed. "I'm beginning to wonder if you're both still too young for this conversation. Perhaps this is all too much for one day."

Leis protested immediately, "Just because Teine isn't..."

Amagorra cut her off with one pointed warning finger and resumed speaking to her brother. "If this is going to become all about him owning you, Teine, you're not ready to hear more or take any oaths. You're going to have to come into your purpose on your own for you to embrace it, I suppose. So, let's move on to other topics for now."

Teine was irritated, but didn't want to let it show. Instead, he clenched his jaw and looked out over the lawn. One of the gardeners had begun mowing the part of the front yard that was enclosed by hedges. The flock of peacocks scattered before the soft snicking of the mower. Darkly amused, Teine watched them strutting and preening, trying to impress the world with their looks alone. They had their job down pat. Maybe he should take lessons from them.

Then it struck him: he'd just blindly allowed Amagorra to withhold information from him, information that was not only pertinent to his job but also supposed to be crucial to the very survival of his master. He'd be a fool to allow that to happen. And worse yet, he'd done so without even questioning her motives. While he was certain that his grandmother had both his and Marne's best interests at heart, allowing her to choose whether or not to disseminate information to him based on her perception of his level of maturity wasn't just ridiculous, it was dangerous as well. Maturity or not, he was already embroiled in the situation and needed all the information he could get. This couldn't be allowed to stand.

"No," Teine said, looking back to meet his grandmother's gaze. "You must tell us everything you know."

"Huh?" Leis questioned. Amagorra raised an eyebrow at him, and said nothing.

"You heard me," Teine told the old woman, steeling himself for battle. He heard Leis draw in a soft gasp of astonishment. Both siblings knew Amagorra was not usually thwarted once she'd set her mind on a course of action. Although Teine knew he was opening himself up for an epic dressing down (at the very least) he continued. "Regardless of what you think of my level of maturity, when you walk out that door and leave here, my job remains the same: to be a companion to and protect that boy." He gestured forcefully with his thumb towards Marne's bedroom. "If I don't make the right decisions because you withhold information from me that would help me, you are culpable. Period."

"Teine, no!" Leis breathed, softly. "Don't be such a j—"

"Hush, child," Amagorra held up a hand to silence her. "I'm thinking."

There were several seconds of uncomfortable silence while Amagorra considered Teine's tirade. Finally, she passed her judgment. Teine steeled himself for the worst.

"He's right." Teine blinked in surprise. "Absolutely correct," Amagorra sighed, folding her age spotted hands in her lap. "I suppose when a person spends most of his or her life keeping secrets, he or she can be reluctant to let go of them. It's probably time for some disclosure."

Flushed with the pleasure of defending his position successfully and being treated like an adult, Teine nodded. "Thank you."

"You have to understand," Amagorra began. "When Marne was born, no one expected him to live. You've seen him." She leaned forward to whisper, and for an instant Teine could see a glimpse of the young girl she was when she first encountered the amazing secret that had been hidden so close. "He's always been frail and sickly, but he just kept hanging on."

"What about his dam?" Leis asked.

"A normal Aoife, but also not in the best of health. From what I hear, she was a lovely woman and very kind, but I never met her. She passed when Marne was but a toddler, and that was well before I was born. At her insistence, news of his birth was kept quiet, which wasn't too difficult to do."

Teine and Leis waited—literally on the edge of their seats—for their grandmother to continue. "It was strange enough that he survived, you understand. But he started manifesting strange abilities before he could even walk. You know that the magics were in full ebb a hundred years ago. Generations of Humans had been born that had never seen any magic beyond a sleight of hand or mere tricks. People were terrified!"

"I can imagine," Teine agreed. Seeing Marne in the dark without his illusions helped him truly understand that fear. Before that he might have underestimated what terror could do to a person. "I've gotten a glimpse."

"Marne was strange enough to make the whole population afraid. They thought he was a demon child, or a changeling. Speculation ran rampant, and it became necessary to entrust his care to a small number of level-headed people only. When his mother died, my predecessor took him into a small hovel in the forest and raised him there for many years. His father was insane from grief and completely uninterested in the boy. It seemed the best way to keep him from prying eyes."

"Be sure you understand," Amagorra emphasized, "He's doing a little bit of actual magic now, mostly imitating things he's seen his uncle do. That alone is remarkable. I don't know what he was doing back then, or if he was even the one doing it, but some of the things going on defy description as 'magic' or 'spells.' From what I heard things were pretty lively out there at that cabin!"

"I can imagine," Teine whistled under his breath.

"Sadly, at the time, Madric had only just been taken by the Church and was still sequestered in the monastery. So there was no one to ask for help without tipping their hand to the Church and having them take Marne away, too." She wrinkled her nose in distaste. "They may say 'sequestered,' but what they really mean is imprisoned. No one wanted that kind of life for Marne."

Both Teine and Leis were silent, waiting for her to continue. Teine's earlier rebelliousness had faded completely as he'd listened to his grandmother's retelling of the events of so long ago.

"I met Marne for the first time in the hospital ward, you know," Amagorra said with a faraway smile. "At the time, Solmurry raised many more children than we do now, and when I got ill, the whole bottom ward was filled with boys getting Cut. And we didn't have magic healers to speed their recovery. There wasn't room for me in the hospital. As contagious as I was, even Humans that had been vaccinated might have been at risk. I was nearly at death's door, and since Aoife don't get scarleteen they moved me up to the room across from Marne's. I was running a high temperature and was delirious. One day I just woke up and he was there. I was so sick I wasn't even alarmed by what he looked like. He had them move his bed into the room with me and he held my hand the whole time."

"That sounds like him," Leis whispered. "He's not much like the other Aoife. He's one of the most compassionate children I've ever met. But, Amagorra? What did you find out about Syndrome from other Humans?"

Teine was eager to learn the answer to his sister's question, as well. It seemed very unlikely that Human gossip would provide answers where Aoife science had fallen on its face.

"I'm sorry, children. I got sidetracked. Happens all the time now that I'm growing older. That's why I need to tell these stories. I need to tell them while I still remember them." She let out another big sigh. "It is good to get this all off my shoulders."

"That's what we're here for," Leis reminded her.

"So," Amagorra continued, "Getting information for helping Marne really all boiled down to luck and nothing else. The right people, the right circumstances, and the right time all converged. It was shortly after I'd taken my job as Marne's companion, and was living out in the forest with him and his head nanny most of the time. I'd been sent into Solmurry proper to pick up a few essentials and had just gotten my allowance. I stopped into the Commissary and happened to listen to a few of the women talking. There was a visitor there, an old Human woman from Hilliard. Apparently the master had won her in a card game and was planning to put her on the coach and send her home."

Teine nodded. Even though he hadn't been impressed with Lord Solmurrian thus far, he could easily conceive him doing the decent thing and sending an old woman back home to her people—at least, in that circumstance.

"Several of the young women had just gotten out of their Women's Studies lecture and were loitering in the Commissary, talking about the 'Drome. The woman from Hilliard heard them and beckoned them close. I was lucky enough to have been passing by, and I added myself into the back of the group so I could hear what she had to say."

"That is fortunate," Leis agreed. "We don't mingle much with the Hilliard people, beyond Marne's little friend Niri and her woman."

Amagorra gave a twisted grimace. "Don't even get me started on Lord Solmurrian's foolish grievances; it'll get me off topic. Now, where was I?"

"Eavesdropping," Teine prompted.

The old woman grinned. "Oh, yes. Anyway, I don't remember all the details, but there have been some that have stuck with me like glue—probably because they were relevant to my specific situation. She said that the Syndrome wasn't a sin or a curse at all. It was something that was happening on purpose, to a very specific end."

Teine frowned, once again gripped by skepticism. "What end could be important enough to justify such wasteful loss of life? Is this the work of the Gods?"

"I don't know," Amagorra confessed. "But she said that one day, a child with the 'Drome would be born and live. There would be others to follow, more and more all the time, and they'd all be gifted and powerful. But the first one would be special. Destined for exile from the Empyrean and a journey of a millennium. And when they returned to their homeland they would put an end to the corruption at the heart of this great nation, and restore Humans and Aoife to a state of equality."

"That's a great weight to lay across such frail shoulders," Leis breathed. "Are you sure he's the first?"

Amagorra nodded, her wrinkled lips pursed into a thin line of certainty. "Absolutely. And I think his journey is going to need to begin within my lifetime."

Chapter 17: Prophecy

Leis' eyebrows flew up like two startled birds. "Why would you say something like that? Marne will be too young to be on his own for a long, long time!"

"Well, for starters," Teine interjected, turning to face his sister's question, "We won't be able to keep him a secret forever. Prior Vihah has already started asking some very pointed questions." Amagorra and Leis shared a significant glance, filled with worry. "And I'm sure there are other people who suspect Marne is a candidate for the Monastery. Also, that illusion bracelet is a neat trick, but Madric's having problems with it. It's far from foolproof."

"Indeed," Amagorra agreed. "It's never been about whether or not he's going be discovered. It's all going to boil down to *when*."

"Oh dear," Leis winced. "Is it that bad?"

"Yes," Teine and his grandmother said in unison. Teine continued, after being sure Amagorra didn't have anything else to add. "The Prior pretty much just asked me, point blank, to spy on him."

It was Amagorra's turn to say, "Oh, dear!" Her hand clutched reflexively at her grey-clad bosom. Teine could tell that his addition to the conversation was a genuine surprise to her. "It's fortunate that it was time for Marne to get a manservant. We women would never have had a conversation like that with the Prior," she told Teine. "You're going to be able to go places, hear things, and discover information that Leis and I would never have had a chance to even know about."

Suddenly all the nameless nervous unease Teine had been feeling over the last few days came roaring to a head. It was all making sense, and it was not the kind of sense that would let Teine sleep well at night. "Ugh," he groaned putting his head in his hands. "I think it might be even worse than that."

Amagorra nodded once more. "I have more to add, but please, Teine, you first."

Honored, Teine hesitated. He knew what he felt, but was trying to muddle through the reasons he felt that way so he could explain himself logically and his observations would carry the weight they deserved. Fortunately, both Amagorra and Leis were silent, apparently understanding his need to think before speaking. "Now that I know a little more, I think Madric could either be a huge problem, or Marne's salvation," he told the women, continuing to keep his voice low so he wouldn't be overheard. "And right now, I'm not sure which one he's going to be."

Raising her eyebrow and giving her grandson a sharp look, the old woman demanded, "Why do you say that? I've known Madric all my life, and up until this minute would have bet Marne's life, my life, and the future of our entire nation on Madric's loyalty and love for his nephew."

"I don't know how it used to be," Teine explained apologetically. He could see the stubborn loyalty on his grandmother's face and could understand it himself. He genuinely liked Madric and wanted nothing more than to believe Amagorra's feelings on the subject. But something hadn't set right with him, and he was learning to pay attention when that happened. "I don't know how it used to be," he repeated. "But I believe Madric is starting to be jealous of some of Marne's abilities."

"Madric, jealous of Marne?" Amagorra gasped, with disbelief. "Teine, that sounds so outrageous it's very hard to believe. What makes you think it's so?"

Gesturing the women to lean in close, Teine explained as quietly and succinctly as he could. He recounted the incident in Madric's Tower when Marne had shown them all the inner workings of the magics on the ancient ring, and the expression of jealousy and longing he'd seen on Madric's face. He also told them about Marne's casual use of an actual spell, in mending the candle, and how he seemed to have been able to do these things without any formal instruction whatsoever. And then, for the finale, he told them about Hamoni, and how she was doing the bulk of the work that was making Madric famous while he was taking credit for it. When he was finished, both women were speechless.

"I know," Teine soothed. "There may be a time someday when Madric is tempted to harness Marne, just as he's put Hamoni to work. He could easily do this under the guise of keeping Marne safe. He might even believe it himself. There's a huge potential for further exploitation, here." As frightened as they looked, he was elated to know that he hadn't been overreacting. Their concern was the ultimate validation. "And I don't know how much this plays in," he added, "But Madric hinted that the Doyen Prince was especially interested in the Solmurrian family—something about the Capite and their famous ancestor who rose from the dead. The Prince is watching them, too."

"If that's true, it's even worse than I feared." Amagorra's lips were set in a tight grim line. She reached out and patted Teine's hand. "Teine, son, I know that this wasn't the life that you'd foreseen for yourself, and I'm truly sorry. But can you understand now how fortunate it is—for all of us—that you've been assigned to Marne? You're perceptive enough to get meaning out of your casual observations, and be aware of potential threats to his safety and..." The old woman trailed off, her eyes shining as she searched for words to convey what she hoped to say.

Teine nodded. He'd already started feeling the weight of genuine responsibility on his shoulders for the first time in his life. It seemed there was really no way out. Fate had stacked the deck against him—or for him. Either way, things were never going to be the same. "I understand," he answered simply.

"I wanted to let you know that the Hilliard woman was no idle gossip," Amagorra told him. "I stayed in touch with her until her death, and she told me everything. After she passed, she had some things of hers willed to me and delivered here. She had a massive collection of historical documents and accounts on Syndrome, and even some ancient drawings that had been made to tell the story in case we Humans were ever rendered illiterate."

"Rendered illiterate?" Leis wondered aloud.

"Yes." Amagorra glanced back at the girl as if she'd forgotten she was there. "Everything that we learn now, we learn at the pleasure of the Aoife. If they suddenly decide to stop schooling our children, we Humans can be reduced to complete illiteracy within less than a century."

"That's not good," Teine observed.

"And just like discovering Marne, it's not a matter of if. That, also, is a matter of *when*." Amagorra scowled, a fire coming to her eyes that Teine had not seen before. "You children are far too young to remember, but even in my day, we Humans had many more freedoms that we took for granted and are now gone."

"Like what?" Leis asked. "I have to admit, I'm a little skeptical about this literacy thing. It's in the Aoife's best interest to make us useful. They put an awful lot of emphasis on schooling if their ultimate plan is to make us ignorant."

"This is Solmurry," Amagorra said simply. "Things are different here. Your education is more about showing our stock to be trainable than teaching us to actually think for ourselves. Things really are changing. When I was a girl, Humans used to be able to refuse a post if we hated it. A woman could also refuse any breeding assignment she didn't agree with, without suffering any kind of penalty. We used to be allowed to read anything we liked. And we also had two television stations of our own, with programming written by and for Humans. And these are just a handful of examples. I could get much more specific."

"We don't get the real news now on the radio," Teine added, echoing Marne's sentiment from the other day. "They save that for the television, and give us whatever watered down drivel they want on the radio."

Amagorra chuckled, "You've been listening to the young master, haven't you? He's a little too aware for his own good sometimes."

"He lays out a compelling argument," Teine countered. "Once he pointed it out, I realized that all the broadcasts I've heard seemed to be packed with fear-mongering crap…"

"Easy, son," the old woman warned. "Remember your place. Talk like that can get you in a lot of trouble, possibly even beaten or sold, if it's heard by the wrong ears."

Humiliated, Teine looked down at his hands while his face burned with shame. Amagorra was completely right. Expressing such disapproval of the Aoife's management was serious business indeed. However, it still stung to be scolded. After all, he wasn't his friend Seymour, who was always saying the wrong thing. He was just about to apologize when the three of them were startled by a light tapping on the glass window, then the click of the door as Madric opened it and stepped out onto the porch.

"I'm going to head to town for a bit. Is Marne-?" the Aoife magician said, then froze in his tracks with an incredulous expression on his handsome face. "Silvia, is that you?"

Amagorra smiled, rising slowly to her feet. "Yes, Madric. It's very good to see you. How long has it been?" Teine noticed his grandmother's cheeks were flushed, he thought from nearly getting caught at such seditious conversation.

Surprisingly, Madric crossed the balcony in several swift steps and took the old woman's hand. "Far too long, my dear friend. You look very well. How have you been?"

"Other than old?" she giggled, sounding for all the world like a schoolgirl. Teine and Leis both exchanged confused expressions. Was she *flirting* with Madric?

Whatever she was doing, Madric seemed not to mind. The two of them strolled over to the balcony, where Madric threw the curtains wide. There, they stood exchanging the gossip like old friends, which Teine supposed they probably were. Sliding over to Leis, he watched the two with disbelief for a second, before leaning in to whisper to his sister, "I wonder what the story is with them?"

"They were lovers, once," Leis replied, speaking so softly that even Teine could barely hear her. "She was known as a great beauty when she was young. And Madric is pretty lonely in his tower."

Teine could do nothing but blink. And stare. Then, he caught the glint of mischief in his sister's eye.

She chuckled, "You should have seen the look on your face! It was priceless!" Her giggles turned into full blown gales of laughter, and Teine couldn't help but smile sheepishly when Amagorra and Madric stopped their conversation and turned to look. "Don't mind us," Leis chortled, "My brother's just a gullible prat."

"Most brothers are, you know," Madric observed. He smiled amiably, and Teine realized how comfortable he'd grown in the Aoife's presence over the last few days. At first, he'd thought how nice it was to know an Aoife he actually liked as a person. But even though he enjoyed Madric's company, he was beginning to realize the genuine danger of the situation.

The thought made Teine's head hurt.

Chapter 18: Room to Grow

Madric's unexpected arrival had put a real damper on the intense conversation. And the Aoife magician showed no signs of leaving anytime soon. He loitered, chatting up Amagorra for the better part of the next half hour. She eventually suggested that Leis take Teine and show him his room. And just like that, Teine realized his window of opportunity for gathering more information was closed.

"Oh, I'm sorry," Madric told the siblings. "I do go on, monopolizing your Amagorra. Please forgive me."

"It's all right, Madric," Amagorra interjected. "We don't get to see each other often, and it's so good to catch up. I've just been filling their ears with old lady gossip. They're probably grateful you rescued them." She smiled winningly at Madric, but shot the children a look that suggested that they make themselves scarce.

"I really do need to unpack," Teine replied with what he hoped sounded like genuine reluctance. "I haven't even seen my room yet. But it was good to visit with you, Madric. I really enjoyed my stay at the tower."

"Any time." The Aoife was so casual, he seemed the height of sincerity.

"So, Madric, how is Pasha doing? Is she still cooking for you?" Amagorra chimed in. Teine took that as their cue to leave. He sketched a polite bow, then grabbed the curtsying Leis by the hand and led her through the glass door back into the main room.

"Do you think he suspects anything?" Leis asked, looking nervous. She didn't hesitate long in the main room, but immediately led the way toward the door to Marne's sleeping chamber.

"It's hard to tell." Teine was partially relieved and partially frustrated that Madric had interrupted them when he did. Although he knew much more about the situation now than he had before, he would have liked to have gotten the entire story. He was certain Amagorra hadn't yet shared all she knew. But even with the incomplete information he'd received, it was still a lot to digest all at once. In the course of a couple hours, Teine's life had managed to get even more complicated. He was beginning to notice a trend.

He followed Leis across the great room, hesitating only as her hand was on the door to Marne's room. "Are we supposed to be in there?" he whispered.

Leis nodded. "We're not only supposed to be in here, we're expected to be," she told him. "Both our rooms open onto his, but he's a very heavy sleeper when he's tired. It takes a lot to disturb him. Come on, I'll show you around."

Teine mentally willed himself to switch gears and tried to enjoy the experience. After all, he was about to see his new room—his first private room of his life! They slipped through the double mahogany doors that separated Marne's bedroom from the main areas. The curtains were pulled tight so the boy could sleep. The room itself was mostly filled with a very large, plush bed with rich velvet curtains tied in at each of the four corners. An electric fan whirled silently overhead. Only a thin draping of pale gauze surrounded the mattress, and Teine thought he could make out Marne's slight form nestled in among the pillows.

Stinky grinned and thumped his tail at them as they passed, not bothering to get up from his upholstered cushion on the floor at the foot of Marne's bed.

"Here it is," Leis whispered, gliding soundlessly across the floor and sliding a pocket door open. "I hope you like it, but I'll take it if you don't."

Teine stepped around his sister and walked into the room that Amagorra had proudly decorated years ago. It had rose and mauve wallpaper with stripes and flowers, along with a dainty four-poster similar in style to Marne's but smaller and more delicate looking. Lace and ruffles dominated the comforter set. There was a large stand-up wardrobe in the corner, and a dressing table with an upholstered bench and a chair, all painted to match the bed. As promised, a cut glass door led out onto his own private section of the balcony. As Phoebe had mentioned, Teine's beautiful new trunk and a couple of duffels of his possessions were already waiting for him. "It's very pretty," he told her.

"It's not too feminine, is it?" she asked, hopefully.

Looking around, Teine took in the delicate rose and mauve furnishings and the wall art that looked as though it'd been carefully selected to go with the wall paper. "We'll see," he told her, trying to keep a straight face. "I really like the balcony, but let's have a look at your room." It was obvious his sister was completely smitten with this room, and Teine figured if he gave in too easily he might lose the opportunity to get a favor he could cash in later. Having her owe him one could come in handy.

The siblings crossed Marne's chamber again, this time heading to the other room. Leis slid the pocket door open, revealing a much larger space done in blues and dove grey. This room also looked bare and unlived-in, as Leis was naturally tidy and had only been in residence full-time for a few days. Teine looked the room over, admiring the writing desk, generous padded window seat with shelves underneath, plush bed, and black lacquered furniture. It even had a closet with shelves, built in drawers for underwear and socks, a rack for weapons storage, and space to hang many more articles of clothing than Teine could ever see himself owning.

To Teine, the room was nearly perfect. The only thing problem was his honey-colored wooden trunk didn't go well with the rest of the decor. He supposed he could leave it in the closet. There was no one to impress.

"The closet is really nice," Leis sighed. "If I could take this closet, and stick it on that other room, it would be perfect. But you'll probably end up with more clothes than I have, anyway."

Teine shrugged. In light of this room, he was feeling generous. "If you really want to switch rooms, it's all right with me, as long as Marne doesn't mind." Leis made a happy squeaking noise under her breath and hugged him around the ribs. Teine was glad there was no one around to see. "How did you end up in here, anyway?" he asked. It was beyond obvious that this room had been designed with a manservant in mind, not a nanny. As Marne had been so good at anticipating Teine's wishes thus far, Teine found it strange that the observant boy would slip up with the room assignments.

"Amagi hadn't moved out yet when I got here," she explained. "Now that she's had her room assigned in the dorter, one of the work crews moved her things there while you were away. Not that she's seen it yet—she's in the hospital wing waiting for the new baby!" The girl twirled with delight, then pounced on her gear to get ready to change rooms. "Just think—a new baby brother or sister!"

Teine was privately less than enthused. The last time he'd seen their dam, she'd looked positively exhausted and had large bags under her eyes. Normally, she'd been the kind of woman to practically glow when she was with child. Teine was beginning to suspect she was getting too old to keep bearing children every other year without it taking a high toll on her health. Rumor was that even the master had confirmed that this baby would be her last. To quiet his unease, Teine stepped up to help his sister organize her belongings.

"Isn't this fun?" Leis enthused. "Living so close by, and seeing each other every day! We'll get to spend a lot of time together now. I bet we get even more done with our story writing."

Leis seemed very sure the room switch was, as Teine's friends would say, "a done deal." It seemed a reasonable request that no one in their right mind would have reason to refuse, but Teine didn't want to be presumptuous and possibly get in trouble. Or worse, somehow manage to get Marne in trouble. "You don't think Marne will mind?" he felt compelled to ask.

"Mind what?" Marne asked from the doorway. His fair hair was all askew, and he was rubbing one of his eyes with a balled up fist while his other arm was companionably resting across Stinky's withers. "That you're changing rooms? I expected as much, and truly don't care one bit. Do what makes you happy."

Leis squealed with delight, and bounded over to hug Marne and kiss him on the cheek. "Oh, thank you!" she gushed. Teine was amused to notice Marne's reaction was similar to his—sheepish embarrassment.

"I thought Teine might like to have the wall space to put up some of his own art," Marne explained, ducking the last half of Leis' barrage of affection. "The Rose Room is pretty, but it wouldn't make as good of a gallery." He idly scratched the wolfhound under the collar before continuing, "I have a few things I need to get done today, so why don't the pair of you sort your rooms out and enjoy the rest of the afternoon? We'll get into a routine starting tomorrow."

"Thank you," Teine responded. The thought of putting up some of his favorite art pieces made him want to drop everything else and get settled in as soon as possible! He did a quick mental accounting of his funds and fervently hoped the Commissary would have picture frames in the right sizes without having to specially order them. "Is there anything you need done that I can take care of? I'll be making a run to the Commissary."

Marne shrugged, looking him in the eye for the first time since the beating. "No, truly," he told Teine, a sincere expression on his angular face. "The only thing I have planned is some unstructured free time." He cracked a shy smile. "We Aoife get in the habit of sounding busy, even when we aren't. I just was planning to goof off, preferably out-of-doors. Might ride a pony or two. I haven't decided yet."

Teine was amused at the boy's candor. "Certainly, sir. We'll get our rooms sorted out, but feel free to summon us if you need anything."

Dismissing them with a wave, Marne turned and withdrew from their suites. "He's probably going to get a snack," Leis observed. "Amagi says he's always hungry after he's been ill."

"Well, let's get to work then," Teine urged. "If we hurry, we can get all unpacked and still make it to the Commons in time for dinner with the rest of the gang. I'd love to tell them what we've been up to, the last few da—"

"You know you have to be careful what you tell them," Leis cautioned, speaking under her breath to avoid being overheard. "I know Amagorra was going to remind you of that before she was interrupted. She's always said young people are a threat because we talk before we think, especially to our frien—"

It was Teine's turn to interrupt. "Do you take me for a fool?" he whispered. "I know we can't even hint at most of this, or write anything—even for fun—that might make people wonder how we got the idea. Of course I'll be careful!"

Leis seemed mostly convinced, Teine thought. She didn't bring it up again as they worked in tandem to empty Teine's new room of Leis' belongings and carry them to the "Rose Room." Soon, both siblings were installed in their new quarters, unpacking and settling in.

By the time Teine had finished unloading his trunk, choosing which pieces of art he wanted to display, what size frames he'd need and where he'd place them, Leis was long finished with her room. He came out of the suites to see her sitting at one of the worktables in the great room, scratching away at a letter. Teine noticed something that made him raise his eyebrows in surprise. Outside, on the balcony, Amagorra and Madric were still lounging and talking like old friends, even though a couple of hours had now passed. The glass door was closed, so Teine couldn't hear a word that was being spoken. But he couldn't help but wonder what they were speaking about and observe that they seemed to be having a fine time.

"I'm writing to Samia," Leis announced when she saw him. "If you want to scribble a quick note, I'll add it in with mine and save the postage."

"No, thanks," Teine responded, slinging the book bag containing his sketchbook and notes on framing supplies over his shoulder. He immediately regretted his words, though, seeing the sad expression his sister's face. "It's not that I don't want to write to her!" he amended quickly. "I just have errands to run, and don't want to write a short note when I know she'd rather have a long gossipy masterpiece. I don't mind spending the stamp."

Leis seemed unconvinced. "She's going to be homesick, you know," she urged.

Teine couldn't help but wonder if Leis' insistence on letter-writing had more to do with *her* loneliness at having her younger sister gone than it had with Samia being homesick. It seemed to Teine that Samia might have plenty to do to keep her busy, and lots of new company, too. "I'm going to the Commons for supper to see my Cohort," he volunteered impulsively. "If you're worried about me spilling the beans, why don't you meet me there? We can all sit together. It'll be fun!"

She seemed to weigh the options for a moment before answering. "Not that I'm eager to spend any more time than I have to around your dumb boy-friends," she began, wrinkling her nose with distaste. "But it might be a good idea if I were there. I could make sure you don't slip up and reveal things you shouldn't."

"That, too," Teine agreed amiably. "Besides, since Vosh has gone, I don't think you've sat with us even once. And he was the one that teased you the most."

Leis blushed to the very roots of her strawberry blonde hair. "That dumb Vosh," she grumbled. "It's a good thing he got drafted to play fabal. He's too thick to do anything involving his brain."

"So I'll save you a seat," Teine assured her as he headed for the door. "See you then."

Chapter 19: Thicker Than Water

After wandering the halls for at least ten minutes trying to find a way out of the Demesne, Teine was growing more frustrated. "I swear, I'm going to need a map," he complained to Andreas, the second of the pair of middle-aged Humans who served Lord Solmurrian directly, when he passed him in the hallway. "If you don't help me get sorted out, someone will have to send in trained dogs to find me!"

"I got lost too, my first day," Andreas confided. "It's not that bad. No one will fault you for drawing a map if you feel you have to. But my guess is that in the time it takes to draw one you'll have already gotten your bearings."

Teine grinned, eying the other Human's well-worn but tidy Solmurrian livery. "Thanks for the encouragement." Normally, Andreas and Lesmar would be attending Master Solmurrian at the flat he kept in Empyrea. "Where's my sire?" Teine asked. I don't think I've seen him since we first returned from the tower. Is he out keeping an eye on Willis at the stable?"

The big man nodded his affirmative. "Yes, he is. He thought I might see you before I did." He produced a neat square of paper and handed it off to Teine before continuing. "Normally we'd have tagged along to the shipyards to attend the master there. Instead, he offered us some recreation time, and left us to oversee the lads who will be doing the bulk of Willis' care."

"Any word on how she's holding up?"

"Her condition is still stable, but her injuries are so extensive Clinician Nocdoramus has decided to keep her sedated for a few days. Looks like she'll pull through, though."

"I hoped that might be the case!" Teine immediately thought of Marne, then realized that the young master would probably be one of the first people to know. Chances were that Marne might already be at the stable himself. He glanced at Lesmar's note to see if it had any other information and was pleasantly surprised to see a postscript. "Oh, he wants to get together for a visit later! How long will you both be here at Solmurry?""

"Until the lord gets back from his tour of the shipyards," Andreas replied. "Or maybe longer. Aside from keeping tabs on our patient, we each have a few breeding assignments to attend to. Though, technically, we're on leave and can do as we please. We still have plenty of time on our hands. Why, did you have something in mind?"

Thinking fast, Teine ran down his mental list of things someone new to the Demesne might like to do. He was eager to get to know his sire better, and Andreas was a good source of information. Teine was sure that Leis would also be curious to meet Lesmar. As far as he knew, she never had. He made a mental note to tell Samia, as well, when he wrote to her. "Does he like to play cards?" he asked. "And do you think he might like to meet another of his get? Leis, my full sibling, is also free this evening. She works as Marne's head nanny. I know she'd be delighted to meet him."

"I'm sure he'd find that an enjoyable way to spend part of the evening." Andreas nodded. Teine smiled, remembering the approval he'd seen on his sire's face earlier that day. Andreas continued, "He's very proud of all his offspring. But you, especially, must feel honored. The young master chose you for Display! You'll have to keep us informed of all your preparations. I bet it's changed a lot since our day!"

"I wouldn't know. I was only assigned a of couple days ago," Teine admitted. "Maybe Lesmar can tell me more about it. I'd better go invite him." Excited, Teine turned to go, but Andreas caught his arm.

"No need to rush off. I'm headed to the stables myself."

Teine caught the gist. Producing a sketching pencil from his knapsack, he flipped Lesmar's note over and scrawled his reply and invitation on the back. "Can you see that he gets this?"

"Of course."

They parted ways, with Teine's mood far more buoyant than it had been previously. He was going to play cards with his sire! Andreas had made it sound as though Lesmar would readily accept the invitation.

Like most of the Human boys at Solmurry, Teine kept his own calendar. He'd meant to get in for a haircut about two weeks previous. With his tight natural curls, he liked to see the barber regularly; otherwise he'd look scruffy and ill-kempt. He hustled past the smithy, sizing up the status at the cozy barbershop next door. There didn't seem to be a wait. The small two-story shop was even devoid of loiterers in the rocking chairs on its deep, shaded porch. The sign, reading "*Snippy's Snip 'n Shine*" swung back and forth in the light breeze, creaking softly. Teine supposed most people had scheduled their appointments right before the Eoaster festival so they could look their best for potential mates. It stood to reason there wouldn't be a line now.

As he approached, Teine could see that the shop door was propped open, and he could hear a waltz playing on the radio. Solmurry's resident barber was probably on duty, so he rapped loudly on the door frame and walked in.

"Hello? Snippy?" he called, grabbing one of the newer fabal magazines off the rack. He planted his derriere in the patent leather barber's chair and gave it a spin out of habit, enjoying the whirling feeling of disorientation. Generations of Solmurry Human children had been getting delightfully dizzy in Snippy's chair while waiting for their haircuts. It was practically a tradition.

"Be right down!" the barber called. Teine could hear Snippy's heavy footsteps from above, then the creak of stairs as the half-breed joined him in the front room.

Teine shoved his foot against the floor and spun the chair once more, grinning. "How are things going, Snips? How are you doin', ya big elf?" Normally the racial slur would spur any half-breed to fight, as they generally had inherited their hot tempers from their Aoife parent. In this case, though, "elf" was nothing more than the usual opening gibe in their habitual banter.

"Right as rain, little son, right as rain," Snips answered, returning Teine's grin in kind as he pulled scissors and comb from a jar of clear fluid and shook the excess off over the sink. "So, I hear you're going on to Display, huh?"

"Yep," Teine nodded. He put his feet down to stop the chair so he could look the barber in the eye. "Thanks for reminding me to get in to get my ears lowered. I've been looking a bit shaggy."

Snippy ran the comb through Teine's thick auburn curls, eying them critically. "Don't knock it, kid. Most of the girls I see would kill to have hair like yours. So, how are you liking your new job?"

Teine sighed, then wondered exactly what he could say, or couldn't say. "It's not what I'd hoped for, or planned for, but it is what it is and I'm going to make the most of it. Now..." he said, pointing back at his unruly mop. "Make me pretty so I make the girls swoon, eh?"

Snips made a show of looking over Teine's hair, even taking the boy's face in one of his hands and turning his head this way and that. Teine submitted to the examination, searching the barber's face for any hint of his assessment. Snips, (his given name long forgotten) despite being mixed-race, was one of the few freemen working at Solmurry.

Few Human girls could resist his exotic good looks coupled with the green diamond that announced his sterility. Seymour had once commented that Snips couldn't get any more action if he wore a welcome mat for pants. Like many of the boys his age, Teine had always looked up to the half-breed and had often talked with him about his own problems and pursuits.

The only half-breed Teine had ever seen up close, Snips was fascinating to look at. In some ways, he had been the inspiration for Miriam, the half-breed main character that Teine and Leis had been writing about in their stories. Snips was as tall and nearly as powerfully built as a Human man, but far less ponderous in his movements. The old Lord of Solmurry, Marne's grandfather, had gifted him with a bit of their longevity, pointed ears, and an angular face, but he had gotten his soft half-beard from his Human ancestry. To Teine, Snips looked like Madric around the eyes. Rumor had it that Snips was well over two hundred years old, but it didn't stop Leis' friends and many of the older Human women from fawning over him.

"So," Teine began, hesitantly, falling back into the comforting role of the youngster asking a trusted elder for advice. "What do you think I should do?"

"Leave it," Snippy replied, mussing Teine's hair playfully. "We could shape it up a bit, but at this stage, a trim isn't going to make you any better looking."

"Oh, ha ha!" Teine laughed, trying to fend him off. "No, seriously..."

"I am serious," the barber answered, turning his back to Teine and pointing to the bobbed ponytail cascading down his own back. "It's time for you to start growing it out. It'll look like hell for a few months, but you'll want it long for Display. Best to start now."

Teine frowned. Long hair sounded like a hassle, not to mention an open invitation for teasing from his friends.

"Trust me," Snips assured him, getting to work on a few shaping cuts. "Don't even bother coming back for four or five months, unless you absolutely can't stand it and are willing to part with some coin for a potion. That's one I can make on my own, for the record." The barber wore an amused and slightly self-deprecating grin before he hurriedly continued. "But don't go telling everyone. I'm not cut out for life in the Monastery. In the meantime, though, if anyone gives you any grief tell them that *I* said you should start growing it now for Display. That will get even Lord Solmurrian off your back. In fact, I'll tell him myself the next time I see him."

Teine remained unconvinced, but wisely kept his mouth shut while the half-breed plied his scissors and comb. Teine wasn't sure why, but it seemed that somehow Snips had lost some of his authority since Teine had seen him last. Was it because he'd been spending more time with the Aoife and had finally seen what *genuine* authority looked like? It was an unsettling notion, and it made Teine wonder if he was being disloyal. He pondered his uncomfortable thoughts to the whooshes and snips of the barber's comb and scissors.

Soon enough, Snips finished with his haircut. Teine shook the stray hair bits off his tunic while Snippy put his tools away. Then he swept Teine's hair into a pile while humming along with the radio. Teine was just about to tip him, thank him, and leave, but Snips held up a finger thoughtfully. "I might have an idea," he said. "Have you met my half-brother, Alain, Lord Solmurrian, in person yet? How is he disposed to you?"

Forgetting Leis' warnings, Teine hooked the neck of his shirt and pulled it out, exposing his healing lash marks.

Snippy whistled in amazement. "You too, huh?" He pulled up his own shirt, and sure enough, the faint marks of a long-ago beating marred the fair skin of his back. "Yours won't scar, of course," the half-breed assured him. "They want to keep you pretty, so you were seen to in time." With no further ceremony, he went back to sweeping. "So, what set him off?"

Teine summed up the whole of his interactions with Master Solmurrian, omitting anything that could be a danger to Marne, but including the basics of the incident that had culminated with him getting a beating in Marne's stead. He felt vindicated when Snips winced. "So," he finished, "I don't think he likes me much."

"Alain's been a real crank lately," Snips nodded. "But it has nothing to do with you, other than you catching flack because Marne went against his wishes." The barber looked as smug as a cat who'd eaten a canary. "You may not know this, but Solmurry has some financial troubles. It sounds like he's just taking his frustrations out on you."

"May be," Teine agreed, trying not to sound glum.

"Here's my suggestion. The next time you see my esteemed half-brother, *you* bring up the haircut and ask his advice."

"Hmm," Teine murmured, unable to keep the skeptical part of his mind silent. "Won't he be annoyed that I bothered him with something so trivial?"

"Certainly!" Snips grinned. "In fact, you can count on a round scolding for it. But you have to look at the bigger picture. Going to him will also send a message that he'll like."

"How do you mean?"

The half-breed leaned on the counter with one elbow and stroked his soft, fine beard. "It shows you defer to him, and you asked *him*, not Marne. Makes him think you're in his pocket and he can count on you."

Teine tried not to make a face. Although he wasn't crazy about belonging to Marne, he knew where his loyalties were. The boy, whatever kind of creature he was, had a kind heart and tried to do the right thing. But Teine didn't think anything so positive about Lord

Solmurrian. He was about to say as much when there was a rap on the frame of the open front door.

"Come in!" Snips called.

Two girls a couple of years older than Teine walked into the shop, all smiles and fluttering eyelashes. Although they said they were there for a trim, Snips hustled Teine out of the shop. The next thing he knew, Teine was standing on the front porch of the barbershop, listening to muffled giggles through the closed door. He suspected that one or maybe both of the girls weren't going to leave with haircuts after all. The thought was both irritating and a little arousing, so Teine hurried off to tend to his errands.

Chapter 20: Framed

Teine's next stop was the Solmurry Commissary, a rambling building attached to the Commons by a breezy covered walkway like a giant porch. The "C&C" was always crowded with off-duty Humans ready to dine, recreate, or spend their sentas. Teine had many chances to smile and nod as he made his way into the Commissary—so many, in fact, that he began to wonder if everyone at Solmurry now knew who he was and the details of his new status. It was a strange feeling, being recognized, both exciting and a little embarrassing all at once. He expected he'd probably be exposed to escalating levels of scrutiny as his status increased and he became even better known.

Shopping at the Commissary was easy but time-consuming. The building was large and reasonably well stocked with everything from basic clothing staples to toys and specialty foods. Teine threaded his way past several tempting displays of merchandise on his way back to the housewares department, where the picture frames were kept.

Unlike some of the other Humans, Teine wasn't one to spend every penny he earned. To further distinguish himself, he even carried a positive balance on his account at the Commissary so he needn't be bothered with remembering to carry coin if he decided he wanted to make a purchase on the fly. But this time there was a good chance his purchases for decorating his room would exceed his balance, so he had his pouch along with him, just in case. It was important to him to mark his new space as his own. And he realized that the faster he could get his own art up on his room's blank walls, the faster it would feel like *his* room. Choosing exactly the right frames for his art seemed to be crucial to that goal.

He pulled out the crumpled piece of paper where he'd jotted notes and sizes and began to look through the selection to see what frames might match each of the pieces of art he'd most like to display. There were many kinds of picture frames, from the inexpensive large ones for preserving posters, to ones made of intricately carved wood made by the artisans of Solmurry. Teine began making his selections, examining each style of frame carefully. The poster frames, though cheaply made, actually seemed to be a real bargain; they looked decent enough and had the added bonus of being both durable and easy to use. Teine decided to get three of them. He wanted two for full-size pieces, and then another as fun way to display collages of his current. He took a brief moment to congratulate himself on his frugality, then took a deep breath and stepped down to the end of the aisle where the custom frames were kept.

The custom frame section didn't carry complete frames. Instead, the selections were for matched sides only, so an intrepid decorator could buy the frame pieces that best fit the dimensions of whatever he wanted to feature. There were many choices, and Teine carefully considered his options for each of his favorite art pieces before deciding. While he was ruminating on his choices, one of the clerks quietly wheeled a basket up behind him for his selections. "Thanks," he muttered as he consulted his list again, figuring out what hardware he'd need to assemble the frames and hang the assortment of pictures.

Soon, his wheeled basket was piled high, and Teine was ready to check his merchandise at the counter and pay.

"Mercy!" the middle-aged Human woman behind the counter exclaimed when she saw his overflowing cart. "Are you putting on an art show?"

"Something like that," Teine admitted with a grin. He was privately horrified at the potential expenditure he was about to make. He'd never spent so much money at one time in his entire life, even though he'd always been generous with his holiday and birthday gifting.

When the woman started calculating his purchases, Teine removed the necklace with his identification chit to give to her. "I keep an account with a positive balance, but I have coin if I've gone over."

"Positive balance, indeed," she commented, pausing from her accounting to peek in the ledger. "You were gifted twenty binna earlier today." She eyed his cart of framing equipment shrewdly. "You should order glass for those. You can easily afford it."

Twenty binna. Teine couldn't help but blink at what was, to him, such a princely sum. But, realistically, it wasn't much for any of the Aoife, even Marne. Likely the young master was his benefactor once again.

"Yes, I think I'd like to order the glass," he agreed, handing over his list of frame measurements. "And these," he added, impulsively grabbing a bouquet of fresh flowers and a recently released paperback novel by his dam's favorite author. He hesitated for an instant, hand hovering over a gift-wrapped box of very expensive chocolates, before sweeping them into his pile, too. "My Amagi's in the hospital wing having a baby," he explained.

"Aren't you the sweetest thing?" she cooed. "I wish any of my get were so thoughtful. Do you want the rest of this delivered?"

Teine nodded, pleased at the prospect of not having to lug all his purchases back to the Demesne. "Yes, please. Everything but these." He pulled the chocolates, book and flowers out of the pile. "I'll put the frames together myself and you can leave me a post when the glass is ready."

Soon Teine was striding across the Commons yard, unencumbered by the largest bulk of his purchases and whistling a jaunty tune. There were benefits to reaching the next stage of life—home delivery being one of them. The new batch of youngsters who filled the bunks at Mastiff and the other Cohorts would be the new "fetch and carry" kids. Teine hadn't minded messenger duty when he'd been the one performing it. In fact, he had always enjoyed trying out *any* new chore, even the messy ones. Novelty was fun. But it was good to know that he was moving on to bigger and better things.

"Oy, Teine! Want to knock a few?" Seymour's yell caught him by surprise, and he turned to look. "We have one color left!" Some of the newly minted Men were setting up a croquet set, and Seymour brandished the yellow mallet, beckoning him to join in. Teine wished he had time. Croquet with the boys was more of a full-contact sport than the official rules suggested, and he really wanted to blow off some steam with a little playful scuffling.

"I'm off to see my Amagi," he replied, holding the flowers high. "But maybe I'll see you later."

"Mamma's boy!" Seymour retorted. "Apron-clutcher." The rest of the guys broke into laughter and catcalls. But Teine didn't mind. He knew their jests were meant in fun.

"Sorry! What?" Teine held up a hand to his ear, as if he'd suddenly grown hard of hearing. "Sorry, I can't hear you over how much fun I'm having and how busy I am!" He grinned to himself. That was really poking the bear. Anything that hinted Seymour might be missing out on something was sure to drive him nuts.

"Pompous ass!" the dark-haired boy hollered in his wake. "Sycophant toady!"

"With a mouth like that, you should be playing Scrabble!"

With that, Teine quickly ducked around the furthest corner of the C&C to be sure he'd gotten the last word.

Chapter 21: Marked Man

Before long, Teine had made his way across the closehold and was at the hospital wing. As he came through the door to the main floor infirmary, he was suddenly hip-deep in a swarm of nurslings. The Human children milled around the room, examining everything while under the watchful eye of their four nannies.

"A bit of a field trip today," Clinician Nocdoramus explained. Although still dressed in her customary white doctor's coat, the Aoife woman had her long golden hair back in a ponytail and was wearing a casual dress that still had bits of hay clinging to the hem from checking in on Willis in the stable.

"So I see." Teine ruffled the hair of a tow-headed boy who he'd almost stepped on. He remembered his field trips to the infirmary at that age. They'd done a lot to dispel the fear and suspicion of going to the hospital for him and his classmates. It was a sound strategy on the part of the Aoife. Once the mystery was removed, fear lost a lot of its potency.

While he was speaking with the Clinician, Sigolier Zan breezed into the room, carrying a tray with a variety of implements. Her merry eyes lighted on Teine and her delicate, pixie-like features creased into a delighted smile as she turned to Nocdoramus. "Oh, you got one! How lucky!"

"Lucky indeed," Clinician Nocdoramus agreed, speaking loudly to be heard over the chattering children. "I didn't even need to send for him. He's here to visit his Amagi."

Teine gave the pair of Aoife women a worried look, wondering what he'd just gotten himself into. His eyes then darted to his Amagi, who he could see in the far corner of the big room. A bag of clear fluid, suspended on a rolling rack next to her bed, was dripping into a tube that was attached to a tape-stabilized needle in her hand. Amagi was napping soundly in the very bed Teine himself had occupied a few days previous, her swollen feet elevated on several pillows and her distended abdomen pushing up the covers like a giant dome tent. Teine had never seen anyone look so pregnant, not even poor Phoebe!

"Looks like she's sleeping," Teine pointed out to the Aoife women. "What do you need?"

"He's always such a good sport," Nocdoramus told the Sigolier. "Never a complaint about him."

Teine flushed from the praise, but didn't say anything. "Good!" Zan enthused, setting her tray down. Then she looked up at Teine. "Would you mind letting the children see me update your sigil record?"

Teine breathed a huge sigh of relief. "That's it? I thought it was going to be something worse! The last time I was in here I had my pants down around my ankles in front of an audience!"

"Yes, that's all," Zan assured him. "Most of this lot will be due for their first updates soon. Because none of them remember getting their sigils in the first place, many are fearful it's going to hurt since it's oh-so-scary magic and all." Zan waved her hands at the children, as if she were doing something spooky. Her playful sarcasm went over well with the kids, and the room erupted with giggles.

"Happy to oblige," Teine shrugged, peeling off his shirt. "Where do you want me?"

Sigolier Zan retreated to the countertops at the front of the room, then patted one. "Right here," she instructed. "And I'll stand on a stepstool so they can all see."

Teine waited patiently while the nursery teachers mustered their pint-sized troops into an orderly group and the Aoife women made the preparations. After spending a few days with Madric, Teine found himself looking at Sigolier Zan from a brand-new perspective. She was a practitioner of magic, just as surely as Madric was. Had Zan been forcibly admitted to a monastery or nunnery once her talents manifested? Or was it different for women? He longed to ask, but knew it would be inappropriate.

Teine turned his attention to the shield-shaped magical tattoo on the left side of his chest, just under his collarbone. It was the Solmurry heraldry, a stylized tall ship riding the crests of the rolling waves with the sun peeking out from behind its sails. Even if there hadn't been a minor enchantment that made the waves, sails, and ship seem to move, Teine would have still thought it was a beautiful design. But even though it was attached to his skin, Teine rarely thought about it. The sigil had been a part of him for as long as he could remember. Everyone born at Solmurry had the same design, from the lowliest Human to the Lords themselves.

"Right then. Children, gather around!" Sigolier Zan said, her musical voice commanding. The Human children stopped visiting and immediately joined the group gathering at the front of the room. "Today, we're going to demonstrate a sigil update. Teine, here, is my lovely assistant."

Teine grinned, and fluttered his eyelashes at her, simpering like a girl at her first party. The children all giggled, as if on cue.

"Now, now—you're not *that* lovely!" Zan teased, swatting him playfully on the arm. "We need to stop giving you so many compliments, or we're going to have to grease the sides of your head to get you out the door." She turned back to the Human children. "So, can anyone tell me what a sigil is for?"

Several hands shot up, some attached to children so eager to be called on they stood on tiptoes and bounced up and down. "Melanie," Zan called, selecting a freckled girl with pigtails in front.

"Sigils are for identification," Melanie said. "In case a person's papers get lost, or they get lost or kidnapped."

"Very good!" Zan told the girl. "What else are sigils for?" She scanned the crowd of children again, and selected a tall, lanky boy with mousy brown hair. "You, there—I'm sorry I don't know your name."

"I'm Daniel of Bellamore," the boy announced, his polite smile exposing a gap where his front teeth were coming in. "And I've only been here for a few days, so I'm pretty new."

"Welcome to Solmurry, then!" Zan cheered. "I bet your sigil looks different from everyone else's. Would you mind showing the class?"

Daniel shrugged, an excellent imitation of Teine's nonchalance, then shuffled up to the front while pulling his shirt off. As he stood on the stepstool Zan had surrendered, the other children crowded around to see his sigil, which was very striking. The stylized red heart with a sword and an arrow through it was far more memorable and interesting than the Solmurry tall ship.

Not everyone was as impressed. "His doesn't move," one of the girls complained.

"Not every lord puts as much care and artistry into their sigils. Solmurry's sigil is unique in that *everyone* gets an animated one," Zan explained. "The static sigils are much less expensive to create and update when they need it. Both Daniel and Teine here have recently changed hands. Teine's transfer will cost the young master five binna to update his sigil, while Daniel's will only cost Lord Solmurrian fifteen senta." She paused to let the children consider and murmur to themselves. "So, Daniel, tell me, what else are sigils for?"

"They're a record of who has owned you, and what you know," Daniel told the class. "They can tell where you were born, what classes you've passed, skills you've learned, and whose household you've been a part of."

"Excellent, Daniel," Zan said. "We're going to update Teine's sigil now, so everyone can see. Teine's passed his general studies, and made the Cut to be considered as a stud. Someday, if all goes well for him, he will be the father of *many* babies!" The children murmured their congratulations and approval before the Sigolier continued. "Also, Teine has been chosen by the young master as his Centennial birthday gift, and will be shown in the Displays." There were gasps of excitement from the children, and a small scattering of applause. Now that Teine was a bona fide celebrity, most of the youngsters seemed far more interested in him.

The noise woke Amagi. When Teine caught movement out of the corner of his eye, he glanced to the back of the room and saw his Amagi struggling to sit up in bed for a better view.

While the children watched, Zan made the cantillations and prepared the special ink for Teine's sigil. Like Madric, she used material components, some of which Teine thought might be berries, plant leaves, and charcoal. Zan added items into a pestle, mashing them into a fine paste with a mortar. The sharp, almost antiseptic scent made Teine recoil at first, but it soon mellowed into a strong but not unpleasant floral smell. The Sigolier used a fine-tipped paintbrush to apply her concoctions to Teine's sigil directly. In contrast, Madric's chanting seemed to be the direct catalyst for his magics. From what little Teine had seen, Madric rarely needed to physically touch anything. Teine watched Zan as intently as the children did, if not more so. He did his utter best to hold as still as humanly possible, even though the paint brush tickled.

Zan herself was silent, deep in concentration, and Teine noticed the Aoife woman had a habit of sticking the tip of her tongue out the corner of her mouth as she painted. He caught himself smiling down at her. Truly, he couldn't help but think Zan was adorable, but his feelings were anything but lusty and therefore completely appropriate. He reflected back on his interactions with both the Sigolier and Clinician, then came to an interesting conclusion. Sexually speaking, Aoife women didn't even register, but the lingering glance of a busty, full-figured Human girl could practically light him on fire from the inside out. His attraction to Hamoni had far more to do with her accessibility and station in life than anything physical. Teine had, on some level, suspected this even though he'd been unable to put his finger on it at the time. The revelation left him knowing that everything was right with him and his place in the world.

"*Sha-havree, itzen*," Zan whispered, cupping her warm and dainty hand over the still-damp sigil on Teine's chest. "Let it be on record. All right, children, gather 'round."

The nurslings crowded in, and even Teine had to look down when the tingling sensation spread from a point right in the center of the tattoo to engulf the whole thing. As they all watched, gasping and murmuring in wonder, the symbols in the shield shape around the Solmurrian crest began to glow. Like inkblots on a waterproof piece of paper, the symbols ran into each other, doubling, making new shapes, while the Solmurry ship bobbed on the ocean, waves lapping at its planks and the sun shone in the sky. Then Teine felt a prickling as the new configurations melted into his skin. The record of his transferred ownership was complete.

Zan patted him on his bare shoulder and handed him his shirt. "So, how does it feel to be someone's number one?"

Teine considered for a moment. He'd heard most Aoife were very sentimental about their first Human, giving them extra consideration and status throughout their life. Even Master Solmurrian had several portraits of his first, Nazaire of Solairn, scattered throughout the Demesne. Teine's thoughts turned automatically to Marne and his old dog Stinky. The boy put his arm around the old dog even when he smelled bad—because he took care of his own, and understood loyalty. "Good," Teine finally answered. It was a surprise how *right* it felt. That, in itself, was another revelation. "Very good."

The Sigolier pressed a purple lollipop into his hand, thanked him, and dismissed him. "Now, Daniel, how about you?"

Teine hopped down off the counter to make room for the younger boy while catching his Amagi's eye. She waved and beckoned him closer. "Never a dull moment here," she sighed as he approached. "So, how's my boy?"

Chapter 22: Mother's Day

Leaning in, Teine hugged the woman who had given birth to him and tried not to worry. Up close, she looked terrible. Bruise-like dark circles created shadows under her eyes, and her ankles were so swollen they looked like they belonged on an elephant. To Teine, Amagi appeared to have aged ten years over the course of this most recent pregnancy. Even her red hair was now cabled with streaks of wiry white.

"I'm good, Amagi, very good," he assured her.

"So, how's my *other* boy?" she pressed. "I was sleeping when he came by earlier. You two getting on alright?"

It took Teine a moment to realize she was talking about Marne, and to notice the flower arrangement, box of chocolates, and paperback at her bedside. "Fine," he muttered, annoyed at how his own master had managed to show him up. With a sigh, he unwrapped his flowers and added them to the vase with the larger bouquet already there.

Amagi laughed, "Oh, don't be such a sour-puss. It was sweet of both of you."

Teine handed her the chocolates, trying not to look like he was sulking.

"I just think it's funny that you both brought me the exact same things," she teased. "The *exact* same things."

"He needs to get his *own* Amagi," Teine grumped, only half joking. "And not steal mine."

Amagi swatted him with the box of chocolates. "Don't be such a brat!" she scolded, but it didn't carry much weight as she was trying not to laugh. "*We're* his family! More than his own flesh and blood, that's for certain."

Her knowing expression spoke volumes to Teine about her understanding and awareness of Marne's situation, and how they all fit into it. Whatever kind of creature the child really was, he'd managed to root himself deeply into the loyalties of all the women in Teine's bloodline. *And he has my loyalty, too,* he thought, *even if I am a little irritated with him at the moment.* His stomach did its familiar little flip-flop of unspoken anxiety as he wondered what this loyalty might cost him—or his line—in later years. They were a strange little family, and like it or not, Marne was somehow included under the hens' wings as surely as if he'd hatched out of one of their eggs.

"You seem to have a surplus of chocolates," he observed, an expression of angelic innocence on his face. "I can help you with that."

Amagi grinned and tossed him the box he had brought. "Get that open and we'll start fixing that problem."

The rest of their visit was pleasant. Teine, unlike Marne before him, "helped" Amagi devour a good number of chocolates in the box while they talked candidly about what was going on with themselves and the other people they cared about. She asked how Leis was doing without Samia, and Teine had to admit he didn't know. Leis was the kind to have a tight rein on her emotions most of the time. Other than the few minor cracks in her composure, Leis seemed the same as ever. He vowed to find out more and be more supportive.

Far too soon, Clinician Nocdoramus came around with the tray of medicines and announced it was time for Amagi to get some rest. Teine obediently rose to his feet, kissed his mother on the cheek, and promised to visit again at his next leisure period.

"You might have a new little brother or sister to kiss by then," Amagi suggested.

Teine glanced at the Clinician for confirmation and was disturbed by the quiet worry he saw reflected in her wrinkled brow. "I hope not," Nocdoramus said. "That's a bit too early, in my book. I'd really rather see you hold out for another couple of weeks."

Amagi sighed wistfully as she waved Teine goodbye. "Ah, perhaps someday I'll see my feet again," he heard her quip to the Clinician as he left the room.

Far from ruining his appetite, the expensive chocolates Teine had shared with his mother only served to awaken the raging beast that was his hunger. He ended up running all the way to the Commons, only to realize that Marcus, Seymour, Billy, and Abel were on their way, as well. He sounded off a joyous whoop, then charged in their direction.

All four boys waved, but only Marcus met him halfway. "You got your trunk?" Marcus asked, "It was a very strange feeling to bundle up all your things and then hand them off to strangers."

"It all arrived safely," Teine assured him. "Even the spare key. Thanks!"

"So, how did your trip to the tower go?" Marcus fell naturally into step with Teine, and the two boys walked together toward the Commons, a bit behind the others. "I heard you got in trouble and had a beating, but, knowing you, I figured it was all just talk."

Chapter 23: Not Far From the Tree

Teine blinked, then realized Marcus was still searching his face for answers. He'd forgotten to reply. "Where in the world did you hear that?" he demanded.

"Oh, I'm so glad!" Marcus breathed. "I was afraid it might be true. I just heard some girls talking."

"I didn't say it wasn't true," Teine muttered under his breath. He could feel the painful heat of a blush prickling his face and ears. "I just wanted to know how you could have known. I only told..." Then it hit him. He'd spoken candidly to Snips, and then those girls had come in right after him. Either the girls listened for a while before walking in or the barber had casually passed along his tidbit of juicy gossip. "Arghh!" he groaned, grabbing his face with his hand.

"Are you alright?" Marcus persisted, lowering his voice as they caught up to the slower-moving group of boys they'd been following.

Teine sighed, "Fine, fine. Just as stupid as can possibly be. Yes, it happened." At his friend's stricken expression, Teine continued hurriedly, "No, it wasn't me that was in trouble. Have you ever heard the phrase 'whipping boy?' Well, let me assure you, the practice is alive and well at Solmurry."

Marcus said nothing, staring with his mouth open.

"And apparently *everyone* I trust with the details of my life isn't as good at keeping confidences as you and Vosh," Teine added, trying not to sound as bitter as he felt.

"Was it… *Leis* that told everyone?" Marcus seemed completely aghast at the idea.

"Oh, no!" Teine waved that possibility off. "First of all, I haven't even told her about it, and although Marne might have, I sincerely doubt it. He feels too bad." He paused, considering for the briefest moment that he might be wrong. Then he dismissed the thought. Leis had known about Marne's big secret for an undetermined amount of time without telling him. Even when it became something that would directly affect him, Leis hadn't told him anything because it wouldn't have been appropriate for her to share. "Leis understands discretion like no one else I know," he explained simply.

Now that they'd caught up to the other boys, Seymour was slowing down to join them. Seeing the wicked grin on the dark-haired boy's face, Teine braced himself for the worst.

"So, took a beating, did you?" Seymour asked, then continued without giving Teine a chance to counter, confirm, or even respond. "I think it's ironic how you're always telling me I overstep my bounds and am going to get in trouble, and then *you're* the one to get a strapping from the master himself! Ha!"

Teine was completely taken aback by how gleeful Seymour appeared to be at his misfortune. He'd never known Seymour to be unsympathetic to anyone's troubles, but there he was, practically gloating. It was a side of him Teine had never seen before. "Duly noted," he replied, as casually as he could. Teine felt strongly both he and Marne had been punished unjustly, so he didn't plan to share any more details of the incident with the boys. Instead, he decided to simply leave it at that, in hopes of giving Seymour as little ammunition and encouragement as possible.

Seymour opened his mouth to continue taunting, but Marcus pointed a stern finger at him. "Shut it!" he growled.

Teine wasn't the only boy to blink in surprise. Seymour didn't have a monopoly on acting out of character. Marcus had never attempted to exert his will on anyone or anything before, but Teine was very grateful his friend was doing so on his behalf.

Seymour kicked at a tuft of grass on the lawn and sulked. "I was just saying," he pouted. "Ironic."

"And none of our business." Marcus told him, then grinned playfully at the other boys and raised his hands as if he were conducting an orchestra or leading a class in recitations. "Repeat after me: *None of our business! None of our business!*"

The others laughed, then repeated after Marcus in chorus. Although Marcus managed to change the conversation to a heated discussion on draft choices for next fabal season, Seymour continued to sulk all the way to the Commons.

By the time they arrived, a line was already forming for dinner, so the five of them diverted course to check their mail. Each Human and Aoife had an individual box at the Solmurry Postal Exchange Depot, which was affectionately called by its acronym, SPED. The SPED acted as both Solmurry's main post office and bank, and had its own room in the Commons, right off the main lounge. Each resident of the Demesne had their mail hand-delivered from the SPED if they hadn't picked it up by close of business each day, but everyone else had to stop by and check their boxes regularly if they wanted to stay up to date. Almost everyone subscribed to at least one magazine for their trade or hobbies. Allowance and privilege chits were also deposited into each person's SPED box.

"I hope that steam engine book arrived," Marcus whispered while they were waiting in line. "I can't wait to get my hands on it!"

When their turn came, Teine waved Marcus ahead. He was pleased to see the book his friend awaited had arrived. When the clerk caught his attention, he was still looking over his shoulder at Marcus, who'd already begun to flip pages.

"Ahem," she coughed, then snapped her fingers. "Hey, next up!" Her full red lips were pursed just between a pout and a smile.

"Oh, sorry," Teine grinned sheepishly. "Teine of Solmurry, box 329."

She was new, a pretty young woman with curly dark hair and an exotic olive complexion. As she checked her list, Teine admired how nicely her gold hoop earrings set off her dusky skin tone. "It says I need to verify ID," she told him, wrinkling her nose with a cute grin. "Looks like someone is getting a raise."

"He belongs to the young master now," Seymour chimed in. "So, soon he'll be too good to check his mail here."

Teine shrugged, glad he'd stopped at the Clinic to get his sigil updated. While the girl and his friends all watched, he unlaced the front of his shirt so the clerk could see his name on his sigil.

"Now we want to see *your* ID!" Seymour added, leaning on the counter and staring boldly at the girl's ample bosom. Then he gave her a suggestive wink. On Seymour, though, it looked more like a nervous tic or a grimace. Behind them, some of the boys groaned in embarrassment.

While the new clerk didn't blush, the boys had all been trained from earliest childhood on how to speak to women. There was a brief playful scuffle as several of them gently picked Seymour up and deposited him outside.

"Sorry, Miss," Billy crooned as he swaggered back inside and leaned casually on the door so Seymour couldn't get back in. "Our friend isn't from Solmurry originally, and sometimes he doesn't remember how to talk to ladies. We're educating him."

Seymour rapped his knuckles on the glass of the window, and Billy pulled the blind down to a chorus of laughter from his mates inside. The clerk shook her head and turned away from the boys and their roughhousing. She then moved into the back of the office, skirts swinging, while the boys looked on appreciatively. Teine suspected she was really more flattered than put out.

She returned with a postal bin piled high with a small stack of magazines, a couple of boxes with brightly colored pictures of food on them, three books, and some new chits. "I think you've struck the motherlode," Marcus murmured, looking up from his own book. "What *is* all that?"

"Pay raise," the girl said, pointing to the new chits. "I'll take your old one to turn back in. Did you want to cash this in right now or bank it?"

Teine shook his head no, his ears flushing red. The last thing he wanted to do was pull out any kind of pay raise in front of his old friends while things were still uncomfortable. Mercifully, another clerk came from the back and started waiting on Billy, distracting the others from his show of good fortune. "Can you just bank it all, please?"

She smiled knowingly, and Teine noticed she had the most brilliant sea-foam green eyes. "Certainly, Teine," she told him, pulling the pay chit from the stack. Teine fumbled with the leather thong around his neck that held his old meal chit. The knot wouldn't come undone. Holding out her hand, she beckoned, "Here, let me."

Teine did as she asked, pulling the thong over his head. Rather than even attempt to untie the knot, the girl pulled a small knife off her belt and trimmed it away. The old token slid off the leather easily, but she had to wet the end of the thong by putting it in her mouth and then rolling it between her fingers to manage to poke the strand through the hole of the new chit. He watched the process, as dumb as an ox.

"What's your name?" someone blurted out. It took Teine a second to recognize his own voice.

"Zandra," she replied, without looking back up with those enchanting eyes. Teine sadly realized that the fascination was far from mutual. "Like Sandra," she said, "But with a Z. Sign here, please."

He did as he was told, then tied off the end of his thong with the new chit while she deposited his allowance chit and gave him a receipt. When she was done, he grabbed his mailing bin full of loot and bolted for the door.

Marcus caught him outside. "She's new."

Teine nodded. "Yes, I think so."

They decided not to wait for the other boys, as they were all just going to end up in the same line anyway. Apparently Seymour had the same idea because he was nowhere to be found. When they cut back through the main lounge, they saw him standing in line far enough ahead to have been there for a while.

"Cuts?" Marcus called out hopefully.

Seymour responded with a rude gesture.

"He sure is grumpy today," Marcus sighed. "You know, he's been acting oddly since we all got Cut."

"He'll get over it," Teine told him. He'd known Seymour long enough to know he just hadn't had enough time to cool off. "Give him an hour or so."

Marcus held Teine's place while he went into the cafeteria and selected a spot to plunk down his bin of mail. Then the two of them waited in companionable silence punctuated by the rumbling of Teine's stomach. "Good gods," whispered Marcus. "Don't they *feed* you at the

Demesne?" Teine made a mock ferocious face at him and ignored the question.

When their turn in line came, the boys showed their meal chits and selected trays off the rack in the same color as their chit. Marcus still had his old red chit, but Teine's new one was orange. When the friends went down the line and made their selections, the cafeteria workers gave them portions sized correctly for the color tray they carried. Although anyone could spend their own coin on snacks, the chit and tray system ensured that everyone got the basic nutrition that was appropriate for their needs. Teine had never given the system much thought until the first huge blob of mashed potatoes hit his plate. "Hey, are you sure that's right?" he asked. The cafeteria lady only chuckled and added a second blob, as mountainous as the first, then poured a river of rich rib tips and gravy over the two.

"If you're still hungry after that, I'll be amazed," Marcus laughed, eying his smaller portions. "Hey!" he chided the lady. "I'm bigger than he is! Hand over the victuals!" He brandished his tray hopefully, but got only an added portion of greens and was waved away.

"I think Marne plans on working me hard," Teine told him as they finished filling their milk glasses at the dairy station. They moved to the table where their friends and Teine's belongings waited. As they were sitting down, they saw Seymour and Billy had both taken boxes from Teine's pile and were reading the contents. "Hey!" he snapped at them, indignant they were pawing through his things before he'd even had a chance to look at them. "Lay off, all right?"

Billy looked at Teine's tray and whistled, shoving the box he was examining toward Teine. "It's supposed to be some kind of nutritional supplement, but from the looks of your plate, I don't know why they think you're going to need it."

"He's a little small for Display," Marcus teased, elbowing Teine while snagging a piece of meat off his friend's plate. "They need to feed him a lot so he can catch up."

"Good grief," Teine sighed. He was amused by Marcus's mock bravado because he knew it was all in jest, but Billy and Seymour could get on his nerves in a hurry. "You," he began, gesturing to the whole lot of them. "Are as barbaric as Islanders."

"Look at these gents!" Seymour hooted gleefully, interrupting Teine's impending tirade. He'd helped himself to one of Teine's new magazines and was holding it open to a page. "Is that a Man, or a beef steer?"

All the boys, including Teine, leaned in for a closer look. The Human man in the photograph was listed as the "Nationals Finalist" in Open Display from three years ago. To say he was enormous would have been an understatement. He wore only a loincloth, and was posed and oiled to show off musculature so overdeveloped it seemed almost ridiculous.

Teine's stomach recoiled with a feeling of inadequacy, but he didn't have a chance to say anything, as Leis was suddenly at his side. She cheerfully shoved her way in between him and Abel. "That's no steer, boys. That's a *bull*," she grinned. "The loincloth confirms it!"

They all roared with laughter, and Teine was laughing so hard that he had to bury his face in his hands. "That was crass," he chortled, putting his arm around his sister and squeezing her roughly. Trust Leis to one-up the boys when she had to.

She grimaced, but didn't have the chance to answer before Billy chimed in, "You're late, Fleecy Leis-y! You almost missed eating dinner with us. Some of us don't lead lives of leisure. We have to do homework for the new classes that started today!"

"It's been a busy day," Leis replied, properly cutting a bite of meat. She squirmed a bit in her seat on the bench to encourage Teine and Abel to make more room. "I've been so busy doing Amagi's job that I haven't even been down to visit her."

"She's doing fine," Teine assured his sister. Now that he'd started eating, he was surprised at the appetite he'd developed over the day. Taking a cue from his sister, he finished chewing and swallowing before he continued. "I went to see her, but Marne had been there first."

"That doesn't surprise me," Leis nodded, continuing with her very proper table manners. When she'd swallowed, she continued. "Marne adores her like she's his own Amagi. I think it's good she's retiring. She's getting too old to keep having babies."

The other boys at the table had lapsed into awkward silence, turning their attention to their meals. Normally, things were quiet when they all got down to the serious business of eating, but Teine could feel a change in the air. Uncomfortable seemed to be the new order, and Teine could only assume it was his new position. Before long all the other boys except Marcus had finished eating, but instead of staying to chat they cleared off one by one. Teine continued to work diligently on clearing his plate, with a bit of help from his larger friend. Leis ate slowly and thoughtfully while quietly keeping to herself.

As the minutes ticked away, Teine grew more and more unsettled. Dinner had always been a happy occasion, marked by lively wit and cheerful banter. The silence was unnerving. If Marcus hadn't been there, Teine could have shared some of the details of his last few days with Leis, as long as he kept his voice down. If Leis hadn't been there, he and Marcus could have talked about sports or extolled the virtues of the pretty new clerk at the SPED. He couldn't help but wonder if he was going to end up completely dislodged from his usual social circle, with only Leis and the young master for company.

Finally, it hit him! He had the perfect conversation starter that would engage both his sister and his friend. "So," he began, trying to achieve the right tone of casual nonchalance. "I spoke with our sire today."

Both Leis and Marcus stopped chewing and stared. Teine privately congratulated himself on a win.

"And I invited him to play cards with us tonight," he continued, attempting to look as though he arranged such unlikely gatherings every day. "I hope you can make it."

"Who's your sire?" Marcus asked.

"Lesmar of Solairn," Teine replied, with a grin. "He's on leave here, helping to look after Willis and waiting for the master to get done touring the shipyards."

Marcus squeaked, "He's your sire, too?" The other boy seemed thunderstruck.

"Sure. Nice chap. He has some breeding assignments, but he should head this way after dinner. Care to join us?" Unable to stop himself, he glanced at Leis, who was still staring, stunned.

"You're our sibling?" Leis asked Marcus, an incredulous tone in her voice.

"I know we have different dams, so I'm only your halfs, but yes!" Marcus nodded, brimming with enthusiasm. "Everyone always says how much I look like him. Isn't that great? We're all sibs!"

Chapter 24: Three of a Kind

Leis surprised both boys by squealing with unabashed delight and throwing her arms around Marcus' neck. "Another brother!" She was rewarded with a goofy smile.

Meanwhile, Teine reflected back to the time in the Infirmary, only a few days ago, when Marcus had wished out loud for siblings that he could be friends with. He chuckled to himself, hiding his smile behind his hand as he admired the irony. *Be careful what you wish for*, he thought—but Marcus didn't seem to mind Leis' behavior at all. The pair were already enthusing over the shared aspects of their pedigrees. The two of them had always gotten along well. Now they had even more reason to continue doing so.

Now Teine was beginning to understand why Master Solmurrian had been so insistent in urging his son to choose Marcus for Display instead of himself. Marcus did resemble Lesmar in the face and the build while Teine took more after his dam's side of the family tree. Lesmar had a long and decorated Display career before retiring to be the lord's personal valet.

While Teine had only a passing familiarity with Marcus' dam, a large strapping woman with enormous hips and bosoms, he could see her contribution to Marcus' makeup very clearly. She made their Amagi look practically dainty by comparison. She had passed on her statuesque physique and good nature to her son as surely as their Amagi had passed on her pretty face and quick mind to her progeny. Marcus' dam was known for being a bit shy and introspective and, like her son, was said to have a gentle way with the animals. Marcus had been assigned his dairy shift at her behest, but had always favored the horses over the cattle.

Although Marcus had many fine qualities, Teine just couldn't imagine the other boy dealing with the hidden pressures of his job. Marcus would have welcomed being chosen by Marne and he was certainly bright enough. But Teine was fully aware that his friend had no talent for deception and even less appetite for conflict. As much as Marcus would have enjoyed Marne's companionship and all the educational opportunities the position would afford him, Teine was sure the other boy would have been beyond miserable once he knew the whole story.

Leis interrupted Teine's musing by snapping her fingers in front of his face. "So, how did your journey to the tower go? Other than getting a strapping, I mean?"

Teine blushed beet red again. "Good gods, does *everyone* know about that already?"

"Probably," she shrugged. "I heard about it from Melissa on my way over. If she knows, trust me, *everyone* knows. Sorry." She patted him on the shoulder, attempting to console his hurt feelings. "But never mind that. What's done is done. Tell us about the tower!"

"Never mind that?" Teine grumbled. As if he could forget so easily. "Hmph!"

"And Madric!" Marcus added. "I've heard he's got a magic workshop with hundreds of books and he keeps other magic people chained in his basement!"

Teine paled. Marcus had no idea how close he was to the truth. "Well, you're right about the workshop." He threw Marcus that bone, eager to divert him from the second half of his rumor-mongering. "He has almost as many books as the library, and all kinds of vials, tubes, and devices for enchanting items." He paused, wishing he could make a snide comment about Hamoni doing most of the heavy lifting, but he restrained himself and took a second to mentally fish around for anything completely amazing he could tell them, without breaching any secrets. "I even saw a magic plant that eats rats... oh, and people made of water!"

The minutes ticked by and other diners came and went as Teine enthusiastically recalled the parts of his adventure he could safely share with his eager audience: the wild carriage ride, meeting Willis the guardian Holidocrith, and the famous painting. He described the afternoon on the beach as an excursion of relaxation and enjoyment rather than a frantic flight from government clergy, and carefully spoke of his evening in the basement with Marne as one of providing companionship for a sickly child.

While he was telling them about Hamoni (the *censored* version) and Kenneth and "the Louts," Teine realized that he was thinking about Marne. Remembering his conversations with Madric about Marne's magic bracelet, he suddenly wondered if it was still working. He couldn't even begin to imagine the consequences if it stopped projecting its altered image of Marne.

To cover for the lapse in his train of thought, Teine changed the subject as deftly as possible. "To answer your first question about Madric," Teine began, pausing to sip a glass of water while he stalled to decide what to say next. "The very first thing he did was take me into that workroom and test me for magic!"

Leis' eyes widened in alarm. "*Are* you?" she squeaked, leaning forward. "Oh, Teine if you are, please tell me you haven't bragged abou—"

"Not." Teine scowled. "If I were, do you think I'd really be dumb enough to blurt it out all over the Commons?"

"Well, you were dumb enough to tell someone you'd managed to get yourself strapped," she countered, her expression icy. "So I thought it was a fair question. Fool."

"That wasn't even my fault!"

Leis shook her head. "If you got strapped, it was your fault. Period."

Marcus looked back and forth between the two of them, worry wrinkling his brow. "You two still like each other, right?"

"Of course we do," Leis snapped.

Teine glanced over at her, then rolled his eyes. He couldn't help but begin to laugh. Soon the other two joined him. "Welcome to our weird little family, Marcus," he chortled.

When the giggles had died down Marcus shook his head ruefully, leaning in to the others to keep the conversation as private as possible. "I hate to continue on such a sore subject, but honestly, Teine, what happened? Why did you get strapped?"

Teine sighed, resting his elbow on the table and drawing a line through a ring of condensation where a glass had rested. *How to present this?* He still didn't really understand what Marne had done that was bad enough to warrant a beating. The only answer that came to mind every time he considered it was that Lord Solmurrian was dangerously unbalanced. And he simply could not give voice to that suspicion. "I'm not sure," he finally answered. "He must have already been angry with Marne for something, and he just blew up—and I got Marne's beating."

A shadow darkened their table, and the three looked up in unison. They'd been so intent on their conversation that they hadn't noticed Lesmar approaching their table. Their tall sire was carrying a leather poker kit under one arm, and a tray holding four glasses and a stoppered blue bottle in his other hand. Conversation ceased as he set the tray down and pulled over a chair to join them.

"Marne is a very willful child," Lesmar began, ignoring his progeny's stunned and shamefaced expressions at being caught gossiping about their betters. "And this trait has been exaggerated by his being left alone so often with only the company of Humans. He doesn't really know or trust his sire, and that is the heart of most of their conflicts." The big man sat down, his expression serene. "Now let's move on to a more suitable topic. Who's playing?"

While Marcus and Leis excitedly focused on setting up the card game, Teine burned with curiosity about his sire. Exactly how much did he know about Marne? He watched Lesmar as he smiled and chatted casually, all the while wishing the gods would grant him the power to read his sire's mind.

"So, you must be Leis?" Lesmar paused for the girl to nod her blushing assent. Then, he turned toward Marcus, his lips pursed thoughtfully, "And... Marcus? Am I right?"

"Yes, sir!" Marcus beamed with pleasure at being recognized with absolutely no introduction.

"Good guess." Lesmar also looked pleased at being correct. "They tell me you look like me," he told Marcus. Their sire leaned back in his chair and folded his arms across his chest, as if to admire the three of them with the smug satisfaction one can only have for his or her progeny. "Well, well. Three of a kind! Do you youngsters want to drink a little mead while we play?"

"You have *mead*?" Teine asked incredulously. In response, Lesmar pointed at the bottle. "But it's only for—"

"Eh, I didn't need it." The big man waved the question off. "We'd met before, and she's the kind of girl who doesn't need any extra persuasion."

Teine's ears felt hot, and he hoped he wasn't blushing too obviously. But a quick glance at Marcus confirmed he wasn't the only one who knew what mead was reserved for. Teine was relieved to not be the only one thinking of it.

"So, what's the mead for?" Leis asked, leaning forward to pick up two cards. Obviously she wasn't privy to that bit of "boys' knowledge."

Lesmar answered without missing a beat. "We're issued a bottle of mead to share with a woman the first time we meet her for a breeding assignment." His manner was matter-of-fact and confident, completely befitting his status as a senior stud.

"Oh!" Leis exclaimed, tilting her head as if she were thinking about it. "That would make sense."

"It gives us time to talk, get to know each other, and relax before being expected to just... proceed with our assignment," Lesmar paused, glancing at each of the children to measure their level of interest before he continued. As all three were listening with rapt attention, he decided a little more explanation was in order. "It can be a little strange, being expected to be intimate the very first time you meet someone. The mead is almost a ritual, and part of that social contract. It makes it easier." Teine found himself admiring the way their sire explained things, and grateful for the information. He hoped Lesmar would be in charge of the upcoming Men's Studies sex education class that all the IMs would be taking in the fall. Teine already felt like he could ask him anything. He'd probably be an excellent teacher.

"So, is it alright if we share your mead?" Marcus interjected. "I don't want to get you—or us—in any kind of trouble." Ever the proper one, Marcus was always concerned with doing things the correct way.

"The mead's mine to share, and you're all of age—or at least close enough," Lesmar confirmed. Teine noted that it looked like their sire approved of the question. "You probably shouldn't make a *habit* of drinking alcohol until you're a bit older, but it's fine for a special occasion. And this is a special occasion—at least for me!" As big as a mountain and as warm as the sunshine, Lesmar smiled again. "This is the first time I've ever sat down with three of my progeny at one time!" Teine was suddenly amused to realize where Marcus got his tendency to grin so much. Then he caught the expression on his own face and realized that Lesmar might have passed that trait along to more than just Marcus.

Teine watched Lesmar carefully as he reached for the tray with the glasses and mead, trying to decide if anyone could really be *that* happy. After a while Teine had to admit that constant exposure to Lord Solmurrian didn't drive *everyone* mad. Lesmar seemed to be immune. Or perhaps their sire was only so cheerful because his master was *away*. Teine watched as Lesmar poured each one of them a drink from the blue bottle. The boys got about two-thirds of a glass, Leis got a half, and he poured himself a full one. As Teine, Leis, and Marcus tasted the mead in their goblets, Lesmar broke out the card kit, set a rack of ceramic chits of different colors on the table, and began shuffling one of the decks.

"It's *sweet*!" Leis exclaimed with delight after her first sip. "Oh, this is wonderful!"

Teine had been looking into the cup, admiring the rich, golden color of the liquid—nearly the red-gold shade of his sister's hair—and enjoying the beverage's honey-like scent. Emboldened by Leis' praise, both Teine and Marcus took sips from their cups while Lesmar looked on with relaxed joviality. Teine swished the amazing beverage around in his mouth, carefully savoring it for several seconds before swallowing. "I think I like that as much, if not more, than I like chocolate." Marcus was nodding in enthusiastic agreement.

"That's why it's rationed so tightly. Otherwise there would never be enough to go around. Solmurry makes almost a third of all mead in the Empyrean, and our mead is sought after for ceremonial use as well. Tradition is the only reason we Humans even get a taste."

"Tradition?" Marcus asked, finally swallowing his first sip.

Lesmar nodded. "Indeed. It's been a vital component of fertility rites and rituals for the last two Ages. Chances are, the next time the three of you will be tasting mead you'll be experiencing First Rites, too."

Teine raised his glass high. "Here's to tradition!" They all joined him and then took a sip in lighthearted solidarity.

Lesmar raised his glass right afterward. "Here's to blood kin. I salute you, my children. May your bonds to each other remain true and bring you nothing but contentment and happiness."

Teine glanced around at their faces, noticing that there wasn't a completely dry eye among them. There was something unspoken and solemn in this toast, and even as Teine raised his glass and drank, he couldn't help but wonder at his kin's ability to connect to each other. Where might this ultimately lead them? After all, Humans had been raised from birth to believe that their strongest relationships weren't meant to be based on family ties or romantic relationships, but on relationships with workmates and friends. Blood ties were seen as almost exclusively an Aoife sentiment. But before he could dwell on the thought too long, Lesmar spoke again in his deep, rich voice. His weathered face crinkled as he grinned proudly at his offspring.

"So, who wants to *deal* these cards?"

Chapter 25: Educational Opportunity

"**S**poilsport!" Marcus sang out as Leis stood up from the table hours later. "Come on! The night is young, you still have plenty of chits, and there's still lots of popcorn with peanuts!"

Leis only smiled and gestured at the clock. "Oh, it's too late for me. I'd usually have tucked Marne into bed a couple hours ago. He'll be missing me if I don't at least check on him."

Lesmar rose to his feet, and took both his daughter's hands in his. "Leis, dear one, it's been a distinct pleasure to meet you. Hopefully this will be just the first in a long line of pleasant visits."

The girl didn't hesitate. She wrapped her arms around him, burying her face in his chest. "I'd like that," she whispered. "We're so lucky to know both our parents and for them both to be so wonderful."

Teine tried not to roll his eyes. Leis could be so sentimental and far too responsible at times to be fun. "*I* don't have to go back yet," Teine volunteered. He didn't want anyone thinking that he was ready to quit just because she was. "Marne said I was free for the night."

"You're just not indispensable yet," Leis returned, primly gathering her things. "I'd remember that, if I were you." Then, as if to illustrate, she snagged the arm of a boy passing by with his friends. "You. Get these boxes and come with me to the Demesne." She snapped her fingers, and gestured to Teine's pile of mail from the SPED. Just like magic, the boy and his friends each grabbed a parcel and fell into step behind her as she walked away.

Lesmar's bass chuckle rumbled his amusement. Teine could feel it as much as hear it. "Little girl, you're a firecracker," he called after Leis' retreating form.

"Don't you know it!" She waved over her shoulder. "Now Teine, don't stay out too late or get into any trouble. And don't wake Marne up when you get in."

"All right, I get it!"

"And don't step on Stinky! He could be sleeping anywhere!" she added before ducking out the door.

"Can we still play with just three?" Marcus asked. He sounded as though he was worried he'd never have another opportunity to play cards again for the rest of his life.

Teine scanned the Commons, which was far from deserted, even at such a late hour. Another enthusiastic group was playing something fast-paced that apparently required lots of swearing and roars of laughter. An impromptu band was playing their instruments on the slightly raised stage, and fortunately, they weren't terrible. The night kitchen staff was dispensing tea and warm ciders, as well as the beer and ale on tap. There was an enormous circle of ladies of all ages doing needle-crafts and knitting. Several couples were tucked into couches and alcoves, whispering, kissing, and otherwise pursuing their own romantic agendas, and a slow but steady stream of traffic came and went. "We might just be out of luck for a fourth," Teine hated to admit.

Just then, a dark-haired woman with an olive complexion, a curvy silhouette, and an exotic peacock-colored dress swept in. She smiled directly at Teine, and started in their direction. "I was hoping I'd find you here," she said, holding her arms open wide.

Marcus, who had been playing with and chewing on a drinking straw, dropped it on the table as his jaw went slack. Teine felt himself flush all over when recognition suddenly hit him. It was Zandra—"Sandra, with an Z"—from the SPED where he'd gotten his mail earlier that day. "N-nice to see you, too," he stammered, embarrassed he'd been caught so off guard.

But before he could open his arms to accept her embrace, she ducked around him like he didn't exist and leapt onto Lesmar's lap to plant a passionate kiss on his lips. Lesmar started to rise to his feet to greet her, but her exuberance pinned him back to his chair. "Hello, Handsome!" she gushed. "I was wondering how long they'd make me wait before I could see you again!"

It was Teine's turn to stare, slack-jawed. Lesmar, however, had the situation well in hand. Or in lap, as the case was. "I'm glad to see you too, Ocean Eyes. These are two of my boys, Teine and Marcus. I've been enjoying an evening of cards with them. You just missed Leis, one of my girls. I believe you two would get along famously."

They should, they're about the same age. Teine grumbled to himself, trying not to let disappointment show on his face. "We've met," he replied instead. It was hard not to feel completely cheated.

"A pleasure to see you both again, as well." Zandra was still perched on their sire's lap and was curling her fingers in his hair. Teine didn't know what was more irritating: her eagerness or the fact that Lesmar was acting as if gorgeous women threw themselves at him every day. *Maybe because they did!*

"Did you want to leave right away or would you mind being our fourth for a few hands?"

Zandra turned back to Teine and Marcus and blinked. "Oh, cards! Yes, that would be fun. I don't mind sharing you for a couple of hours as long as I get you to myself later." With that, she slid out of Lesmar's lap, and took her place in Leis' chair. She assumed the other girl's diminished pile of chips with only an appraising glance. "So, I'm losing? Here, hand those over. I'll deal first." Then she began shuffling and bridging the cards with all the finesse of a professional gambler. "Anyone got a beer or a smoke?"

"Zandra came from a pleasure house casino in Port O'Prye. That's my girl." Lesmar beamed and signaled the attendant for a round of beer. "On me!" he called. The serving lady nodded and went to get the mugs. "We don't smoke in the Commons," he told Zandra. "But we do have snacks." He pushed a bowl of salted shelled peanuts her way.

"Ah. That'll do." She passed the deck to Marcus. "Cut."

Marcus blinked, looking as uncertain as a newborn calf, but he did as he was told and slid the deck back to her. Without missing a beat, the girl swept up the cards and dealt them out quickly and efficiently.

"I'm glad we're just playing for chips," Marcus gulped. "You're kind of *scary.*"

Zandra winked at him.

Teine was about to begin ribbing his half-brother, but then the beer arrived. He'd never had one before. It was a huge mug, tall and foamy with frost coating the outside. While the others considered their cards and made their wagers, he sniffed his beverage carefully, wondering at the strangely bread-like yeasty smell. Finally, he grabbed the mug by the handle and took a swig, just as the a little voice in the back of his head told him this was probably a bad idea.

"You're both too young for a second round," Lesmar chuckled. "So you'd better make this one last. Oh, and I fold."

Teine couldn't answer because he was too busy trying not to gag. "Uuugh," he shuddered. "That's... that's—"

Marcus nodded, with a grimace. He'd taken a cautious sip while Teine was struggling to describe his.

Lesmar chuckled while Zandra gave the boys a wicked, sidelong grin. "I had a feeling they'd be too young to enjoy it."

"We, uh… we enjoy it," Marcus lied, choking down another sip. It's just an—"

"Acquired taste," Teine offered.

"Well, if you can get it all down, I can acquire us something better for the next round. On me," Zandra offered. "After all, I know all the best… everything. Er, *drinks*." She winked seductively at Lesmar, right before she flashed her full house. Teine barely noticed when she raked in the chips. "After all, this used to be my *job*."

Lesmar patted her arm. "Gently now, lover. Go easy on the boys. I was planning to make tonight into a life lesson in responsible alcohol use."

"Couldn't we just turn it into a life lesson on the many dangers of peer pressure? That'd be more fun!" Her green eyes sparkled with mischief as she knocked back her beer. Then she batted her eyelashes at Lesmar. Teine was astounded, marveling to himself, *The girl drinks as if she were a strapping day laborer and not a young woman!*

"Barkeep? A round of ciders!" she trilled, raising her mug above her head.

Teine glanced over at Marcus to get his take on things. Normally his good-natured half-brother was a solid moral compass in just about any situation. But this time, Marcus only shrugged as if to say "Why not?" The pair exchanged a resigned look, wrinkled up their noses, and took another big swig.

"Well, I suppose people choose their own life lessons," Lesmar mused. He reached out to gather the cards while Marcus and Teine worked on getting their beers down. As he shuffled, the big man leaned back and settled into his chair as if he were there to enjoy a comedy.

"Far be it for me to keep someone from their chosen path towards wisdom." With a big sigh and a lopsided grin, he began to deal.

Chapter 26: Nocturnal Adventures

Teine walked the path from the Commons to the Demesne automatically, lost in his own alcohol-muddled thoughts and swirling emotions. He'd begun the evening hoping to spend more time speaking with Lesmar. But instead he'd had to watch as the girl he was interested in threw herself at his father. And it seemed that all of his old friends, except Marcus, were snubbing him. And, as if things couldn't get worse, it looked like he might end up having to take orders from his little sister!

Just then, it struck Teine that all the drinking he'd done that night might be a factor in his dismal mood. After all, according to health class, alcohol *was* a depressant.

He wondered if his life would ever make complete sense to him again. It was hard not to feel a little fearful in the face of that uncertainty. Plus, now he was frustrated, more than a little jealous of his sire, and entirely out of sorts because he was out later than he'd ever been in his life. And he was still a little tipsy. On top of everything else, he was walking to the Demesne instead of the barracks. *And* he was planning to walk right *into* the Demesne like he lived there. Because he did.

It all just felt *wrong*.

As much as he tried to rationalize, Teine still couldn't shake the feeling that he was merely an actor who had wandered onto the wrong stage. His life no longer felt like *his*. It hardly resembled his old life at all, except for cameo appearances from some of his old friends. He felt adrift with no one to go to for guidance and he couldn't for the life of him figure out what he had done to end up in such a situation. "It's just not fair," he muttered.

"What's not fair?" a breathy voice whispered from behind him.

"Gah!" Teine squawked, and whirled to face a gangly, freckle-faced, and bespectacled Human boy behind him. "Who are *you*?"

"Dillan of Solairn," the lad answered. "Just transferred up from Port William." Although he was also slightly cross-eyed and didn't have the most appealing looks, Dillan sounded well-spoken and seemed bright enough.

Teine eyed the youngster, feeling suddenly old—and gigantic. He absolutely towered over Dillan. The new kid looked to be about ten or so, with the pale, freckled, and parchment-like skin of a true redhead. He was about the age that Teine had been when he'd transferred into Mastiff Cohort. In fact, this kid could be living in his old room, sleeping in his old bed, living his old life. "Hmpff," was all Teine could think to say. He was *so* entirely ready for the day to end.

"So, what's so unfair?" Dillan pressed, trying hard to match strides with Teine and keep up without jogging.

Fuming to himself, Teine tried to be polite. "My life."

"You going to work in the kitchen, too?"

"No. To bed."

Dillan gave Teine a wry grin. "Cry me a river," he taunted. Teine blinked at the harsh words, but couldn't hear any rudeness in the tone. Then he realized the kid was teasing him. "You think your life is unfair? You're going *home*—in this big, gorgeous mansion, probably in your own room with a feather bed. Am I right?"

Teine grunted, not sure whether he was amused or annoyed, and the unfortunately favored little fellow was still staring him down.

"While you lay your pretty head on those soft pillows, think of me. I'm starting my first day of work in a job I'll probably hate, and likely die still doing."

Teine suddenly felt about two inches tall.

As they approached the Demesne, Teine was surprised to see the lights on and activity in the kitchen. A pair of middle-aged, bleary-eyed Human women were firing up the ovens, putting on the kettle, and getting the kitchen ready. Teine supposed they were bakers. He'd heard somewhere that the cooks who did the baking had to get up incredibly early to have morning pastries ready for breakfast. "You're a baker?" Teine guessed.

"Probably till the day I die."

Teine thought a second, surprised by the other boy's pessimism. "You know, you're only just getting a few chores while you go to school. It's not as though you'll be stuck in the bakery if you don't like it. Just study hard and do well. Solmurry has all kinds of opportunities."

"I don't take school," Dillan panted. The effort of trying to keep up with Teine was wearing him out. "Can't read. No one ever taught me."

Teine blinked in utter shock and automatically slowed his pace. *Another illiterate one?*

But Dillan wasn't done. "Yeah, and your lord didn't even pay for me. Just took me in out of kindness. It was just too hot down there, and the sun was so bright. I sunburned every time I went outside and got some little sore spots they had to cut off. Since I couldn't work outdoors there wasn't much for me to do. So they gave me away up here. Hey—don't look so glum! It's my misfortune, not yours."

Teine couldn't stop shaking his head. This kid—according to Solmurry standards—was *worthless*. The fact that they weren't bothering to educate him at all was so telling. Teine just didn't know what to say.

"Hey, it's not that bad. I'll get to eat the overdone pastries, at least!"

The thought of pastry—or any food at all—suddenly set Teine's stomach to a slow roll, and a wave of queasiness washed over him.

"You don't look so good. Hey, where are you going?" Dillan called after him. Teine didn't even recall telling his legs to move, but somehow he was on the run, trying to put as much distance between himself and the kitchen, the pastries, and the hopeless-case kid as possible.

The cool night air helped him breathe, and he began to feel better. More clearheaded. He vowed to look into Dillan's situation and keep some kind of an eye on him later. He was just rounding the corner of the Demesne, into the luxurious side lawn on Marne's side of the house, when a furtive movement caught his eye and froze him in his tracks.

Marne, clad in a dark, hooded cloak, was carefully climbing down the flower-laden trellis that decorated his second-floor balcony. The young master was carrying a small pack and wore a metal canteen on a strap over his shoulder. He had on riding leathers, and seemed prepared for some type of clandestine night-time activity. Teine watched for three whole seconds, his mouth agape. *Sneaking out? The young master was* definitely *sneaking out!*

"That's a nice reverse cat-burglar impression you've got going on," he whispered. "But they usually break *in*, not *out*."

Marne squeaked with alarm, momentarily lost his hold on the trellis and nearly fell. "What?" he hissed irritably at Teine, clinging with one hand and clutching his stomach with the other. "What the holy hell are *you* doing out here?!"

Perhaps it was the alcohol still in his system, but Teine found the whole unexpected scene outrageously funny. He was sneaking in. Marne was sneaking out. Neither of them were being a model of the responsible good citizen. And it was hi-lar-i-ous! He put both hands over his mouth to stifle the stream of drunken guffaws that threatened to slip out like the call of a braying jackass. Instead, he snorted loudly.

"Shh!" Marne snarled at him. "Do you want us to get caught? It will scuttle the mission! We can't let him free if we get caught. They'll make me give him back." Marne, gesturing with his hands, completely lost his grip on the trellis and fell the last six feet. Like a cat, he twisted in mid-air, but still landed in an ungainly sprawl on top of the rose bushes.

Teine went from amused to alarmed in a fraction of a second. When he bent down to help Marne up, he could feel the heat radiating from him before he could even offer him a hand. He cupped his charge's chin in his hand and looked him in the face. Marne's glassy eyes and unusually rosy cheeks completed the picture. The boy was sick. Again. Or maybe it was still. Either way, something was obviously wrong. "Hey, you don't look well."

"Doesn't matter." Marne shook his head, vehemently, shaking off Teine's concern like a dog shakes off water. "Need to leave. Once they figure out he's missing they'll take him away. He needs to be free."

Delirious? Teine wondered. From what he'd heard from Marne's other caregivers, it wouldn't be the first time. "What are you talking about, little marse-man? Who needs to be free?"

"Well, *me*, for starters," Marne grumbled, practically climbing up Teine to get back on his own two feet. "But that's not a project for tonight. Tonight I need to let Spritz go." He held out the canteen and thumbed the pop-open top as though he were going to take a drink. As Teine watched in amazement, a miniature watery hand reached out, then *waved* at him.

"What?!?" Teine couldn't believe what he'd just seen. "You *stole* a water elemental?"

"You can't steal a person," Marne told him, his chin jutting out in pouty, child-like defiance. "You can only liberate them from slavery if they're being held against their will, or kidnap them if they don't want to go with you. He wants to go with me. It's legal. I looked it up."

That was it. Teine had heard enough. Without further ado, he bent down, recapped the flask, and swooped Marne up over his shoulder. "Whoa, now. Settle down there." he whispered, remembering Madric's conversation with Clinician Nocdoramus earlier that day. "You're not going *anywhere* tonight." He hoped he'd managed to pull off a commanding adult tone, or at least keep his young master from realizing exactly how much drinking he'd done that evening. "You look just awful, Marne. You need to rest. We'll debate the ethics of elementalism later."

"But my horse is ready!" Marne protested. "Everything's all in place! We won't have another chance as perfect as this."

"What if I did it for you?" Teine offered, trying to feel out the situation. "Where did you want to let him go?"

"The ocean. We have a private beach and a nice little cove. It's about ten miles from here." Marne ceased struggling as he considered Teine's offer. "Too dangerous for you to go by yourself."

"And not too dangerous for *you* to go by *yourself?*" Teine snorted. "Really?"

"You don't know where you're going. I do. And have you ever even *been* on a horse?"

Teine paused to consider. "Touché, little master. I can't do it for you. But I also can't allow you to do it, either."

"You're not the boss of me!" Marne growled deep in his throat, a buzz that was too cute to sound menacing. "I'm the boss of *you!* You have to do what I say! Let me go!"

"I may be new to how things work here in the big house, but I'm not dumb." Marne's struggles were weakening already. Clearly the child either wasn't as recovered as they'd thought or was ill with something brand new. Teine did his best to soothe the boy while still holding firm. "I won't get in trouble for this. There isn't a single adult here who would let you just wander around at night with dangerous people on the loose. And face it: you're sick again, too."

"They'll take him away," Marne whispered, finally giving up. He hung limp in Teine's arms, exhausted from his brief resistance. "He needs to be free. I promised. And it has to happen soon! I don't know if my spell will hold and he needs more water. Plus, Madric will notice he's gone when he gets home!"

"No, he won't." Leis' voice rang like a soft, clear bell above their heads. "Now you two hush up and get inside before someone *else* hears you!"

Teine made a conscious effort to whisper. "What? Why?"

Leis sighed, audible even from two stories up. "Didn't you hear? Brigands looted the tower about an hour after you left. In broad daylight, even! Madric went home to see what the damages were as soon as he found out."

Both Teine and Marne shared a glance of astonishment at the boldness of the brigands, but Marne spoke first. "Let me down, or I'm going to be sick."

Teine immediately set him down, since that was a threat Marne could actually make good on. "Was anyone hurt?"

"Come inside," Leis answered cryptically. Teine's stomach twisted in alarm, instinctively aware that more bad news was on the way. Thoughts of Madric's staff—many of them either young and tender like Hamoni and the Louts, or old and frail like Pasha and Kenneth—flickered through his foggy brain.

Then, without warning, Marne threw up on his boots. The boy collapsed on the ground, retching. The mingled scent of vomit and blood wafted up to Teine's nostrils, making him powerfully queasy.

"Good grief!" Leis yelped. "I'm coming down."

Teine was profoundly grateful she was already gone from the window when he threw up in the rosebushes next to Marne.

Teine, Marne and the rest of the folks at Solmurry will return in True, Book 3 of The Gilded Shackle *series, scheduled for September, 2016.*

Chapter 1: Infirm

"You're drunk! I don't approve of drunkenness, you know." Marne scolded weakly, then rolled over on his side to dry heave.

Poor little guy sounds like he's turning inside out, Teine thought. Oddly, he felt better himself after he'd gotten some of the alcohol out of his system. He wanted to ask if Marne was feeling better too, but it was obvious that the boy was in far worse shape. "Here, here," he said, crouching next to Marne. "What's all this about?"

"Dunno." Marne's voice sounded tremulous, slurred, and more than a little fearful. "I had some little blisters in my mouth right after dinner, and then about a half hour ago I had stomach cram—" He began to retch again, and tears streamed down his face from the effort. "I felt bad right after dinner, but I thought it was just nerves until I threw up."

Teine was surprised that the odor of Marne's sickness wasn't still making him throw up too. However that worked, he was simply grateful. Bending down, he scooped Marne up in his arms. The boy instinctively wrapped spindly limbs around him. He was weak and feverish and smelled of vomit, but there was definitely an additional odor of blood that Teine hadn't just imagined. He couldn't think of a single thing he could say to comfort his charge, who was still clinging and writhing from the pain.

Teine didn't recall ever feeling so helpless in his entire life.

Suddenly, they heard a door open and a rectangle of light appeared down by the kitchens where the mudroom was. Leis was silhouetted in the lit doorway, and Teine immediately started carrying Marne to meet her. "Hold the door," she hissed to someone inside. "If it closes we'll have to go around the front, and this needs to stay secret." Running lightly and almost silently on the balls of her feet, she bounded up to them, holding her arms out for Marne. Teine didn't mind handing him over, but he was surprised at feeling weak in the knees with relief. Leis had *presence*. "What's wrong, little man?" she asked.

Marne recounted what had happened, and although Teine had planned to listen something caught his eye. When he'd walked toward the mud room and kitchen entrance to meet Leis, he'd gained a better view of what was going on inside. A wiry figure, draped in a rich red and gold velvet dressing robe, tottered into the room and sat down at the kitchen worktable while the kitchen staff continued their ballet of breakfast preparations around him.

"Prior Vihah!" Teine hissed. After his conversation with Leis and Amagorra about the old priest, he was fully aware that the Prior was probably the person most dangerous to Marne that he knew. Seeing the Aoife priest unexpectedly like that—well, Teine couldn't have been more alarmed if the Demesne had been on fire.

Leis, still clutching Marne to her chest, peered around him to look. "Ohhhh. That's not good."

"At least I have my bracelet. He can't see the real me."

"Thank the All-Mother for small favors," Leis snorted. "How are we going to get past him?"

"We will probably ha—" Marne coughed and sputtered, trying not to be sick on Leis. "Go through my father's quarters. Private entrance."

Teine nodded his agreement. Even Lesmar wasn't going to be there. "Good idea. Go around. I'll come in through the kitchen, all drunk, and be sure the Prior doesn't—"

"It's locked," Leis whispered. "After the raid at Madric's Tower, they locked everything tonight. The only reason I can get back in right now is there's a new kid. He's holding the door for me and is too new to ask any questions."

Teine foggily tried to recall the freckle-faced kid's name, and exactly how the mudroom opened onto the kitchen. It seemed that with the way the mudroom and hallway were configured, there would only be an instant that someone hurrying in through the mudroom into the hall would be visible to people in the kitchen. "All right. I have a plan."

"You distract him, and we make a run for it?" Leis offered, an uncharacteristically sarcastic tone in her voice. "Absolutely brilliant strategy, genius. How much did you need to drink to come up with that?"

"Be mad later," Teine told her. "Believe me, this is its own punishment."

"Yeah, I can smell."

Marne whimpered, and the two siblings fell silent, glaring at each other. Just then the mudroom door opened a crack, and there was...

"Dillan." Teine staggered toward the door, deliberately exaggerating his level of inebriation. "Lemme in."

"I heard it all," Dillan smiled, his slightly crossed eyes merry behind his thick spectacles. "I'll let them in right after you."

Teine couldn't decide which eye of his to look at when speaking to him, and the thought set off another genuine wave of queasiness. "All right, then. It's showtime." And with that, he threw the door open, making sure it banged, and then deliberately tripped over the threshold, staggering into the kitchen.

The three plump cooks and their two skinny scullery maids all started in alarm as Teine careened into the kitchen, bumped into the Prior, and made sure he spilled the tea all over both of them. "Uuugh, so sorry, Prior," he slobbered, inwardly grinning at the women and how they all sounded like frightened hens. To enhance his performance, Teine grabbed a towel out of one of the maids' hands, then seized the elderly Aoife priest by the shoulders. Pivoting Vihah into the light, he arranged him so that he couldn't see the doorway. Stunned by all the unexpected activity, the elderly Aoife allowed himself to be steered and blotted by the towel.

"My son," the priest began, aghast. "Have you been drinking spirits?"

"Not… very much!" Teine denied. Teine could see Leis peering around the corner in his peripheral vision, but focused his gaze on Vihah's ruined robe. It was time for the show stopper. "Uuugh, I think I'm going to be…" He snatched one of the baking bowls and hunched over it, doing the best impression he could muster of natural-sounding dry heaves.

The effect was magical. "Oh no!" the head cook exclaimed. Suddenly Teine had the full attention of everyone in the room, leaving an opening for Leis and Marne to make a run for it. Teine smiled to himself and fake-retched again. Sadly, he underestimated how he really felt and ended up throwing up for real.

"There, there, son." Prior Vihah patted Teine on his shoulder with his bejeweled and bony old claw. "Get it all out of your system and you'll feel better."

Teine let tears come to his eyes, groaned, and ceased the acting job. "Uuugh! I was so stupid. This girl, she was gorgeous, she kept buying me drinks, and I didn't want to look like a baby."

"I think most young men have a bad experience with alcohol their first time."

One of the cooks chuckled, still sounding like a hen. "Not *just* young men. I'll put on a spot of tea for you. Some chamomile will settle down that tummy." She waved a wooden spoon at him, her round cheeks flushed and smiling. "I hope you learned your lesson. You're lucky the master wasn't home tonight."

"Lucky, indeed," Teine agreed. "Believe me, I won't be making a regular habit of this!"

Prior Vihah continued to pat him on the back. "I have a prayer that cures most non-magical poisons. I'll use it to remove the effects of your hangover, if you promise to behave with more self-control the next time."

The old Aoife looked so wise and kind, Teine had to remind himself how dangerous he was. Then, he nodded, the very picture of meek and embarrassed obedience. Intensely curious to feel the workings of an actual clerical spell, he watched the priest closely.

"You'll feel better in just a moment," Prior Vihah told him. Then the old man closed his eyes and began to chant, almost like a song, in a language Teine not only didn't understand, but didn't think he'd ever heard before. He could barely count to three before every single trace of his inebriation and sickness had passed.

"Like magic," he whispered, completely astonished.

"Like *prayer*," the Prior corrected. "All good and lawful things serve the will of Vuaren."

Teine only stayed long enough to drink his tea and make an exit that looked natural. He didn't want to mess up a perfect plan by arousing suspicion. Fortunately, the entire ploy had worked like Krunal clockwork—especially with the added touch of realism Teine left in the bowl. The "secret ingredient," so to speak.

Once he had made his excuses, Teine headed upstairs to Marne's quarters as fast as his wobbly and exhausted legs would carry him.

Although he'd seen Marne sick before, there was something about this particular time that gave him a feeling of deep uneasiness.

He burst through the door to Marne's quarters like a horse leaving the starting gate. "How is he?" he asked Leis, who was standing in the middle of the main room, wringing her hands and looking as though she was waiting specifically for him. He could hear Marne groaning in the other room.

"This is *bad*," Leis said, almost in unison with his question. "It's happened before, but never this severe. We know it's some kind of poisoning, but we've never figured out what causes it. We need the Clinician, and we need her *now*."

"What do—should I—?" Teine held his hands out helplessly. Just hearing Marne was terrifying. Normally, he was a stoic little fellow. If he was carrying on like that, Teine knew he must be in agony.

"Go," Leis pointed toward the door. "Go now. No need to be stealthy."

Teine wheeled and was about to blast off, but then he heard it. "Teine! I want Teine!" Instead of heading out the door, Teine ran to Marne's bedside. "Teine!" Marne was writhing on the bed in his underwear, his sheets already soaked through with sweat. His illusionary face was twisted with pain, yet he sat up and looked Teine in the eye and spoke. "Get the canteen! Spritz can't stay in there. I tried to do the spell but it isn't very good. He'll need a bigger vessel and some more rainwater from the storms."

"Oh no! He's delirious!" Leis was wringing the hem of her apron as she looked on. Even Stinky the Wolfhound had lain his head on Marne's bed and was whining softly.

"How big of a vessel?" Teine snatched up the canteen out of the pile of blood and vomit-spattered clothes Leis had tossed into the wicker hamper. He couldn't believe Leis had simply dismissed everything Marne had just said as mere delirium, but he had no time to devote more thought to it.

Marne's face was all clenched up, and tears welled out of his closed eyes. "The biggest thing you can fi—the tub! Just use the tub!"

Teine ran into Marne's private bathroom, uncapping the flask as he went. Once he got there, he unceremoniously dumped the contents right into the tub, where it barely made a puddle. Spritz stirred and rippled the water, roiling it up into a miniature foamy ocean. He could only assume the elemental was agitated. "What now?"

"Go get the Clinician, now!" Leis ordered. "I can do whatever else Marne needs, but I can't run as fast as you."

"Please hurry," Marne whispered.

Teine followed his hunch and went to the stable, and was rewarded by finding Nocdoramus there. The young Aoife doctor was curled up, fast asleep under a horse blanket, on a folding cot in Willis' stall. He hated waking her, she looked so rumpled and exhausted, but it was necessary.

"*Beyond* necessary," she insisted, as he apologized for the sixth time while they were running, side by side, back to the Demesne. "He's had this before and it's just horrible. I hoped it was a fluke at the time, but I'm afraid not."

It had only been a few minutes since Teine left the Demesne, but word had traveled. The lights were on in the main hall, and several more Human servants were up and about, dressed in bathrobes and nightclothes. Clinician Nocdoramus made no pretense of congeniality, running past them towards Marne's rooms. Teine followed, hard-pressed to keep up with her and trying not to jostle the heavy doctor's bag that he carried for her. Within a minute she was by Marne's side, taking his hand and feeling his forehead.

"We've... we've got to stop meeting like this," Marne whispered, the faintest of smiles on his illusionary face. If it was possible, he looked even worse than he had just a few minutes earlier. "People will talk."

The Clinician's eyes filled up with unfallen tears. She whirled, pointing a finger at Teine, who'd only just caught up. "Bar the door. Don't let anyone in. I need to take his bracelet off to see what's really happening. That damn illusion..."

Suddenly Teine understood. Nocdoramus was in on it. Of *course* she was in on it—she'd have to be! According to Leis and Amagorra, the Clinician was practically the only person who knew Marne's entire story who wasn't either a relative of his or a full-time Human caregiver. Teine barred the door to their quarters.

By the time he returned to Marne's bedside, the Clinician had already removed Marne's bracelet and set it aside. Leis stood nearby, hovering helplessly. Without the bracelet and the illusion it carried, Teine could see that Marne's face was livid. He lay very still, veins visible through his pale skin, and there were blisters around his mouth. Nocdoramus was examining the boy, looking down his throat, pressing on his gums, all while shaking her head with a grim expression on her face.

"I'm certain you've been poisoned again. Think. Think! Was there anything different you came in contact with today? Anything?" Marne blinked slowly and wrinkled his nose with concentration, which caused one of the blisters near his mouth to burst.

"I can't remember."

She reached for her bag, pulling out a syringe and vial. "I'll run some blood tests, but without knowing what he might have been exposed to, it's all just guesswork." She worked as she talked, drawing a small vial of odd, bright orangish-red blood from Marne's unresisting arm.

"It's my strange anatomy making things difficult again." Marne sighed weakly.

"It's not your fault." She took his hand. "You know you're my favorite patient."

"I'm your own private freak show," Marne sighed, raising his head shakily. "Have you ever considered that perhaps I'm sick all the time because I'm not meant to live?" Teine could see the resignation on Marne's alien face and understood the boy wasn't just being dramatic.

Clinician Nocdoramus flushed, and her eyes filled with tears. "No, Marne. It's not like that at all." But Teine didn't need to hear her say it to understand that Clinician Nocdoramus was very afraid that Marne might be right after all. She was going to lose her patient. The thought made Teine dizzy to think of it.

Suddenly an idea popped into Teine's head. It was sneaky. It was risky. And it was so obvious he doubted that it hadn't been thought of before. "Can we speak for a moment?" he asked, touching her arm. "Out in the playroom?"

Nodding, Nocdoramus rose to her feet. "I'll be back in just a moment," she told Marne. Teine beckoned for Leis, who started as if she'd been in a trance and then followed them.

Teine led the way, then closed the door behind them. "First of all, is the situation as desperate as I think it is? I have to know."

The Clinician hesitated, then nodded. "The last time this happened, we almost lost him. And this time it seems to have come on faster, and frankly, it looks even worse."

"I have an idea. If you've exhausted what medical science can do for him, maybe it's time to try magic." Nocdoramus' eyes widened, as if Teine's thoughts were contagious. "Get his bracelet back on. I'll go get Prior Vihah."

Dictionary/Pronunciation Guide

Age of Majority: The time when a young Aoife is considered a full adult; at 140 years of age.

Alemis (Al-LAY-mus): Ersan goddess of nature, "Mother Nature." Also called the "All-Mother."

Amagi (Ah-MAHDG-ee): Honorific for "mother" in the Empyrean.

Amagorra (Ah-Mah-GORE-uh): Honorific for "grandmother" in the Empyrean.

Aoife (EE-fuh): Slender, "elf-like" humanoids with pointed ears, oblique-set eyes, and angular features. The dominant species in the Empyrean.

AF: Abbreviation for "Altered Female." A Human or half-breed female who has been surgically rendered sterile. Much more rare than an AM.

AM: Abbreviation for "Altered Male." A Human or half-breed male who has received a vasectomy and is sterile.

Awakened: An item or animal that has become either sentient or magically active, when it wasn't before.

Besom (BESS-um): A low-born, trashy woman.

Bess: A slang term for a working woman, with positive connotations (i.e., "She's a hardworking Bess.")

Cantillate (CAN-till-ate): The act of casting magic with the aid of gestures or the spoken word. Proper usage: cantillating, cantillation, to cantillate.

Capite (Cap-EET): A grant of land from the Emperor that can never be divided or sold.

Castellar, The Kingdom of (CASS-tell-ar): A neighboring Human kingdom, where the ruling class is magically active. They have trade relations with the Empyrean.

Centennial: An Aoife's 100th birthday, signifies their entry into an adult role. They are allowed to marry at this age.

Closehold: The lands immediately surrounding the Demesne or Estate (the close-in yards, formal gardens, etc.)

Cohort (CO-hort): A group of young Humans of the same age, usually boys. A name for the barracks living arrangement of young Humans grouped by age, usually given a mascot name like Mastiff or Falcon.

The Cut: A rite of passage that marks the start of adulthood for young Human men within the Empyrean. They are evaluated and then given a circumcision. If they are not needed for breeding they also receive a vasectomy and become AMs. The boys who will go on to sire children receive a circumcision only and are left as IMs.

Demesne (Duh-MAIN): The main Manor house of an Estate.

Destrier (DES-tree-er): A war horse.

Display: A beauty pageant for Human slaves where breeding stock is evaluated and judged.

Dorter (DOR-ter): The dormitory buildings where most adult Human women live. Each woman is assigned their own private room with other amenities, such as a private bathroom, available as a perk for exceptional service.

Doyen Prince (DOY-un): A prince who is the acknowledged heir of a kingdom/empire. The one who will inherit and take over the duties of the Emperor.

Driller: A coach and/or certified physical fitness specialist, in charge of making exercise assignments and goals for Humans.

Eaoster (EE-stir): A spring equinox holiday sometimes celebrated as fertility rites in some Ersan cultures and as the resurrection of their deity in others.

Elementals: Extraplanar creatures stuck on Ersa that can be forced to perform services through the use of magic.

Elf: An insulting slang word that Humans from outside the Empyrean use to describe Aoife.

Emmett: The closest small borough to Solmurry lands. Population about 1500. Between Solmurry and Hilliard lands, on the peninsula.

Empyrea (Im-PEER-ee-uh): Capital City of the Empyrean, also referred to as Capital City.

Empyrean (Im-PEER-ee-un)- The wealthy secretive walled Empire run by Aoife. Also known as "The Elvish Empire" to outsiders

Empyrean Gazette: The big newspaper that covers the Empyrean's Capital City.

Enchantment Feeder: A magical device constructed to aid in enchanting other items.

Eos (EE-yos): Ersa's sun.

Ersa (UR-suh): The planet/world.

Espaliered (Es-PAL-yerd): A tree or other plant grown to entwine itself to a flat surface, such as a wall or trellis.

Fabal (FAY-ball): A rough team sport with some similarity to football or rugby, with the egg of a dragon as the ball.

Greeves Academy: A respected school for the study of magic, in the Human Kingdom of Castellar, a neighboring nation of the Empyrean.

Grudge: A gladiator that answers challenges to their house.

Holidocrith (Ho-LID-oh-crith): A large, intelligent, usually psi-active warm-blooded native creature of Ersa that has dragon, horse, and dog-like features.

Hospitality: A hotel reserved for noble travelers and their staff, a resort.

IM: Abbreviation for Intact Male; a male Human who has been circumcised but has not been given a vasectomy. Another term for Human male breeding stock.

Inquisitor: An agent of The Church of Vuaren, usually a magically active member of the clergy, whose duties consist of uncovering illegal magical practitioners, securing confessions of their wrongdoing, and incarcerating them in the Monasteries for re-education.

Inspector: An agent of The Church of Vuaren, usually a non-magically active member of the clergy or an Inquisitor-in-training, whose duties consist of regular follow up and welfare checks on legal magical practitioners.

Madric's Tower: An ancient lighthouse and watchtower on Solmurry's coast built centuries ago by contracted Krunal stonemasons. Now houses the magician Madric Solmurrian and his people.

Marse (Marss or Marz): Slang for "Master." Normally used as a term of affection. Boss.

Port Chandler: Coastal city in the Empyrean.

Port O'Prye (Oh-PRY): Large, freeport bordering the Empyrean and the wild Northern lands and servicing ships from many different nations.

Prior (PRY-er): A priest in service of Vuaren, the Lord of Light.

Sea Dragon: A native creature of Ersa that has both a saltwater and freshwater lifecycle. Adults can get to be hundreds of feet long. They like the taste of wood, and occasionally attack ships and lifeboats. Their freshwater larvae are considered a delicacy.

Sigil (SIG-ill): A magical marking that denotes bloodline, place of origin, ownership, identity, pedigree, and schooling on Humans within the Empyrean.

Silderwort (SIL-der-wart): A plant with an extraplanar origin used in many magical preparations.

Sin of Drome: See *Syndrome*.

Sire and Get: A class entry in a Human Display show where a male Human is shown with several of his offspring to showcase his quality as a breeding specimen.

Solmurry (SAUL-meury): One of the largest land holdings within the Empyrean, the Solmurry estate is protected by an Imperial decree of Capite—meaning it cannot be divided or sold. Passed down through the noble Aoife of the Solmurrian house, the estate is currently under the care of Lord Alain Solmurrian, to fall to his sole heir, Marnariel Emerys Solmurrian upon his demise.

SPED: Abbreviation for Solmurry Postal Exchange Depot, the post office within Solmurry proper, attached to the Commons building.

Swiving: A curse word for sexual intercourse.

Syndrome: A specific set of "deformities" that plague Aoife newborns and result in death.

Theia (THEE-uh): Ersa's moon.

Titan: A slang word that Humans outside the Empyrean use to describe Empyrean-bred Humans.

Vuaren (VUAR-en): Empyrean God of Law. Sometimes worshipped as a Saint in other monotheistic cultures.

Wiydon (WHY-don): A leggy, stork-like seabird.

Wiydon Isles (WHY-don): A Theocratic Human Kingdom across the sea from the Empyrean.

The People of the Gilded Shackle

Abel of Bartheim (BARTH-heim): AM Human, sold to Solmurry by his previous master because he wanted to work at the Solmurry shipyard.

Alain Solmurrian (Ah-LANE Saul-MEURY-en): Male Aoife, younger brother of Madric, father of Marne, Lord and Master of Solmurry.

Aleric Solmurrian (Al-ERR-ic Saul-MEURY-en): Male Aoife, historical figure who accidentally turned himself into an undead.

Amagi/Selene of Solmurry (Ah-MODGE-ee/Si-LEEN): Female Human, mother of Adina, Teine, Leis and Samia.

Amagorra/Silvia of Solmurry (Ah-ma-GORE-uh/SIL-vee-uh): Female Human, mother to Selene, grandmother to Adina, Teine, Leis and Samia.

Andreas of Mahoney (Ahn-DRAY-us of Muh-HO-nee): Male Human, Senior stud who works with Lesmar of Solmurry to attend Master Solmurrian directly. Their duties vary but could be compared to a valet.

Mr. Aylmer (AIL-mer): Male Aoife, newspaper reporter for *The Empyrean Gazette*, bought Samia as a handmaiden for his wife.

Billy of Mahoney (Muh-HO-nee): IM Human, purchased as a stud prospect, from Peregrine Cohort, about Teine's age, is acclimated to life at Solmurry but still keeps in touch with his relatives at Mahoney.

Clinician Nocdoramus (Nock-door-AM-us): Female Aoife, young up-and-coming physician.

Daniel of Bellamore: Nursling Male Human, potential stud prospect. Acquired in a partial trade during the Eaoster Day auction. The Bellamore sigils have a stylized red heart with a sword and an arrow through it.

Dillan of Solairn: Cohort-age Male Human, given to Solmurry to get him to a cooler climate.

Driller Goran/Goran of Solmurry (GOR-un): AM Human, retired Grudge, now in service as Solmurry Driller.

Ebric Hilliard (EB-rick HILL-yerd): Male Aoife. Lord of Hilliard, father of Nirilemi/Niri.

Earl of Broshenford (BROSH-en-ferd): Male Aoife. Business associate of Lord Solmurrian. Has a widowed daughter with a young son.

Edgar of Solmurry: AM Human, middle-aged master silversmith at Solmurry.

Hamoni Falshaad (Huh-MOAN-ee Fal-SHAHD): Female Aoife, apprentice to Madric Solmurrian, works in exchange for training and keeping her talents hidden.

Haneesha Falshaad (Han-EE-sha Fal-SHAHD): Female Aoife, Courtesan, professional seductress and older sister of Hamoni Falshaad.

Kenneth Blank: AM Human, Madric's groom and stable hand at the Tower.

Leis of Solmurry (LEES): Female Human, younger sister of Teine of Solmurry, granddaughter of Silvia of Solmurry, daughter of Selene of Solmurry and Lesmar of Solairn, head nanny of Marne Solmurrian.

Lesmar of Solairn (LESS-mar of Sau-LAIRN): IM Human, senior stud at Solmurry, Headman of Master Solmurrian, sire of Teine, Leis, Samia, Adina, Marcus and many other Solmurry Humans.

Madric Solmurrian (MAD-rick Saul-MEUR-y-en): Male Aoife, eldest brother of Lord Alain Solmurrian, talented magician, works from Madric's Tower.

Marcus of Solmurry (MAR-cuss): IM Human, half-sibling of Teine and Leis of Solmurry, son of Lesmar of Solairn.

"Marne" Solmurrian (MARN): Heir to Solmurry, son of Alain and Brigid (d.) Solmurrian.

Miska of Solmurry (MISS-kuh): AF Human, shepherdess who works the back pastures. Believed to be simpleminded.

Nirilema (Niri) Hilliard (Neer-ee-LEE-muh/NEER-ee): Female Aoife, daughter of Lord Ebric Hilliard, fascinated with magic, Marne Solmurrian's secret best friend.

Pasha of Solmurry: Elderly Human woman who works at Madric's Tower in the kitchen.

Phoebe of Solmurry (FEE-bee): Female Human, senior housekeeper at the Solmurry Demesne, currently pregnant.

Prior Vihah (PRY-er VEE-hah): Male Aoife, High Inquisitor for the Doyen Prince. In charge of capturing, sequestering and "educating" people within the Empyrean who are found to be practicing magic in secret.

Samia of Solmurry (SAM-ee-ya): Female Human, youngest full sister of Teine and Leis, sold as the Special Reserve to Mr. Aylmer, a columnist for *The Empyrean Gazette*.

Seymour of Cartierscross (SEE-more of CAR-tee-ears-cross): AM Human, friend and cohort-mate of Teine and Marcus.

Sigolier Zan (SIG-oh-leer): Female Aoife, common-born. Works in Records Department of the Empyrean. Is trained in the care, updating, and maintenance of the magical tattoos that identify each Human and noble-born Aoife in the Empyrean.

Silpa of Cartierscross (SIL-puh): Female Human, nanny to Nirilema Hilliard.

"Snippy" Solmurrian: Half-breed sibling to Madric Solmurrian and Master Alain Solmurrian. A freeman, he operates Solmurry's barber shop.

Stinky the Wolfhound: Favorite pet of Marne Solmurrian and the staff of the Solmurry Demesne.

Teine of Solmurry (TYNE): IM Human, full-sibling of Leis, Samia, and Adina, son of Selene of Solmurry and Lesmar of Solairn, grandson of Silvia of Solmurry. Has been given as a gift from Lord Solmurrian to his son, Marne Solmurrian, in celebration of Marne's Centennial.

Victor of Solmurry (VICK-tor): IM Human, friend of Teine and Marcus.

Vorogu and Volsney (VORE-oh-goo and VOLE-snee): Male Aoife twins, elder common-born Aoife men who have worked for Solmurry in an accountant/docent role since before Madric and Alain were born.

Vosh of Solmurry: IM Human, best friend of Teine. Professional Fabal player.

Willis the True (WILL-iss): Female Holidocrith. Highly decorated wartime mount for Lord Alain Solmurrian's father during the last Wiydon Isles invasion.

Zandra Blank (ZAN-dra): Human Female, born outside the Empyrean in Port O'Prye. Previously worked in a floating pleasure house/casino before being purchased by Lord Alain Solmurrian for his favored Human manservant, Lesmar of Solairn.

About the Author

A long-time fan of sci-fi and fantasy, C.T. Griffith began developing the world of *The Gilded Shackle* in the 1980's as a setting to run Dungeons and Dragons games. She has a total of nine books planned for project, which will be the first of many other series set in the world. An avid tabletop roleplaying gamer and artist, she still plays and draws when she can.

Ms. Griffith lives in the Midwest with her three borzois. You can see a list of her other works and her upcoming publishing schedule at www.ctgriffith.com or find her on Facebook at www.facebook.com/author.ctgriffith.

www.ingramcontent.com/pod-product-compliance
Lightning Source LLC
Chambersburg PA
CBHW020604180626
46810CB00007B/2641